W9-BCE-772

"I shall keep to my own bed after the sham vows are recited, and you shall keep to yours!

"Or anyone else's bed you fancy, for all I care!"

"Are you saying what I think you're saying?" Nicholas demanded, his eyes angry.

Emily propped her fists on her hips. "Well, if you didn't understand what I said, my lord, perhaps it is *you* who needs a governess. Since we are to have a loveless union and it is all for outward show, there will be no consummation of it. Do you understand that, sir, or need I make it plainer still?"

For a long moment fraught with tension, Nicholas said absolutely nothing. "I did promise that you could have whatever you wanted," he at last said softly. "Whether you believe it or not, I am a man of my word. Just be certain you really want what you demand...!"

Praise for Lyn Stone's recent books

The Highland Wife
"…laced with lovable characters, witty dialogue,
humor and poignancy, this is a tale to savor."
—*Romantic Times*

Bride of Trouville
"I could not stop reading this one….
Don't miss this winner!"
—*Affaire de Coeur*

The Knight's Bride
"Stone has done herself proud with this
delightful story…a cast of endearing characters
and a fresh, innovative plot."
—*Publishers Weekly*

**DON'T MISS THESE OTHER
TITLES AVAILABLE NOW:**

#599 THE LOVE MATCH
Deborah Simmons/Deborah Hale/Nicola Cornick
#600 A MARRIAGE BY CHANCE
Carolyn Davidson
#602 SHADES OF GRAY
Wendy Douglas

LYN STONE
MARRYING Mischief

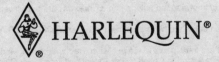

HARLEQUIN®

TORONTO • NEW YORK • LONDON
AMSTERDAM • PARIS • SYDNEY • HAMBURG
STOCKHOLM • ATHENS • TOKYO • MILAN • MADRID
PRAGUE • WARSAW • BUDAPEST • AUCKLAND

If you purchased this book without a cover you should be aware that this book is stolen property. It was reported as "unsold and destroyed" to the publisher, and neither the author nor the publisher has received any payment for this "stripped book."

ISBN 0-373-29201-5

MARRYING MISCHIEF

Copyright © 2002 by Lynda Stone

All rights reserved. Except for use in any review, the reproduction or utilization of this work in whole or in part in any form by any electronic, mechanical or other means, now known or hereafter invented, including xerography, photocopying and recording, or in any information storage or retrieval system, is forbidden without the written permission of the publisher, Harlequin Enterprises Limited, 225 Duncan Mill Road, Don Mills, Ontario, Canada M3B 3K9.

All characters in this book have no existence outside the imagination of the author and have no relation whatsoever to anyone bearing the same name or names. They are not even distantly inspired by any individual known or unknown to the author, and all incidents are pure invention.

This edition published by arrangement with Harlequin Books S.A.

® and TM are trademarks of the publisher. Trademarks indicated with ® are registered in the United States Patent and Trademark Office, the Canadian Trade Marks Office and in other countries.

Visit us at www.eHarlequin.com

Printed in U.S.A.

Available from Harlequin Historicals and
LYN STONE

The Wicked Truth #358
The Arrangement #389
The Wilder Wedding #413
The Knight's Bride #445
Bride of Trouville #467
One Christmas Night #487
My Lady's Choice #511
The Highland Wife #551
The Quest #588
Marrying Mischief #601

Other works include:

Silhouette Intimate Moments
Beauty and the Badge #952
Live-In Lover #1055

Please address questions and book requests to:
Harlequin Reader Service
U.S.: 3010 Walden Ave., P.O. Box 1325, Buffalo, NY 14269
Canadian: P.O. Box 609, Fort Erie, Ont. L2A 5X3

This book is dedicated to my good friends
Julie and Mike Hammersley, and their incredible band,
Auburn. You have England on the dance floor.
Nashville's next! Thank you so much
for your friendship, encouragement and inspiration.

Chapter One

Southern Coast of England—1856

She had only meant to tug the gate open. Yet here she stood with the old broken latch in her hand and the rotten boards of the neglected little portal collapsed at her feet. She peeked inside. Emily Loveyne could scarcely believe that she, the vicar's own daughter, was breaking into the Bournesea Estate.

With a disgusted sigh, she raked away enough of the overgrown ivy and morning glory vines to squeeze through. Obviously no one had used this as an entrance or exit for years. She had when she was a child accompanying her father on his Sunday afternoon visits when her ladyship still lived.

The small gardener's gate had been the nearest way in on their approach from their cottage, and had led them directly past the roses, once inside. Her father did love roses. They still enjoyed the beauties grown from cuttings Lady Elizabeth had given them for their own garden. Good thing, too, she noticed. No one had tended the par-

ent bushes for quite some time. What a weedy, overgrown tangle!

These days she supposed everyone went in and out the
front or side entrances. Unfortunately, both of those were
closed, their decorative wrought-iron gates locked tight
as a sailor's hitch. Staunchly guarded, too, by burly,
bearded ogres she did not know. Judging from their attire,
they were clearly seamen.

She shook her head in consternation as she rounded
the tall hedges flanking the walls and made for the servants' quarters. That's surely where her brother would
be, not in the manor house itself. She was infinitely glad
she wouldn't have to approach that place. As familiar as
she was with it, she had no wish at all to enter there and
risk an encounter with the new earl.

How dare he keep Josh on duty here now that the ship
had laid anchor. The double-masted brig had been there,
well off the coast, for at least two days before she heard
of it or she would have come sooner. Why, she wondered, was it not in the harbor?

Her brother was only thirteen and must be homesick
after more than six months away. Their father needed to
see his only son, and Emily had missed Josh terribly.

No matter how much she had objected at the time,
Father had allowed Josh to sign on as cabin boy with
Captain Roland for the unhappy voyage all the way to
India. They had gone to inform Lord Nicholas of his
father's death and to bring him home to assume his du-
ties.

Lord Nicholas. He had always possessed the honorary
title, of course, since he was the earl's son. Now he had
inherited the earldom and, things being as they were, she
must remember to call him *lord* if she ever saw him
again.

But, earl or not, the man had no business keeping her little brother under lock and key in this place, and would do that no longer if she had to bring it down around his noble ears. Why the devil were there guards on the gates? They had told her nothing. They had just stood at a goodly distance behind the lacy ironwork and ordered her away.

She lifted her skirts a bit higher, stepped around the puddles standing in the gardens and made for the door to the outer building adjacent to the carriage house.

Other than the guards she had seen, no one was around, she noticed. Today's village gossip held that the skeleton staff remaining after the old earl died had been ordered away when Nicholas arrived.

No one in the village had seen him yet. Isolating himself this way seemed to be taking his grief a bit too far, considering the animosity between father and son. Must be Nicholas's guilt working, she reckoned, and was glad of it. He ought to feel guilty, leaving as he had.

She pushed open the door to the half-timbered, two-story building that she knew was home to the male servants in the earl's employ.

"Anyone here?" she called hesitantly, ducking her head in all the rooms that stood open. Nothing but dusty furnishings. Then she heard voices down the hallway.

Never a shy mouse, Emily quickly headed in that direction. As she did, she passed a chamber with the door ajar and stopped to peek inside. There on the bed lay her brother, sound asleep. Imagine that, in the middle of the day!

He was not even dressed. His sleeveless undershirt revealed his skinny arms and shoulders. So pale, she noted.

"Josh?" she said softly, so as not to startle him awake. When he didn't answer, she went straight to the bedside and put her hand on his arm, shaking gently. "Darling? Are you ill?"

His eyes flew open. First he appeared overjoyed, but then his expression turned to one of stark horror. "Em, get out of here!"

"Nonsense, I've seen you in your smallclothes before and—"

Two men suddenly rushed in and grasped her by the arms. Without a single word of explanation, they hurriedly dragged her out of the building and across to the manor house.

Terrified that the entire place had been invaded by a horde of pirates and thieves, Emily fought them all the way to the door to the kitchens and across the hall inside the main house. "Let me go!" she screamed, struggling and kicking to no avail.

One let go of her arm long enough to open a door and the other thrust her unceremoniously into the earl's library.

She grew still when the men no longer held her and looked around.

The man behind the huge cherrywood desk rose. She almost did not recognize him. He looked so much older, so much larger, so absolutely furious that she was here. Blue eyes that had held such warmth seven years ago now rivaled arctic ice its chill. Dark brows lowered, giving him an almost menacing appearance. The beautifully shaped mouth that had once pressed so fondly against her own drew into a firm and disapproving frown. His nostrils flared.

"Nicholas?" she gasped, unable to credit how much he had changed.

"What the hell are you doing here?" he demanded,

his expression promising retribution for her trespass. "Who allowed her in?"

One of the wretches who had dragged her here cleared his throat. "No one admitted her. She sneaked in somehow, milord. We caught her in young Josh's room out back."

Nicholas grimaced as if in pain and pressed his temples with a thumb and forefinger. "Damn!" His deep voice grated on the vehement, solitary word.

"Well, damn you, too!" she exclaimed, her own ire rising to meet his. "I had not expected to trouble you with my presence, my *lord.* I merely came to fetch my brother home. If you will kindly excuse me, I shall do just that."

"You cannot," he said, his voice gruff.

"Watch me," she replied, whirling around to leave. The men blocked the door. "Move aside," she ordered in her best schoolmistress voice. She had been practicing it for her new position and thought it quite effective. It obviously did not work on adults. They stood firm.

Nicholas had come around the monstrosity of a desk. Emily heard him move and could now feel his presence there, invading the space just behind her. She jerked around to face him.

"Emily, we must talk. Would you please have a seat? Wrecker, pour us a brandy," he said in an aside to one of the men.

She propped one hand on her hip. The other rested at her throat, hopefully hiding the rapid pulse in her neck. "You know very well I do not take spirits, my lord. Say what you have to say, then permit me to leave and bring Josh home with me. He looked ill when I saw him."

He reached for her hand. She ignored the gesture. His frown grew darker. "Leave us," he said to the two men, "and find out how she got past the guards. See that no one else does, or you will answer for it."

She heard the door close. "Now what will you do?" she demanded, determined to show no fear even though she felt very nearly petrified. This was not the Nick she knew. That smiling, witty suitor had disappeared. In his place stood this disheveled, intimidating stranger who frightened her silly.

"Please sit down, Emily," he said.

She did not. Instead, she swiftly stepped around him, afraid of his nearness.

He must not have shaved his beard for several days and was in his shirtsleeves. Those sleeves were rolled up to his elbows, exposing strong, sun-browned forearms. His rich dark hair fell tousled across his brow and curled over the back of his collar. That same collar stood open at his neck, revealing a glimpse of chest covered with a mat of even darker hair.

The forbidden sight perturbed Emily. Never before, even in their youth, had she seen him look so rumpled. Like an unmade bed. Thinking of Nicholas in conjunction with a bed of any kind upset her even more. For someone she disliked so wholeheartedly, he certainly could provoke some highly dangerous thoughts.

She backed against the desk, putting as much space between them as possible. Her heart galloped like a runaway horse.

His expression changed from anger to what appeared to be regret. "You should not have come here," he told her.

Emily expelled the breath she'd been holding and rolled her eyes. "You need not worry, my lord. It is not as if I came to confront you. Even I have more sense than to hound a peer of the realm for an explanation of his actions, past or present. Get out of my way and I will trouble you no longer,'' she snapped.

''Would that I could believe *that*. Does your husband know you're wandering about the county, breaking into private property where you have no business?''

''My *husband?*'' She laughed bitterly. ''No, I'd reckon not, since I do not have one! Thank God for small favors,'' she added.

''You…have no husband,'' he demanded, as if confirming her words so there would be no mistake.

''Certainly not, and we both know the reason. But I do have a brother, and Josh will accompany me home or I shall know the reason why.''

''Because he is ill,'' Nicholas told her, his voice gentler than before. ''Joshua cannot leave the grounds of Bournesea, and—now that you have entered—neither can you.''

''What? You would hold us here against our will?''

''If I must, that is precisely what I will do,'' he said firmly, yet not unkindly. ''We fear it is blue cholera.''

The breath left her in a choked cry of alarm. Her vision wavered, her knees buckled and she grasped the desk behind her to keep from falling. *Oh, God. Blue cholera? The Asian sort.* Before she could right herself, he was there, his arms around her, lifting. Resisting did not even occur to her.

When he had placed her on the brocade settee, he knelt before her, his hands still on her arms. ''Emily, believe me, I am so dreadfully sorry this has happened. Please forgive my bluntness in the telling. I knew no easy way to say it.''

She brushed a shaking hand over her eyes, then clamped her palm against her mouth and swallowed hard when sickness threatened.

"Breathe deeply," he suggested. "Lie back." Not waiting for her to comply, he pushed her into a reclining position, her head resting uncomfortably against the high, padded curve of the couch arm.

She watched as he rose and hurried to the sideboard. A moment later he returned with a snifter and put it to her lips. "Sip this. It will help," he promised.

Consuming spirits suddenly dropped far down on her list of things to avoid. She grasped the glass and swallowed deeply. The coughing fit almost undid her. Tears rolled down her face unchecked. "Will...will Josh die?" she rasped when she was able to speak.

"No, no, of course he won't die," Nicholas assured her, all sympathy now. "I promise you, he won't. He has been improving every day since we came ashore. In fact, he is keeping his liquids down and the fever is almost gone."

She grabbed his arm with both hands. "Nick, he must have a doctor. Please—"

He smoothed the hair back from her forehead. "He has the best. Dr. Evans is quite accomplished."

Emily sniffed, trying to think properly. "I have never heard of him."

"He is the ship's doctor, who has sailed with Captain Roland for years. I trust him implicitly."

"But *cholera*, Nicholas?" Emily whispered. "I can scarcely believe it."

"It has been epidemic here before," he reminded her. "No one is safe from it."

"Mostly in London and the crowded cities. Not anywhere near Bournesea."

"No, but it does exist now in Lisbon, where we docked on the way home. Apparently, that's where they contracted it."

"In a faraway port?" she asked, her voice breaking.

"Yes, Portugal. There has been no rampant outbreak here in England recently, and this is what I am trying to avoid. Firsthand, I witnessed the devastation it caused in India. So, you see why I cannot allow you and Josh to leave. By coming here, being with your brother, you have exposed yourself to it," he said gently. "Also, I am allowing no possibility that rumors of it will spread and cause panic."

"But Father—"

"Shall be told, of course, when he comes looking for you. Unfortunately, I dare not send anyone out to inform him. When he comes to the gates, I shall speak with him myself from a safe distance. I know I can trust him not to reveal anything."

"He is not well himself," Emily said, "I can only imagine how upset he will be when I do not return home in time for supper. I neglected to tell him where I was going."

Nicholas sighed and sat back on his heels, holding one of her hands. When had he taken it up and why had she not noticed when he did? She should pull away, but she needed comfort from any source available. Even he would do at the moment.

"Does the vicar have someone to do for him in your absence?" he asked.

Emily nodded, still so shocked by what he had told her, she could not gather her wits. Concentrating on something as mundane as the vicar's supper seemed somehow inconsequential. Wrong.

Nick patted her hand. "I shall have my mother's room prepared. She would approve your presence there, I think," he said with a comforting smile.

Here was the Nick she remembered, Emily thought

with relief. At least she knew he still existed inside this sun-kissed, muscled, unkempt rogue who scared her. She tightened her fingers and clasped his hand, holding fast to the only solace she could find.

Josh would be well soon. He had to recover. "What if I sicken from this, Nick? There will be no one to care for my father and Josh. I cannot *afford* to die!"

He tried to soothe her. "Isn't there someone who cooks for you at home? What of Mrs. Pease who used to do that?"

"She is still with us. I only meant that there must be someone to pay for her services once Father retires, which must be soon. And Josh will have to be schooled somehow."

"Ah," he said, taking her meaning. "You need not worry about that. Even if the worst happens and both of us succumb to the sickness, you may rest assured that your family will lack for nothing in the future."

"What do you mean?"

He smiled, the old sweet smile that had convinced her that he loved her all those years ago. But his smile had not signified it then, and she must not mistake the meaning of it now.

"The instant I made a profit in trade that did not apply to my father's business, I placed you in my will, Emily. So, as your next of kin, your family would inherit what I would leave to you."

"Why?" she demanded. "Why on earth would you do such a thing? Guilt?"

Certainly, it was guilt, she reminded herself. *Only* guilt. He had all but seduced a young girl with pretty words, gifts and kisses, then left her the very next day without any explanation, and had stayed away. He had never had any intention of returning to her. A pity it had taken her years to realize that fact. He was no man at all if he felt no remorse for the pain he had caused her.

"Guilt, of course," he admitted curtly. He released her hand and got to his feet. The stranger who called himself Nicholas was back. "If you are recovered enough that I may leave you alone, I will go and see to your accommodations. Please remain in this room. We are keeping everyone as isolated as is humanly possible." He snapped a perfunctory bow, turned on his heel and left the room.

Emily sat up, leaned forward and hugged herself, trying to dispel some of the horror she was feeling. A thousand questions occurred to her the instant he was gone. What were the symptoms? How long did it last? How many recovered? She looked around her. Books. There would be answers here somewhere.

Quickly she scrambled off the settee and began examining the titles. She picked a *Materia Medica* off a shelf at eye level. There was a paper inserted, already marking the section referring to the cholera. Nicholas's doing, she knew. He would have had the same thought as she.

Emily carried the tome back to where she had been sitting, opened it and began to read. There was precious little to learn there, however. Speculation, mostly. Remedies that worked for one, killed another. The cause of the disease's spontaneous occurrence, or how it traveled one to another remained mysteries only guessed at by the learned minds who should have the answers and cures.

Moments later, Nicholas returned. "I see you are using the time productively. Ever resourceful, aren't you?"

She turned a page as she looked up at him. "How long has Josh been affected?"

"Two days out of port after we left Portugal, he came

down with fever and began to behave strangely. Two others were similarly affected, all of their complaints consistent with the cholera. Josh and the two men did go ashore together and must have contracted it somewhere there in the city.''

Emily felt the need to strike. ''You allowed a young boy to carouse in a foreign port with two sailors? What sort of shipping enterprise do you conduct, sir?''

He raised a brow and glared at her. ''One of those *sailors* is the captain, Emily. A man whom you know and respect. I was not aboard at the time. Captain Roland had business in the city and did not think it wise to leave a *young boy* alone on the ship without proper supervision, so he kindly took him along.''

''Oh,'' Emily said, biting her bottom lip. ''The captain has it, too?''

''Unfortunately, but I had sailed enough to chart the course for home, so we headed here. I felt they could not be treated properly at sea.'' He went on, dismissing her contrition. ''I had the three, including Joshua, confined to the largest cabin. Our doctor volunteered to tend them and remain apart from the rest of the crew. We came ashore and directly here after dark three nights ago. There have been no further cases among us, so we are hopeful it has been contained.''

''What of your staff here?'' she asked, wondering why no word of this had circulated within the village.

''I arrived alone and spoke from a distance with the gatekeeper. I simply told him that he and the others were to vacate Bournesea within the hour and hasten to the London house and remain there.''

''And they left? Just like that?''

''They went directly as I commanded. They might be

curious, but they would never question my order or disobey me. Father trained them well in that respect.''

Emily nodded, too disturbed over the issue of the sickness to comment upon the old earl's iron hand with servants. ''The doctor has not sickened from his contact with the men and Joshua?''

''No, and he assures me all three are in various stages of recovery. They are incredibly lucky. Few survive it and many die within hours.''

She heaved a sigh of relief. ''I know. I've heard.''

''No one understands how it is carried from person to person,'' Nicholas replied in a guarded tone, ''but none of us have had close contact with anyone outside the crew since they sickened. I figure another fortnight should tell the tale. If by that time, everyone remains well, we may go about our business and count ourselves extremely fortunate to have been spared.''

''Fortunate indeed,'' Emily replied thoughtfully. She laid the book aside and stood. ''I will see to Josh myself.''

''No!'' he exclaimed, blocking the door as if she were planning a sudden escape. Which she supposed she was, if the truth be known. He visibly forced himself to relax and held out his hands in entreaty. ''Emily, you must give it two days. I beg you. I promise if Josh continues to improve as he has thus far, you may see him then. Your contact with him was brief today. Let's not tempt fate with another visit.''

She understood that Nicholas had her best interest at heart. At least in this matter. ''I suppose you are leaving me no choice.''

''None, I regret to say. And I am also sorry to refuse your request to leave. But a mere two weeks of idleness should do you no harm.''

"Little do you know," she muttered.

"What? What am I asking you to abandon that is so crucial? Tea with the local ladies? Walking out with some local dandy?"

Anger suffused her. She absolutely shook with it. "How *dare* you judge my days of no account, you stupid man! This enforced confinement will cost me my employment so that my father must work on in your employ for who knows how much longer!" She flung herself down upon the settee and dashed the heavy book to the floor. "And there is no *suitor,* thanks to you!"

He smiled, damn his eyes. "No suitor? I'm glad of it, but how did that come to be my fault? I heard that you had one and were about to wed."

"Well, you were sadly misinformed." She stuck out her chin and pinned him with a glare. "After you, sir, I was put off men altogether." Let him find humor in that, she thought with an angry huff.

Her words effectively killed his smile. "This employment you mentioned," he said, deliberately switching topics. "Is it something in the village? Dressmaking or the like? You plied a magic needle, as I recall."

She ducked her head, wishing she had not brought up the matter at all. "Governess," she muttered, then chastised herself for her hesitation. Why should she have any qualms about making him uncomfortable? He certainly hadn't minded her discomfort in times past.

His expression grew sad. "Oh, Emily…"

Disappointed, was he? Because she would be trapped in that strata between well-born and servant and accepted by neither? She knew well what she could look forward to, and thought it small price to pay for what she would gain.

Her only goal in life at this point was to secure an

income so that she could support her family. Father would not last much longer if he continued working so hard. And Josh should be at school instead of racketing around the world on a boat. Now her plans were dashed.

Emily raised her chin and elaborated. "I was to travel to London the day after tomorrow and assume my duties immediately. That was the condition of my employment. Now Lord Vintley will accept someone in my stead."

"Vintley?" he asked with a dreadful frown. "That's just as well, then. He used to visit the Worthings, where I met him and was not favorably impressed."

Emily pinched her lips together. But they would not hold back the words. "Lord Worthing's daughter recommended me. I am certain she will be greatly disappointed to hear I have lost the *opportunity* she afforded."

"Dierdre," he said with deadly calm.

"Just so. Your intended."

"She is not my intended."

"Your father thought differently. He told me that you had been betrothed to her for two years before you went away."

"That is not true. A marriage with Dierdre was his wish for me, never my own."

"So you say." Emily regarded him closely to see whether she could detect a lie. Either his father had been lying through his teeth, or Nick was now. She was disposed to believe Nick, of course, but the knowledge of how he had dashed her trust once before made her cautious.

He propped his hips against the edge of the desk and crossed his arms over his chest. "Since you never liked Dierdre, why, may I ask, would you even consider such employment if you thought it would please her?"

"Remuneration, my lord," Emily answered readily.

"And I did write and thank her for mentioning me. The salary is twice what I could expect anywhere else." For two hundred pounds per year, Emily felt she could endure almost anything. Even Dierdre Worthing's satisfaction.

It was an offer Emily could not afford to lose. The income from it would probably save her father's life if he could retire before his heart gave out completely. And would definitely ensure that Josh received a proper education.

"Even if your father must give up the living here at Bournesea, Emily, you need not work," Nicholas said kindly. Condescendingly, if she were honest in her appraisal. He might as well pat her on the head while he said it. "You have but to tell me what you need and I will gladly supply it. Surely you have always known you could come to me for anything."

Emily pursed her lips and nodded, holding his gaze with her own. "Ah, I see. Add your monthly stipend to the rumors that circulated about our affair and we would have a full-blown public arrangement, is that what you wish? Well, I have worked hard to dispel those rumors, Lord Kendale, and I do not intend to resurrect or augment them in any way whatsoever. Do I make myself clear?"

"We had no *affair!*" he exclaimed, disturbed that she would even call it that. "This is preposterous. I am merely offering aid to a cherished friend and you know it!"

"A *cherished* friend you embraced and kissed upon the lips whilst standing in the midst of the village commons for all the world to see. I was very nearly ruined by that, I'll have you know."

Instantly, he seemed ill-at-ease. Emily wanted him to be. She wanted him on his knees begging her forgiveness.

She wanted his arms around her, pleading for a chance to make things right. She wanted to scratch his eyes out.

"Emily, listen—"

Instead of affording him any chance to explain the inexplicable, she interrupted. "Is the chamber ready where you would have me stay?"

He sighed and shook his head. But the gesture obviously did not agree with his answer. "Yes, the room should be aired by now," he admitted.

"Then, under the circumstances, I suppose manners force me to thank you for your hospitality," Emily said.

"I am compelled by the same to assure you that you are quite welcome. Use the bellpull if you need anything. There are no maids about to dance attendance, but someone eventually will come to bring whatever is lacking."

She swept past him as regally as she could manage and left the library. *Whatever was lacking,* he had said. That was just about everything she could think of, but certainly nothing a tug on a bellpull would provide.

Chapter Two

Nick had known she was not married, of course. His subtle questioning of her brother Joshua aboard ship had relieved that worry before they had begun the voyage home.

The earl had written six years ago that Emily and the pockmarked postmaster were about to be wed. Nick had stayed drunk for an entire week, then vowed with all sincerity to forget the vicar's daughter and her faithless ways.

His father had lied, of course. But Emily had not answered Nick's subsequent letter wishing her well. Obviously she had wanted him to believe that she was settling into a marriage with Jeremy Oldfield.

Nick knew nothing good about the postmaster, who had been a self-righteous bore and a bully in their younger days. Those traits frequently grew worse with age and Nick had worried about Emily because of that. However, his relief in discovering she was unattached was now marred by what she had just declared about his ruining her chances for a happy life. He had never once considered that.

Perhaps she had overdramatized the case because his

leaving had made her angry. Emily always had possessed a talent for exaggeration. That quality, too, might have increased with age.

As for aging, either Emily had changed or his memory was faulty and his dreams had ceased to do her justice. The years had enhanced rather than dimmed her beauty. Blond flyaway curls framed a lovely heart-shaped face that had grown even more exquisite without its girlish roundness.

Her figure looked fuller, more womanly. To be expected, of course, that she would mature and surpass the prettiness he remembered.

And her mouth, so expressive in both joy and anger, stirred him still. He had almost given in to the urge to plunder it as he had done so eagerly that one time. But at the last moment he had refrained from doing so. She obviously wouldn't thank him for it now.

Her eyes were the same clear and guileless blue, framed by softly curling lashes. However, the absolute trust and adoration he had seen in them once had vanished completely over the years. The absence of that hurt more than he would have believed.

In truth, it made him soul sick. If what she said was true, his attraction to her might have ruined her life. If only he had been more circumspect, less thoughtless, but at twenty-two he had not fully realized the impact his interest in her would have on her future.

Now, taking what she had said into consideration, he could see how none of the men in the county would dare trespass on property the earl's son had publicly claimed and therefore declared off-limits. And that is exactly what he had done with that kiss.

The very next day, on the earl's orders and under determined escort, a furiously struggling Nicholas had been set aboard a packet for India to commence learning the vagaries of trade as his father's representative.

Apparently his son engaging in business seemed far less demeaning to Earl Kendale than having him inappropriately engaged with a village girl.

The old man's warning, issued not an hour before the ship sailed, still rang in his ears. "If you return and insist upon continuing your suit of this little adventuress, I shall ruin her entire family. Loveyne will find himself and his two brats upon the road without a quid among them and with nowhere to go."

A horrifying prospect for anyone.

His father had continued. "She's a fair-looking bit of fluff, Nicholas, but not for you. Not even as a playfellow. As long as you stay away, she will be safe."

Nick had objected vehemently even as he realized he had no choice but to do as instructed. The earl's threat had been clear and concise.

His father had laughed. "You'll be set free as soon as the ship's well under way. When you are, you keep my bargain in mind, my boy. Picture our eccentric, good-hearted Vicar Loveyne destroyed by the dismissal. He knows nothing else but tending his little flock, now does he? Even if he does, I'll see him turned off by anyone who hires him. And the girl, Emily? That little baggage can take to the streets."

The earl leaned nearer as if to impart a secret. "Trust me, I'll see to it that she does. And that skinny brother of hers looks just the right size for sweeping chimneys. How old is he now, five or six?"

Nick had known from experience that his father never bluffed nor made idle threats. The Earl of Kendale had possessed the power, the means and the motive to destroy the entire Loveyne family and he would have done so without a qualm.

Though his father had never applied cruelty just for the enjoyment of it, he certainly never blinked at crushing anyone or anything that did not suit him.

Nicholas had his orders. He was to learn shipping from his father's factors in India, see a bit of the world, then come home and wed appropriately. Wed Lady Dierdre Worthing. His father had left him no choice about the first commands, but against that last, Nick had rebelled. He had stayed away from Bournesea and had never seen the earl, nor replied to his correspondence since that day.

Apparently his father had solidified plans for the marriage during his absence, Nicholas recalled with a frown. On arriving home three days ago he had found the contract stating the terms of Nick's betrothal to Dierdre Worthing.

His own name had been forged below Dierdre's. Nicholas was assuming *her* signature was genuine. For all he knew, she could be as oblivious to the entire matter as he had been. He had not heard a word from her in all this time.

Maybe she was already wed. Heartening thought, but unlikely. Unless she'd become betrothed and married within the past few months, he would have read of it in the newspapers shipped regularly from London.

His father had risked a scandal with the forgery, obviously counting heavily on Nick's unwillingness to reveal the deception once he discovered it.

He wished he could attribute his father's dishonest meddling to love and concern for an only son, but Nick knew it was borne of a need to master everyone and everything.

If Emily had shown any interest at all today in resum-

ing what had been begun between them with that kiss
seven years ago, Nicholas would have been perfectly
willing to pursue it. But she had not. Quite the contrary.

For Emily, their former attachment, innocent as it had
been, had proved disastrous. She must hate him. Because
of his interest in her, she was not married and probably
never would be. She had declared quite fixedly she was
through with men altogether because of him. He knew
Emily's determination once she made up her mind.

But Emily, a governess? He shook his head. Vintley
was no saint. Nicholas remembered him well, and
doubted the lecher would treat her with the respect she
deserved. The very thought of her assuming such an unguarded position was unacceptable and that was all there
was to it.

Emily had made her decision, however, and Nicholas
knew he would never be able to sway her on the matter
of taking any financial assistance from him to prevent her
working. He had to admire her for refusing his offer of
support, even while it angered him that she did so.

Even an offer to renew the close friendship they once
enjoyed, she would view as suspect. And probably would
fling something at his head for good measure if he persisted. He would, anyway, of course. How could he do
less? He'd missed her terribly.

He smiled wryly at the thought of her temper. For a
girl reared as a vicar's daughter, Emily did possess a fiery
spirit plus impulsive and headstrong ways. That had
drawn him to her like a lodestone. He had always admired her fiercely independent nature, her zeal, her ready
laughter and lack of artifice. She never did a thing by
half measure, his Emily.

Not *his* Emily, he reminded himself with a heartfelt
sigh. And she never would be. That chance was gone,

destroyed by old Kendale's malice and Nicholas's fear for her future. Perhaps it was just as well, for Emily's sake, since he had fully intended to marry her at the time. Ah, the vagaries of that youthful passion.

Now, however, he could not envision her in the company of those he would find it necessary to socialize with in London when he took his father's place in the House of Lords. No, such a structured and demanding life would have made her miserable.

He considered Dierdre Worthing. She had often indicated that she felt some attraction to him, Nicholas reflected. As he recalled, she had been an accomplished flirt. Of course, she'd been quite young at the time and he had never taken her seriously.

Emily was younger. Nick shook off the thought.

As the daughter of a baron who was very wealthy and influential, Dierdre would have the training required to fulfill the role of a countess.

All he need do was accept the betrothal and refrain from exposing his father's forging of the document. If he did not, then explaining everything to Worthing would be awkward, to say the least. And Dierdre, if she knew about it, would be hurt to think he did not want her and never had. She might have been waiting these seven long years for him to return and marry her, with her father and his assuring her that she and Nicholas truly were betrothed.

Maybe he should go through with the marriage. There really was no point in thwarting the old man's wishes and causing a scandal just for the sake of revenge. That would be childish and unproductive.

Nick was fast approaching thirty and must begin to think of marrying and producing an heir. What difference did it make whom he married as long as she liked him reasonably well, was of suitable birth and could bear him the requisite son?

His only goal in life now was to undo the wrongs his father had wreaked on others. Nick wanted to gain the respect of his peers for himself and the title. As earl, he meant to do his duty as he understood it, not to follow his father's self-serving example. He would live with honor.

But would it be honorable to marry Dierdre when he felt absolutely nothing for her? Not even a special liking? He had outgrown his belief in love, of course, but lust was a fact. So was admiration and the need to protect. Unfortunately, he did not feel any of those things for Dierdre Worthing.

He could scarcely recall what she looked like. Yet he had never forgotten Emily's face. Her sweet, trusting face turned up to his for that kiss that had changed both their lives for the worse when his father had heard of it. Nick knew very well that he still entertained feelings for Emily.

"No," he muttered to himself, shaking his head, glaring at the drawer in which the false document lay waiting for its implementation. "I cannot wed Dierdre."

But something had to be done about the document. He needed to straighten out the matter with Worthing as soon as possible.

Even more imperative to his peace of mind, Nick knew he had to do something to gain Emily's forgiveness for the problems he had caused her. Perhaps if he explained face-to-face why he had left as he had, and then stayed away. Would she believe him then? She had obviously doubted his written words.

The door opened and Nick looked up. Wrecker grinned at him. "She's a goer, that'un, ain't she?"

"Mind your tongue," Nick warned him. "Leave it hanging out like that and you're likely to lose it."

"Beg pardon, m'lord." His gap-toothed grin grew wider. "Y'know, she woulda made straight for th' lad again just now?" He poked his beefy chest with his thumb. "I stopped her. She were stompin' all the way up the stair, mad enough to curse if she knew how."

Nicholas stood and rounded the desk. "I'll go up and see to her."

Wrecker laughed slyly. "Aye, m'lord. I would do just that if I was you."

Clearly the man knew Emily was forbidden game for himself and the rest of the men. But it was also quite apparent that he thought Nicholas intended to take advantage of her unchaperoned presence.

"The lady is my guest while we wait out the quarantine," he explained. "She is the vicar's daughter, Joshua's sister, and a dear friend of mine. One hint of an insult to her or behind her back, and the perpetrator shall answer to me. And I shall not be kind. Is that understood?"

Wrecker shrugged, still smiling. "Aye, m'lord, I understand. We all do."

It was no use. Through fear, he could control what they said, but the men would think whatever they would. There was no alternative to keeping Emily here, however, despite the harm to her reputation. If he released her and she fell ill, the sickness could spread.

He promised himself he would only go to her room this once, just to reassure her again about Joshua's welfare. Then he would leave her alone. The less he saw of her, the fewer rumors would fly when this was over. But some would fly, he thought with resignation.

* * *

Emily tore off her shawl and bonnet in pure frustration and flopped down upon the bed.

The lavish appointments within the countess's chamber did not surprise her. She had been here before, long ago, and nothing much had changed. The rich, rose fabric of the bed hangings and the draperies had faded a bit, the ornate walnut furniture could use a good dusting, but the room was essentially the same as when she had visited here at her father's side. How privileged and grown up she had felt at the time, being allowed inside. Now, of course, she realized she had lent propriety to the vicar's visit to Nicholas's invalid mother.

The room felt at once both comforting and discomforting. It provided a familiar haven, yet emphasized the vast gulf between her station and that of a noble lady.

What a fool she had been to think Nicholas would ever have chosen such as her to wed. To his credit, he had actually never mentioned marriage. But he had made her believe that he loved her. She'd had to guess what he had in mind then, and to her dismay, she had wrongly assumed that his intentions were honorable.

The present indignity was not to be borne, she thought with a forceful groan. That hulk of a seaman who accosted her just now and prevented her going to Joshua, had all but accused her of coming here for the worst purpose imaginable.

"See to his lordship if ye must heal summat," he had said suggestively. "Poor sod could do wif a bit o' sympathy, *hard* as it's been for 'im."

Emily would have dearly liked to slap that silly grin off his whiskered face if she could have reached it. The wretched giant.

Before the sun set this evening, the entire population

of Bournesea would believe Nicholas was keeping her here for immoral reasons.

Was he? Had Nicholas considered it? Did that rough-looking man who had stopped her from seeing Josh know something that she did not?

No, she didn't really believe Nick would deliberately ruin her. Though he had very nearly done exactly that before he'd left for India, he had been scarcely more than a boy at the time. And half the fault of it had been hers since she had not in any way discouraged him from kissing her.

To be perfectly honest, she continued to treasure the memory of that passionate kiss in the deepest, most secret part of her. Wicked of her, she knew, but it was all she had of him or would ever have. She had loved him with all her heart.

A good thing she had replaced those feelings with dislike. Not hate, however. No matter how hard she tried or how much she wanted to, she could never bring herself to hate Nicholas.

Blaming him for the results of the kiss might be highly unfair, but it had helped her get over the fact that he had not loved her. And now it would serve to keep a chasm between them that sorely needed to be there.

If she were honest, she had to allow that he could do little else in this instance but force her to stay at Bournesea. Given a choice, she supposed she would have recommended the quarantine herself.

She couldn't leave poor Joshua here to mend on his own. Nor would she dare risk carrying the cholera outside these walls. Still, she hated being put in this dreadful position.

The soft knock on the door surprised her. She scram-

bled up from the bed and quickly brushed her hands over
her hair. "Yes, who is it?"

Instead of a verbal answer, the door opened.

"Nick—I mean, *my lord?*" she gasped. "What are
you doing? It is highly improper for you to be here!"

He had not bothered donning a coat for the visit. Em-
ploying all her will, she directed her gaze away from his
exposed neck and muscular forearms.

He hesitated a moment, then stepped into the room,
softly closing the door behind him. "I have told you that
you are not allowed in the men's quarters, Emily, yet you
would have gone straight to Joshua only moments after
I said that. Have you no care for your health?"

"I needed to see him," she argued. "And you did say
he was nearly well."

"Nearly, but still prone to the occasional bout of fever
and other symptoms," he explained. "I hope it will not
be necessary to lock you in this chamber to prevent your
disobeying my orders."

She gaped at him in disbelief. "You would not dare!"

His determined expression left no doubt in her mind
that he would.

"Very well, I shall wait to visit him, but not for long,"
she conceded reluctantly, turning away and peering out
the window to keep from looking at Nicholas. The very
sight of him stirred emotions she had believed well conquered years ago.

She jumped when his strong hands clasped her shoulders. Hands she remembered all too well. Hands that had
caressed her face, threaded through her hair, held her
close against him, fingers flexing, tempting, making her
wish...

"I promise on my honor that Josh will be hale in no
time. Have I ever lied to you?"

With that question, fury suffused her body and she whirled on him, breaking his hold on her shoulders. She shoved against his chest with both hands. "Yes!" she hissed. "Yes, Nicholas, you *have* lied, by deeds if not words! How do I know you are not lying now? How could I ever trust you to care for my little brother when you had no thought to care for me?"

"I never lied to you. I regret that you cannot forgive me for leaving the way I did," he said curtly, "but I tell you again, I was left with no choice. And once I was gone, it was necessary that I stay away. For both our sakes."

Emily took a deep breath, her lips firmly closed on the words she would have spat in anger. Necessary, he said. Necessary, because he had always been betrothed to another woman, long before he had kissed Emily. Necessary, because he feared she would expect more than he could have righteously offered. Necessary, because he did not and never had loved her.

He stepped closer and touched her face. In horror and fascination, she watched his mouth lower to hers. Only at the last moment, did he place the kiss upon her cheek instead of her trembling lips.

Oh, sweet heaven, the gentleness, the heat of that mouth. It had been so long since he had touched her, held her. His tantalizing scent clouded her mind and his breath warmed her face. Fire rushed through her veins, obliterating all caution. He had not changed. She had not.

"My dearest Emily," he whispered, breaking the spell he'd woven as effectively as if he had doused her with a bucket of icy water.

She shoved him away. "*Dearest,* is it? Get out of this room, Nicholas. Do it *now!*"

He had the audacity to look surprised. "What the devil is wrong with you, Em? I only meant to—"

"I know *exactly* what you meant to do!" She backed away, her arms crossed over her chest, wishing they could shield her heart. The foolish thing had barely begun to mend from the last time he broke it.

Though he turned to go, he faced her again when he stood in the doorway. "You have no cause to fear me, Emily. I would never do anything to cause you further pain."

She remained silent, far from certain she believed him, and unwilling to lie about it. Though Nick's intention would never be to inflict any deliberate hurt upon her, Emily knew he could do so without even trying, maybe without even knowing.

He searched her eyes for her answer and seemed to find it there. "I did care for you then, Emily. And whether you can accept the truth or not, I still do."

There was little she could say to that. He might still desire her. But hunger was a common thing for a man to feel toward any female. Even if Nick did not recognize the difference, she now knew better than to confuse desire with true caring. At least he said nothing of loving her.

Without further words, he went out of the room and gently closed the door. She heard his measured footsteps on the stairs and felt as bereft as she always did when deprived of his company. That had not altered at all, unless she counted the fact that the deprivation cut even more deeply now.

With Nicholas residing continents away, it had been somehow easier to accept that he did not love her. How was she supposed to bear it when they were living under the same roof?

No matter how much she wished it, there seemed no way out of this conundrum. Though she wanted nothing more than to sneak back out the gardener's gate with her brother and double her efforts to forget Nicholas Hollander, she knew that she and Joshua had no recourse but to remain here until the quarantine was over.

Emily straightened her shoulders and took a deep breath. "Running is the coward's way," she muttered vehemently to herself, pounding one fist soundly into the opposite palm. "And you, Emily Loveyne, have never resorted to such behavior in your life. Where is your courage?"

She had overcome the snide remarks and polite censure of the whole village of Bournesea, as well as that of the old Lord Kendale, when she was hardly more than a girl out of short skirts. Never once had she doubted her eventual success in that endeavor.

Now she was a woman with the blinders of first love torn away and a much better understanding of people in general. Of *men,* in particular. Clearly, she could stand what she must and weather this storm, as well.

There was certain to be one, she realized. No one in the entire county would ever believe she had spent a whole fortnight in this manor with the man she once adored without surrendering to his charms.

It would likely take her more than seven years this time to convince them of her innocence.

Emily used the bellpull, after all. During the hours alone in the countess's old chamber with nothing to read but a well-thumbed book of poetry, she grew desperately bored.

One could only dwell so long on the ramblings of Byron. Was this what Nicholas's mother had endured day after day? Lying abed, pondering the rather pointless meanderings of a dissolute poet? Small wonder she always seemed so glad to greet the vicar and his tagalong.

Emily recalled the occasions she had come here with her father while the countess was alive. Lady Elizabeth's dark beauty had always left Emily awestruck, as had the woman's unguarded opinions expressed so openly to a man of God. Many of Emily's own views of life were colored by that ready candor.

She had also noted that when her father led them in the requisite parting prayer for improvement of the lady's health, the countess neither bowed her head nor closed her eyes. Once she had even winked and smiled at Emily who had been sneaking a look up at her.

Though they had rarely spoken to one another, the motherless Emily had imagined a bond between them.

"Well, here I am again, my lady," Emily said aloud to the room where the countess had breathed her last. "Best lend me some of that wry humor of yours. I feel I might need it when this little visit with your esteemed son is over."

Byron's little book, lying forgotten on the edge of the mattress suddenly slid off and hit the floor with a thump. A chill ran up Emily's spine. "Thank you, that is quite enough to set me laughing," she muttered. "Keep your humor to yourself now."

Lord, here she was imagining ghosts and talking to the dearly departed. If half a day in this place had her speaking to the walls, she could only imagine how she would be faring after two interminable weeks of it.

Unlike some women who said they could not touch a bite of food when in distress, Emily craved chocolate. At the moment she would have wrestled someone to the floor for a cup of the stuff. And cakes to go with it.

It had grown dark outside. For the third time in less than an hour, she gave the intricately braided cord a firm yank, imagining a bell jangling somewhere below. With all of the servants gone to London, she doubted there would be anyone there to hear it. She could not imagine any of the ship's crew hanging about in the butler's pantry.

Though Emily had been fairly well acquainted with the kitchen and service areas of the house at one time, she was not inclined to venture down the stairs and make herself at home there now.

Still fully dressed except for her boots, she curled up on the wide feather bed and drew the coverlet over her. If eventually, someone did answer her summons, she would request her sweets, a stack of books from his lordship's library and a bucket of coal to fuel the small fireplace. It was mid-May, and the evening had brought a chill with it.

A loud knock woke her from a sound sleep. Emily jerked upright and brushed her tousled curls out of her eyes. "Yes? Who is it?"

The door opened. "Emily? I'm afraid the captain took a turn for the worse last evening and I quite forgot to send anyone with your dinner." Nicholas balanced a silver tray on one arm as he approached.

Carefully, but hurriedly, he set it upon the mattress beside her hip and gestured to the room at large. "I also neglected to offer you the use of Mother's things. Please avail yourself of the clothing, writing materials, and anything else you find that you can use."

"Thank you, my lord."

"By the way, your brother is feeling quite the thing today." He began to back toward the door.

"Wait," she said, reaching out, almost upsetting the teapot. "Don't go yet! Tell me more of Joshua, please?"

He stopped where he was. "He is fine, the doctor says. No fever at all last night or this morning. And his appetite seems quite normal."

"I cannot tell you how that relieves my mind." Emily sighed. "Could I trouble you for something to read today? And perhaps some coal?"

"Certainly, anything you wish."

He smiled then and seemed to deliberately shake off whatever had caused his abruptness. "Look, I know this waiting is damned hard for you, Emily. What if I make a compromise and allow you to see Josh for a few moments? Just from the doorway to his room, you understand. Would that help?"

Emily burst into tears, covering her face with her hands.

"No, no weeping, please," he said softly, approaching the bed again. "Hear now, if you hush, I will let you visit him directly after supper."

"Truly?"

"Yes, truly." His hand lightly caressed her hair and rested on the back of her neck. "Shall I take Josh a message from you this morning?"

She nodded vigorously and sniffed. "Tell—tell him I cannot wait to see him again. That I love him so. And that Father and I missed him dreadfully."

Nicholas pushed the tray aside and edged one hip onto the bed, beside her. He pulled her close so that her bowed head rested against his chest while his long fingers brushed over her curls.

"I have a feeling all will be well," he told her. "You know, even after that small setback last evening, Captain Roland feels much better this morning than he has at all since coming down with this? And George Tuckwell, the purser, is nearly as well recovered as Josh.''

"No one else has had complaints?" she asked, looking up at him.

He wiped the tears from her cheeks with one finger. "Not a soul. I have had each man report the state of his health to me three times daily. Other than the occasional gripe of being landlocked, not a one has suffered so much as a bellyache. I believe we have almost weathered this.''

She didn't dare to hope, but she asked anyway. "Will you still insist upon our remaining enclosed here for the entire fortnight?''

"I must, Emily, for safety's sake. Please understand.''

Oh, how she wished they could remain as they were. How marvelous to feel his strong arms around her, his hands cradling her back, her shoulders, threading through her hair. She inhaled deeply, drawing in the scent of him, wanting more...

Carefully, he disengaged himself from her and stood again, replacing the tray so that she could reach it. "Breakfast now, and you may go below. The library is yours for the day. I shall work elsewhere.''

Emily felt dizzy, light as air, as if a huge lead weight had been removed from her shoulders. Surely he did care, at least a little. "Is there anything I may do to help out...my lord?''

He cocked a brow and pursed his lips. "For one thing, you might cease the *my lord* foolishness and call me Nick as you always have done.''

She smiled and busied herself pouring her chocolate. "I should have used your honorary address all these years, but no one saw fit to correct me. Except your father. He was appalled that I should speak of you at all.''

"You talked with Father? When was that? He rarely spoke to *me,* let alone any other child about the place."

She stirred the chocolate and took a heavenly sip, then another before she replied, "Oh, I was no longer a child when he and I had our first and last conversation. He considered me a full-grown Jezebel, ripe for a set-down."

"The bloody old bastard!" Nicholas's sharp intake of breath surprised her, as did the epithet. "I hate that he spoke rudely to you, Em."

"Yes, well, he minced no words." She waved off his concern. "But that's over and done and of no consequence. You have enough to worry about. Go and see Joshua, if you will. Tell him I shall expect a detailed travelogue, so he is to be arranging it all in his mind for the telling. That should occupy him for the day and relieve his boredom."

"A wonderful idea. How wise of you," he remarked.

"My wisdom knows no bounds. Nor my humility. For your information, age has improved me considerably." She daintily set down her cup, shooting him a look that challenged him to disagree.

Nicholas shook his head and laughed. "You have not changed at all, Emily."

She watched him go.

"How wrong you are, Nicky. How woefully wrong you are about that."

Without so much as a jiggle of the tray, the serviette that was perched upright beside her plate tumbled itself over and unfolded.

Emily caught her breath, then exhaled sharply. "Well, it is *true,*" she announced to the spirit she fancied lurking about her. "I am no longer that docile child I was then."

Emily imagined she heard a trill of muted feminine laughter. This time she was not frightened at all for it seemed to ring with distinct approval. And besides that, a properly bred vicar's daughter did not credit the existence of ghosts.

To prove it to herself, Emily wolfed down the remainder of her breakfast, shucked off her wrinkled dress and went directly to the countess's armoire. There she selected an out-of-date morning gown of sky-blue chintz trimmed with delicate white embroidery. On a shelf at the bottom, she located matching kid slippers.

"You see?" she muttered as she dressed. "If I feared you were hanging about to object, I would not dare appropriate anything belonging to a Kendale. Not the dress," she declared, yanking it off the hanger and threading her arms through the sleeves. "Or the shoes," she added, sliding her feet into the slippers.

Or the son? The teasing whisper of thought piqued Emily's mind like a dare.

"Oh, no, ma'am. *That* never occurred to me. Not this time," she said with a roll of her eyes and a short laugh at the fanciful turn of mind boredom had inflicted. "Believe me, I have learned my lesson there."

Chapter Three

The day had crawled by like a fly through molasses, Emily thought as she thumped down yet another tome of dreadful prose. Her patience with the printed word was scant at best, and pared even thinner by the scarcity of anything interesting in the earl's library.

She jumped when the enormous ormolu clock struck the first chime of seven. Would Nicholas never send for her? Surely all the men had eaten by now.

He had promised she could see Josh after dinner. Her own meal had been delivered half an hour ago. The plain fare had little to recommend it, or else excitement had diminished her hunger so that she could scarcely taste a thing.

"Are you ready to visit?" Nick asked as he stuck his head around the door. "That brother of yours is demanding your presence."

"It's about time!" she exclaimed as she rushed to join him. "How is he this evening?"

"Doing exceptionally well, but dreadfully anxious to see you." Nicholas took her arm, more to prevent her unseemly haste than to lend escort, Emily decided. "That blue you're wearing does wonders for your eyes."

"You're very kind," she said, using her most formal tone. Determined to project her most ladylike behavior and do justice to her attire, she adopted a slower, more graceful gait that would have done the countess proud.

When they reached the hallway leading to her brother's room, however, she almost broke into a run. The door stood open and she would have dashed through it to hug him if Nicholas had not grasped her arm. "Wait. You should not approach too closely just yet," he warned. "Let's be prudent."

"Joshua, darling!" she said, so desperately happy to see him, gripping the doorjamb with one hand and Nicholas's arm with the other for support.

How tall Josh had grown these past months! Her eager gaze traveled from his beloved face to his skinny arms and then the length of his legs beneath the covers. She'd been twelve when he was born. With their mother a victim of childbed fever shortly after that, Josh's care had fallen to her. He was more like a son than a brother. And now her dear boy was nearly grown.

"Tell me how you are," she pleaded. "I would hear it from you."

"Well enough." He crossed his lanky arms over his concave chest and deepened his frown. "And I am bound to tell you, sister," he announced, his voice much deeper and more forceful than she remembered. He pinned her with a glare. "You have sealed your fate by coming here."

"No, no, my dear, you must not worry about that," she said, holding out one hand as if she was touching him, soothing him. "Lord Kendale assures me that the danger of contagion is no longer of much concern. You must not fret—"

"Contagion is not the problem I am addressing, Emily," he declared. "It is your very presence among us that will do you worse than a bout with the cholera."

"What do you mean?" she asked. "What in the world could be worse than that?"

He took a deep breath, his glare whipping to Nicholas, then back to her. "You will be damned by everyone you know if he does not marry you. Am I not correct in this, my lord?"

She heard Nicholas clear his throat. At first, she believed he would not answer Josh's impertinence, for the silence stretched on for what seemed too long. Then he sighed. "You have the right of it, Loveyne. Indeed. She has been compromised beyond help, through no fault of her own."

"Or of *yours!*" Emily exclaimed. "Nicholas, you cannot possibly be considering—"

"That marriage between us would solve matters. Joshua has a perfect right to make the demand," he said without inflection.

"But he doesn't understand," she argued. "Josh cannot possibly realize the complications such a *mésalliance* would involve."

"He is your brother, Emily," Nicholas replied as if that justified the matter of Josh's interference. "No one can force you to accept, of course, but I shall make my offer. Will you marry me?"

As proposals went, she found it sorely lacking in emotion. His expression was devoid of feeling, his voice too carefully controlled to betray a jot of either satisfaction or anger. She could in no way discern what Nicholas was really thinking about all of this. Small wonder. He was caught in a trap of her making with only one honorable way out of it unless she refused him.

She should refuse. Her heart sank in despair. On the

one hand, she would have to render useless her brother's demand and risk both his pride and his good opinion of her.

Judging by the look on Joshua's face at the moment, he would never forgive her if she spurned his effort to protect her.

On the other hand, she could agree to a marriage that was almost certain to founder upon the rocks of Nicholas's resentment and their social inequality.

He did not really love her. She had been nothing to him but a youthful indiscretion, easily discarded and all but forgotten.

His father had said that he was betrothed to Dierdre Worthing. However, Emily knew he did not love Dierdre, either, or he would have come back to England and married her long before now. Despite her apparent suitability, that one would make Nick a terrible wife, Emily thought wickedly. How tempting it was to know she could prevent that with a word.

Nicholas's strong fingers tightened on her arm. In warning or encouragement? she wondered.

"Emily, this is *not* open to argument," Joshua declared, sounding for all the world like their father in one of his rare attempts at disciplining them when they were younger. As if he had read her mind, he added, "You know very well what Father will say. You have no damned choice. None."

She gaped at him. "Joshua James Loveyne, you mind your language!"

He glared back. "Then *you* mind your reputation!"

"Here now, there's no cause to quarrel," Nicholas admonished. "Emily will do the right thing. She only needs a few moments to adjust to the idea," he said to Josh, as if she were not there.

"'A few moments?'" she snapped, yanking her arm out of Nick's grasp. "'The right thing'? Since when? It might have been the right thing seven years ago after what you did! Now, I'm not altogether certain I would have you if you went on bended knee and begged, Nicholas Hollander! Oh, excuse me, *my lord*," she said with all the sarcasm she could muster. "I should use your title, should I not? Have you thought of that at all? How do you think I would answer to *my lady?*" She threw up both hands for emphasis. "Your esteemed father vowed I would be laughed out of the country should I even aspire to become a countess!"

"My father would have said anything to drive a larger wedge between us, Emily. You know he had another bride in mind for me."

She shook with rage. "A flaming pity she so conveniently escaped *your* mind when it most counted! I should like to have known of her myself before I fell into your arms like some shameless trollop!"

"Wait! What's this?" Joshua demanded, springing upright in the bed.

Nicholas strode over to him and braced his hand on Josh's shoulder. "You stay right where you are, young man."

"Fetch your weapons, sir," Josh growled, "I demand satisfaction for my sister's honor."

Emily could have laughed at Nick's expression of dismay if she had not been so worried Josh truly would do something foolish. Nick would never allow a duel of any kind, but her brother's beet-red face and clenched jaw told her he would neither forget nor forgive until he had acquired some sort of satisfaction.

"Josh, he didn't—Nicholas did not dishonor me," she hurried to explain. "I spoke only of the kiss. You've known of that for ages. Everyone knows of it. Nothing else happened, I promise. Not ever.''

Except for Nicholas making her feel treasured, acting as if he loved her, actually saying how he would never want anyone else but her. However, she couldn't let herself dwell upon those lies at the moment or she'd be demanding the pistols herself.

''Just the kiss? You swear?'' Josh directed his question to Nick.

''On my honor, I swear,'' Nicholas replied. ''And I would have married her then if circumstances had not prevented it. I will marry her now, so there is no need for all this uproar. Do you want a relapse when you are nearly well?''

He would have married her then? What an outright lie! How dare he say such a thing? She wanted to scream at him for it, but Emily could tell Nick's patience was already thin enough to read a book through. Josh's trembling now looked more a result of exhaustion than anger.

Her brother was not up to this. Nor was she. And Nicholas ought to be more careful where he flung his half-baked proposals.

''When?'' she asked, commanding their sudden and undivided attention.

''Tomorrow,'' Josh answered without pause.

''As soon as your father comes here looking for you,'' Nick amended. ''I regret I cannot allow anyone to go and inform him and request his presence. You both know the reason. He will come tomorrow or the next day, surely, for there are too few places you could have gone other than here.''

''Very well,'' she agreed, sounding as reluctant as she felt. Once they were married, she fully intended to be a good wife to Nicholas, but she could not help regretting how the marriage was to come about.

The main problem was, she had not realized just how frightfully angry she still was with him. For several years now she'd believed she had forgiven him for the most part, and that he no longer mattered so much to her. Now that she'd seen him again, she knew that neither was true.

Pride insinuated its ugly head, as well, she thought. It galled her that he acted as if he had done nothing to ruin her life thus far and was now doing her a huge favor.

Also, she did not relish explaining the necessity of the marriage to her father. It only underlined her greatest fault, her impulsiveness. "*You* will make the explanations," she told Nicholas in no uncertain terms.

"I expected to do so," he assured her. "I will ask for you as is right and proper."

"'Right and proper,'" she repeated to herself, shook her head at the irony of it all, and turned away from the doorway to Josh's chamber. She did not even wish them good-night.

It would serve them both right if they didn't sleep a wink. She was certain she would not be able to close her eyes.

"A moment, Em," Nick called as she crossed the garden to the house. She kept walking. "Wait, I say! We need to talk about this."

"Why?" Emily asked over her shoulder. "You have my consent. What else is required?"

He caught up to her and fell in step. "Look, Em, I am sorry things have turned out as they have. I want you to know—"

"That you wish I had kept myself outside your walls," she interrupted. "I realize that. So do I, but I did not, and now we are stuck with the consequences."

"No," he protested vehemently. "That's not what I mean at all. Marriage is not such a dire fate, now is it? You have already admitted there's no other man whom you wish to wed."

"Ah, true enough," she began sagely, "but there *is* another woman who thinks she is a part of your future."

"There was never an understanding between Dierdre and myself," Nick insisted, running a hand over the back of his neck. "Certainly nothing legally binding. Even if Lord Worthing ever expected a marriage between us, he would say nothing publicly. Fear of scandal would prevent him."

"So one would hope," she said. "And what of the scandal that will affect *your* good name, my lord? A common bride gained under rather common conditions?"

Much to her surprise, he laughed. "Everyone will doubtless assume we're a love match."

"But we, of course, will know better, will we not." She did not ask it as a question, for they both knew the answer.

He reached for her hand and held on, even when she would have pulled away. "Emily, I know how you feel about me now, but marriage will be the best thing. Think, you'll not have to serve as a governess to make your way and support your father and Josh. You may have whatever you need, whatever you want. As a matter of fact, I am nearing thirty and it's past time I wed. So you see? We shall both benefit."

She could not believe what she was hearing from the very man who once oozed charm as if he owned the patent on the commodity. "Convenient, is it?" she asked in a clipped voice.

Nicholas inclined his head thoughtfully. "Yes. Yes, I suppose it is."

He supposed? And she was expected to smile sweetly and open her arms to him now? Surrender all her pride, forget what he had done and thank him for the privilege of becoming his wife? Devil take him!

"Fine!" she announced, jerking her hand away and clenching it into a fist, which she shook at him forcefully. "Then let us make it imminently convenient for the both of us! I shall keep to my own bed after the sham vows are recited and you shall keep to yours! Or anyone else's bed you fancy, for all I care!"

"Are you saying what I think you're saying?" he demanded, his dark brows coming together to make a vicious V over his angry eyes. His lips drew into a firm line and she could see a muscle work rhythmically in his jaw.

She propped her fists on her hips. "Well, if you didn't understand what I said, my lord, perhaps it is *you* who need a governess. Since we are to have a loveless union and it is all for outward show, there will be no consummation of it. Do you understand that, sir, or need I make it plainer still?"

For a long moment fraught with tension, he said absolutely nothing. Then his features slowly smoothed out into an unreadable expression. "I did promise that you could have whatever you wanted," he said softly. "Whether you believe it or not, I am a man of my word. Just be certain you really want what you demand."

He pushed past her and entered the house. She did not see him again until just after the brute called Wrecker came the next morning to summon her to the front gates.

"Good thing ye donned a fancy frock," he told her as soon as she opened the door of her room. "Yer Da is here ta make a honest woman of ye."

Emily gathered up the slightly too long skirts of the

countess's mint-colored muslin morning gown and followed Wrecker down the stairs. She could swear she heard a voice softly singing "Greensleeves" in a sprightly off-key soprano. A voice that the burly sailor either chose to ignore, or else could not hear. It sounded amazingly like the countess.

Emily shook her head to clear it of the fanciful notion, but the phantom sound continued.

"Well, I'm glad *you* are happy," Emily muttered under her breath.

"Oh, aye, ma'am. Nothin' like a good weddin', I always say," Wrecker announced. "Long as it ain't mine."

The moment they exited the house, Emily saw Nicholas waiting beside the gates. He wore dove-gray trousers, Hessians and a dark blue coat. This was the first time in her two days here that she had seen him so impeccably turned out. Somehow it touched her to know he would go to the trouble to dress so nicely for their impromptu wedding.

She was glad she had decided to put up her hair and attempt to make a good show of herself. Also, it had been wise of her to wear one of the countess's dresses instead of her own dark gabardine frock that had seen better days. She would have felt mortified had she attended this appearing like a frump when Nick had gone to so much bother.

In all honesty, she knew she should have felt more compunction about wearing another woman's clothing, but somehow the soft, lovely gowns soothed and warmed her in the same way her gentle mother's embrace had done when she was a child. Strange that should be so when Emily had hardly known Lady Elizabeth.

Two guards wearing crooked, wrinkled cravats, hair slicked down and scarred boots polished, stood nearby.

Dr. Evans, whom she had met only in passing, was there, as well. Through the wrought-iron bars, she saw her father standing alone some yards away.

The familiar shock of white hair, the dreamy gray eyes under wire-rimmed spectacles, and the portly figure contained in slightly out-of-date black attire, made her ache to hug this sweet man she loved so dearly. Would he understand her predicament? Would he approve what they were about to do to rectify it?

She waved as she approached and spoke to him when she drew close enough for him to hear. "What do you think, Father? Have I gone completely beyond the pale this time?"

He smiled, as she'd expected he would, and gestured toward Nicholas with his prayer book. "Moot question, but not to worry, child. His lordship has matters well in hand, my dear. Yes, yes, I'm certain you'll do right well with one another." In an abrupt change of subject that was totally characteristic of him, he asked, "You've seen Joshua?"

Emily brightened, happy to bring her father good news. "Just last evening. I wish he could be out here so you could see him. His health is improving, however, and you'll not believe how he's grown, Da. His voice is so deep and, though he's still abed and 'twas hard to tell for sure, he looks to have grown a foot taller these past months."

"Good, good. Well he should grow, now shouldn't he? Be strange if he didn't at his age."

"Pardon me, sir, but we ought to proceed," Nicholas interjected. "It is misting and we wouldn't want our Emily to catch a chill on her wedding day."

Emily shot him a frown. How dare he interrupt her conversation when she was reassuring her father about her brother's health. But the men already standing there and those who'd just joined them, were watching them as closely as if this were a tennis match. She knew better than to set up a contest of wills with Nick when she had no prayer of winning. She must choose her battles.

The very idea that she could not afford to speak her mind made the urge to do so all the greater, but she kept her mouth firmly shut and stifled the longing. Impulse had been her downfall too many times to give in to it.

"Now, now," her father admonished Nicholas. "No need to rush on account of that. My daughter's as hardy as one of your sailors there. Got a strong constitution, my girl has. Never sick. Never."

Emily almost rolled her eyes in exasperation. Fine thing, her own parent likening her with a seasoned tar. And Nicholas did not have to add insult to injury by allowing his amusement to show. She was already jumpy as a rabbit. Did they both have to make matters worse?

"Let's get on with it," she snapped. She marched forward and stationed herself at Nicholas's left.

"Pretend, Emily," he said, leaning near her ear to speak softly so that only she could hear.

She searched his eyes to see whether he was making sport of her at this particularly inappropriate moment, but it appeared he was now quite serious.

"Stretch those lovely lips into a smile," he ordered, hardly moving his lips when he said it. "And for pity's sake, take my hand. Pinch me if it makes you feel better, but do not outwardly betray your reluctance further or it will trouble the vicar. I have just spent half an hour convincing him that we are well suited."

"Half an hour? A great deal more than you spent persuading me," she muttered. But she did as he suggested. She pasted on the most pleasant face she could manage under the circumstances and thrust out her chin. In a louder voice, she said, "Shall we begin?"

The lines her father read and the vows required were those Emily had heard dozens of times in her years as the vicar's daughter. She had witnessed weddings of great joy and meaning, and those where couples were less than enthusiastic. Never had she been a party to a total travesty such as this. She feared lightning might strike one or the other of them before the deed was done.

Fate would have served her better if she didn't still love the cad, but she did promise to do that much since she had no choice in the matter. God alone knew she had tried for years to banish him from her heart with no success. It seemed he was stuck there like a nettle that could not be pulled free.

And she would be faithful, she thought to herself, almost laughing aloud at the idea of searching out any other man. She'd had problems enough with this one, even when he'd been absent. Heaven only knew how much trouble he'd be now that he was back again. Yes. One man would be more than enough.

When her father mentioned the part about obeying, Emily crossed the fingers of her left hand, hidden within the folds of her skirt.

As for honoring him with her body, Emily stumbled over those words when prompted to repeat them. Nicholas had reached for her free hand and was grasping both now as if he knew about the crossed fingers, daring her to avoid the promise.

She was making it under duress, Emily told herself. Even so, she supposed she would have to live up to it, in spite of her demand that they not share a bed.

However, nothing in the vicar's little book of ceremonies required her to say *when* she must. Nick could jolly well wait until she felt like it.

"I will," she answered.

Nick squeezed her hands and smiled down at her.

She started to say, "Eventually," aloud, but the word would not form on her lips. Too many ears were listening and her courage did not extend quite that far.

Chapter Four

Nick slipped the ring onto Emily's finger. It was not originally intended as a wedding band, but there could hardly be a ceremony without a ring of some sort. He'd been surprised to find that this and the other jewelry had survived. If his father had discovered it, it would surely have been sold. The dainty gold filigree surrounding the sky-blue stones looked perfect on Emily's graceful hand, fitting in every way, he thought.

"By the power vested in me by the Church of England, I now pronounce you husband and wife," the vicar proclaimed in the loud, sonorous voice he usually reserved for the pulpit.

Nicholas closed his eyes for a brief moment. Emily was his now. He had convinced himself it was never fated to happen, that it had never been meant to take place, that she would be long wed with several children by the time he returned to England.

In those first letters to her after he'd reached India, he had poured out his heart to her, vowing undying love like the half-witted fool he was at the time. He now knew that love as described by the poets did not and never had existed. But he had liked Emily so much, felt wildly protective of her and had actually lusted after her with all his might that last year they had been friends. He had wanted her desperately then and, much to his chagrin, found that he still did.

In his letters he had explained in minute detail about his forced departure, assuring her that he had not only her own future in mind, but also that of her family.

She'd not only withheld her forgiveness, but had never offered any response whatsoever. She had intended to cut him from her life permanently.

Her unbending attitude had made him furious with her. Though the worst of his anger had passed long ago, he did admit now that a residue of it remained. It had literally doubled the instant she'd demanded a marriage in name only.

She looked up at him now, obviously steeling herself for the kiss that would seal their union. He wished he could kiss her witless, show her just how alive and well her desire for him truly was.

Emily might no longer trust him, and she might resent having to marry him, but her response each time he touched her was evident. Beneath his thumbs he could detect her rapid pulse. Her breathing grew unsteady as he drew nearer. Heat reddened her cheeks. Her lips trembled.

God only knew how much he wanted to take that impudent mouth and make it his, but he did not. Firmly reining in the impulse, he lowered his closed lips to her forehead and rested them there for an instant.

Did he imagine that hum of disappointment she made deep in her throat? Or had that been his own? He stepped away, still holding her hands.

"There," he said simply as the hesitant applause and

good wishes of his men rent the stillness of the cold morning air around them.

"Thank you, sir," he called out to the vicar. "We will invite you back as soon as is possible."

Emily tugged one of her hands from his and waved at her father as the old fellow smiled at them and turned to leave.

Nicholas stood with her as she watched the vicar climb into his trap and ride off down the lane.

From the road through the wood in the opposite direction, he heard hoofbeats approaching. "Wait over there out of sight," he ordered Emily and nodded his approval when she obeyed. He could see no point in having to explain a wedding in the middle of his courtyard in the misting rain.

The rider halted in confusion when he noticed the closed gates. It was Carrick, his first cousin. The brat had been the bane of Nick's existence and seven years without his company was not nearly long enough.

"Hallo, Nick! Welcome home," the man said, doffing his hat and nodding in lieu of a formal bow. "Are you refusing me entrance?"

"Yes, as a matter of fact, I am," Nick answered with little regret. "You must ride on, Carrick. If you wish a reunion, it must wait."

The outright rudeness seemed to shock even Carrick, who issued a small laugh of disbelief. "Are you going to tell me why you cannot speak with me now?"

"No, I am not," Nick declared with no room for argument. "Do as I say, Carrick, and leave me in peace for the remainder of this month."

"Something's amiss here. I feel it." Carrick paused, obviously expecting Nick to relent. Then he warned Nick, "I shall discover what it is."

Nick said nothing, simply stared him down.

After a long moment of tense silence Carrick nodded. ''As you wish.'' He slowly reversed his mount and galloped away toward the village. No one moved until the distance had swallowed up horse and man.

It ill became an earl to speak so to any of his family or to deliberately slight his own heir, but Nick knew that—even at his worst today—he had been far more patient than his father would have been in like circumstances. He promised himself he would be more civil to Carrick when next they met.

For the time being, however, he would dismiss that small problem from his mind. It was his wedding day and he had other, far more important things to consider. Not the least of which was how he might go about regaining Emily's good opinion.

Nicholas then gestured to her. ''Come, we must go in now,'' he told her as he glanced up at the threatening storm clouds.

He heard her sniff, but she had lowered her head and he could not tell whether she wept or was merely offering a wordless sound of indignation.

In many ways Emily had changed from that sunny girl he had known and believed he loved. He had altered even more than she, he supposed. Only time would tell whether they had grown too far apart in their maturity to reconcile somehow. One thing he did know: they never would find out if they attempted to live together as she intended.

For the duration of their seclusion here, her edict of celibacy made sense. Nicholas would have insisted on it had she not done so first, but their reasons were in no way the same. She expected it to be a permanent arrangement. As it was, the mere fortnight required by his reason would sorely test his resolve.

He would never risk her health to assuage desire. But when the quarantine was over, he feared they would have set the pattern for their life together. That would never do.

His goal at the moment should be to reestablish trust between them and renew their friendship. Then later, the path would be cleared so that he could coax her into his bed. Not much of a plan, but it would have to suffice.

"Our wedding breakfast will be ready by now if you are hungry," he told her, forcing himself to speak amiably. "Even if you are not inclined to eat, we should both make a show. The men will expect it."

"Of course," she replied stiffly. "We would not wish to disappoint. What of the quarantine? How are we to gather for this when you have said there is to be no close interaction by the crew members?"

Nicholas led her up the front steps. "You and I shall take our meal in the dining room. The others usually help themselves from a buffet set up in the kitchens and wander where they will to eat. The only difference for the men today will be in the special dishes I ordered prepared to celebrate our marriage."

"What sort of special dishes?" she asked.

Nicholas almost laughed at her attempt to sound nonchalant. "Leek soup. Fowl stuffed with rice and truffles. Asparagus and the usual peas."

"We have all that?"

He nodded. "Certainly. The larders here were quite full when we arrived. There also will be the obligatory bridal cake with the bean, of course." He stifled a smile as he added, "And lemon ice for everyone if Cook did not find the icehouse empty."

Her hopeful gaze jerked to his. "Lemon ice? You…you remembered?"

Nicholas shrugged. "Hard to forget. You once made yourself ill you ate so much."

To his great surprise, she laughed merrily. "So I did! I cannot credit you recall that incident. I was only eight. Such a little glutton!" she admitted, shaking her head. "Your fault, you know, for stealing it."

He frowned. "You wound me! That was no theft. It was made for *my* birthday, after all. Shouldn't I have had the choice to share it with whom I pleased?"

As they chatted on about their misbehavior, Emily took his arm and lengthened her steps to match his, exactly as she used to do when they were friends. It was an unconscious habit she reverted to, but Nicholas took immense pleasure from it while it lasted.

If she could assume this small intimacy again without thinking, there might be hope that she would one day make another, more profound slip in her determination to keep their marriage chaste. He devoutly hoped so, because even this casual sort of closeness threatened his control.

Did she know that? Was this a subtle form of torment she had devised to make him pay for past deeds? He suspected it was just that. Yet undeserved as it was, he would not wish her to cease plying it.

He spied Seaman Lofton waiting at the far end of the foyer and gave him the signal to get the feast under way. Then Nicholas escorted his bride to the formal dining room.

At every step, he cursed the circumstances that kept him from ushering her on up to the master chamber. And he wished he did not know how stubborn Emily could be once she had made up her mind about something.

Sometimes the very things he liked most about her proved to be the most exasperating.

Happy is the bride the sun shines on. Emily grimaced at the rain now driving against the windows of the dining room. Wishing it away, she trained her attention on the food before her. She tried to ignore Nicholas as best she could, but he made that impossible.

She was heartily sick of small talk. It was difficult to respond to it when the realization that she was a wife now had just hit like a wall falling on her. She felt trapped by it, unable to wriggle this way or that. This could not be undone. It was forever, better or worse. She feared worse. She stared at the ring on her finger.

"I'll buy you another when I go to London," Nick said, obviously following her gaze. "Something grander if you like."

She shook her head. "I'd rather you didn't. I like the design of this one. It will do nicely, thank you."

Fisting her hand in her lap, she glanced out the window again to avoid looking at him. In the distance, through the rain, she could see the spire of Father's church above the treetops.

"I wish we could have married in the church," Nick said as if he read her thoughts. "We should have had the entire county there to wish us happy."

"You dreamer," she replied and almost snorted. "They would have attended out of curiosity to see whether you had lost your mind. I noticed you neglected to break the news to your cousin."

"Carrick? I always have as little to say to him as possible. I admit I was tempted to tell him about the cholera. He's always had an unholy fear of any sickness, morbid or otherwise. We'd never have seen him again." He grinned. "But of course, he would have promptly reported me for making landfall with an infectious disease and had me arrested."

He changed the subject. "Tell me, how is Miss Jocularity doing these days?" He popped the bite of meat into his mouth, chewing vigorously.

Emily watched, spellbound by the workings of his smooth-shaven jaw. Realizing what she was doing, she jerked her gaze away and trained it on her plate.

But he would expect an answer. "Miss Tate? Still worthy of the appellation we assigned her. She frowns through Papa's sermons, castigates every child within hearing distance, and prims up whenever I pass by."

Nick swallowed and pointed at her with his fork. "Surely not. She always liked you best of all."

Emily put down her own eating utensil, sat back in her chair and glanced again at the rivulets of rain. "Not anymore."

When he said nothing to that, she looked back at him. "I forfeited her good graces. Nothing I have done since has restored me in her eyes. And she is not alone in her opinion."

He regarded her steadily. "Because of the kiss," he guessed.

"Yes, because of that."

"You *know* who bears the blame for my leaving, Emily. That public display of ours was foolish and irresponsible. The results inevitable. You must know how deeply I regret it."

"Why should you feel regret? You had what you wanted with none to think the worse of you. Even if you had remained here, my father would never have required you to answer for it."

"I had no choice but to leave."

Nick had mentioned blame. Was he saying *she* should assume it? Emily had to admit she had welcomed his kiss the way a dying woman would greet an extra hour of life. Had she, in her fervor, misread his desire? Maybe he had merely done what he thought she expected at the time. Her kiss must have disappointed him and he worried she would demand that he salvage her good name regardless of that. Why else would he feel forced to leave so suddenly? He said she should know where the blame lay. Where else but with her? His father had said it was so. Nick must think so, too.

"Very well, I believe I understand now," she said, lowering her gaze again.

"Do you?" he asked, offering no reassurances. Not that he owed her any if he was right and it had been all her fault. He had certainly known she would expect marriage, even if her father would not have insisted. Of course he'd felt he had to leave.

"Would you please excuse me?" Emily pushed her chair away from the table and rose, tears perilously close to falling.

"Certainly," he replied, standing immediately.

Before she reached the doorway, he approached and touched her arm. "Emily, wait. You look very pale. You're not feeling ill, are you?"

She shook her head without looking at him. "No. I did not sleep well."

"Go and rest, then." He glanced at the clock on the mantel. "Come down to the library when you awaken. Or I shall bring a tray and join you for supper if you like."

Replying with a curt nod, she escaped, hurried up the stairs to the far end of the third floor hallway and shut herself in the countess's room. Tears of humiliation and despair had overtaken her halfway there and she gave way to them in full once the door was closed behind her.

She threw herself onto the bed and buried her face in a pillow. All these years she had blamed him for abandoning her to the scorn of their small village when in truth, it was she who had caused him to leave his home. Going away then had saved him from having to marry her, a woman he could not love, only to find himself trapped by that very fate because of her most recent folly. He must hate her now. Despite that, he still acted nobly toward her.

"Because he *is* noble," she cried into her pillow, "as I shall never be. It will never work. Never!"

Rarely did she allow herself to weep over anything, but now she could not seem to stop. Rain beat against the windows as if the very skies wept for her. Years worth of pent-up misery spilled forth and she cried until she felt decidedly ill. Her eyes grew swollen and her head ached abominably. Exhausted beyond bearing and steeped in anguish, she finally fell asleep.

Nicholas balanced the tray of tea and cakes on one hand and knocked gently on her door with the other. It was four in the afternoon and he'd not seen Emily since breakfast. Her pallor and near silence had worried him. Angry or happy, she was rarely as quiet as she had been earlier.

When she did not answer, he knocked more firmly. "Emily? I've brought tea."

Still no response. Nicholas tried the handle and found the door unlocked. He pushed it open a few inches and saw her lying facedown on the bed, still fully dressed. "Oh, God!" He flung the door open and rushed in. With a clatter of dishes, he shoved the tray onto the nearest flat surface and ran to her. "Em?"

She mumbled something but refused to move. Nick rolled her over onto her back and cupped her forehead with his palm. *Hot. Burning with fever.*

He grasped the bellpull and yanked it furiously, then ran to the doorway and shouted for the doctor. Immediately he dashed back to her, loosening her clothing, his hands trembling with fear for her.

"Nick? What…what are you *doing?*" she croaked in a weak voice as she batted ineffectually at his hands.

"You're sick, Em. Be still! This corset is—*curse* the damned thing!" He untied and pulled free the laces that held it together below her breasts. At last he parted it, tugged it from beneath her body and threw it aside. He ripped the gown from her and tossed it, as well.

She stared up at him, muddled, speechless and obviously shocked by what he was doing.

"The doctor will be here in a moment," he assured her while he drew the covers up to her neck. The brief glimpse of her clothed in only her chemise barely registered. He was too concerned she would die.

The doctor hurried in carrying his black case of instruments which he deposited on the bed beside Emily. Nicholas had moved out of his way, but quickly rounded the bed so that he could observe. "She has fever," he announced, "and look at her face."

A frightened Emily raised one hand to touch her cheek, but Nicholas grasped it in his and held it. "Be still, my sweet. Just be still for a moment. All will be well." His voice shook, almost broke. He exchanged a look with the doctor who was frowning.

"My lord, I must ask you to leave for a short while."

"No."

"I must examine your wife."

"Go ahead. And hurry," Nick added. "I will stay."

The doctor shrugged and turned his full attention to Emily. "Have you…evacuated in the past few hours?" he asked. "Either way?"

Her eyes rounded. She sucked in an unsteady breath, looked from Nick to the doctor and gasped, "No."

"Good sign," he commented. "You do have a bit of fever. How do you feel?"

She paused to think, Nick supposed, for she did not reply for what seemed an eternity.

Finally she spoke. "My head. It aches. And I feel quite tired."

The doctor patted her hand. "This might be nothing at all, you know. A touch of the ague or merely the excitement of the day. We shall get some fluids into you as quickly as we may, in the event it is the cholera."

He glanced meaningfully at Nick who hurried to the door where Lofton was waiting and ordered up everything liquid he could think to list.

"For now, you'll need this." The doctor pulled a stoppered bottle and spoon from his case and poured a measure of the milky brown liquid for her. Nicholas recognized the smell. *Laudanum.*

His heart sank. Doc must believe she had cholera. The treatment he had given the others consisted of copious liquids and enough of this opium derivative to calm the stomach and digestive tract. He had said he thought that rapid loss of fluids was what killed the patients who died of the disease.

Nick watched with bated breath as Emily obediently swallowed the medicine and closed her eyes. Doc inclined his head toward the doorway, then stepped back from the bedside and headed for the hallway. Nick followed, knowing what he would hear and dreading it with all his heart. "Is it cholera?"

Doc sighed and leaned against the wall outside the bedroom, massaging his forehead with his hand. "I shan't lie to you. Your wife most likely is in the early stages. Some do not develop the worst symptoms until after four or five days. Yet some sicken and die within hours. I just do not know at this point."

"She cannot die," Nick argued, grabbing the doctor's arm in a vise grip. "You saved the others. Now you save *her!*"

"My lord, you know very well I will do everything within my power, but I am not God."

Nick released a breath of impatience and started to reenter the room.

"My lord, you should go below and wait. At least until we know for certain."

"If she succumbs, she will not do so alone or with people she does not know," Nick replied. "I'll not leave this room until I know she is recovering, or…" His voice failed him. He could not say the word in conjunction with Emily. Instead he met the doctor's rheumy gaze with one of steadfast determination.

"So be it, but this will not be pleasant, my lord. You were witness to little of what the men suffered with this. Cholera is an ugly disease. Humiliating for the patient and noisome for the caretaker. I hope you have a strong constitution."

Nick vowed he would have. He'd do whatever it took, bear whatever he must, to help make her well again.

When he reentered, Emily had pushed herself to a sitting position. She was carefully lowering her legs off the side of the bed. Nick grabbed her just in time to keep her from pitching forward on her head. "Where do you think you're going?" he snapped.

She winced at his tone and he was immediately sorry he'd spoken so sharply to her. "What is it, Em? What do you need?"

"I would as soon not say," she whispered. "Could you leave me alone for a moment, please?"

"Nonsense! You need the chamber pot, then say so. I will carry you."

"No!" she answered, very forcefully he thought, for someone who might be dying. "Please leave this room immediately and do not return unless I call for you!"

For a moment he simply stared at her. Her color was high and her anger apparent. "Let me help you behind the screen. Then I'll wait outside. Will that do? Look how shaky you are. You'll fall if I leave you to walk that far."

"It's the laudanum," she explained as if speaking to a thick-headed child. "It made me dizzy. I hate the stuff."

He walked her over to the privacy screen that hid the facility. It was a chair made of oak with a seat that lifted. At least she would have something to brace her upright. With much trepidation, he did leave her there as soon as she was near enough to reach it. She glared at him meaningfully until he turned away and left her alone.

A scant few moments later she reappeared, grasping the edge of the heavy wooden screen with both hands. "Nick?"

He rushed to her from the doorway where he'd been waiting. "Yes, dearest? Could you not manage alone?"

She tried unsuccessfully to focus on his face. "I see two of the bed. Help me to it?"

Gladly he scooped her up and put her back where she

belonged, reminding himself to order Lofton to bring a bedpan. Less than a quarter hour into this sickroom business and Nick admitted he was already a sorry wreck.

Doc checked Emily's pulse, pinched the skin on her arm, then urged her to drink a full cup of the broth Lofton had fetched. He waved Nick to the chair beside the fireplace. "You might as well get some rest while you can. This looks to be a long night ahead."

Nick settled in the chair, rested his elbows on his knees and clasped his hands, leaning his forehead upon them.

Alternately he prayed, cursed, promised and threatened all manner of things. He both vehemently beseeched and ordered the Almighty to allow her to survive, knowing all the while that what would be, would be.

Nicholas had been in dire straits more times than he could count, but never in his entire life had he ever felt so helpless as he did now.

Chapter Five

"Nicholas?" Emily shook his shoulder gently. He remained sound asleep, sprawled in the overstuffed chair beside the hearth, long legs straight out, spine contoured to fit the cushions.

His fine wedding clothes were rumpled and she could see that he had not shaved. When he did not wake, she dared to smooth the tousled dark hair away from his brow, allowing herself the small contact he would never know about.

When she had first opened her eyes this morning, she immediately recalled how Nick and the doctor had hovered over her, concerned that she had contracted the disease everyone so feared.

They had frightened her, as well, with their worry. Still muzzy from all that weeping, with her head aching and her stomach clenching from lack of food, she had thought they might be correct and that she could be dying. However, now she felt entirely too well to be suffering anything other than the residual effects of that dose of laudanum.

"Nick, wake up. You cannot possibly be comfortable here," she persisted, shaking him again.

He suddenly bolted upright, wearing a look of confusion. Then his gaze landed on her. "What...what are you doing up?"

Before she could respond, he swept her off her feet, carried her to the bed and deposited her there. He snatched the covers up to her chin and reached for the cup on the bedside table.

Ignoring her sputtering protests, he put the container to her lips. She had to either drink or drown, so she drank. In all honesty, she treasured the fact that he cared whether she was ill.

He plunked the cup down and yelled for Dr. Evans. When the man didn't appear on the instant, Nick strode to the door and called out again, more loudly this time.

"Nicholas!" As flattering as it was to see him so upset on her behalf, Emily could not let it go on. "Look at me, Nick! I am all right."

But he had already left the room and was descending the stairs in all haste. She could hear the rapid clack of his boot heels on the marble.

Emily collapsed back against the pillows and twisted her lovely little wedding ring around and around on her finger. At least Nick cared about her. Soon enough, he would bring Dr. Evans back upstairs and they would see that they no longer had anything to fret about.

She only hoped they would bring food. She was absolutely famished.

"Hurry, Evans! I think she might be out of her head and should not be left alone!"

"Calm yourself," Doc advised. "You'll do her no good in this agitated state. You say she was mobile?"

"Standing over me, prodding me awake," he related

as he urged Evans upward with a hand on his elbow. "I put her back to bed. Gave her more liquid. But then I—"

The doctor stopped on the landing and grasped Nick's shoulder. "Will you please listen to me, my lord? As I told you early this morning, I do not believe your wife has cholera."

Nick ran a hand through his hair and shook his head. "But you cannot be certain of that, can you? You saw how she was last night."

"Aye, and at the time, I did think it quite possible she could be coming down with it, but there were no further symptoms as the night wore on. You saw for yourself how well she slept. No griping of the stomach, no flux, no vomiting. The slight fever abated almost immediately after I dosed her. To tell you the truth, I think she was merely tired out and red-eyed from crying. Brides tend to weep over the least little thing or nothing at all."

Nick considered that. She had been upset when she went up to rest. Without another word to Evans, he stalked down the hallway ahead of him and entered Emily's room.

She was sitting up, as pink-cheeked and bright-eyed as he had ever seen her.

"Are you ill or aren't you?" he demanded.

"No," she replied, calm as you please. "I tried to tell you. I feel fine except that I'm hungry. Remember, I hardly ate anything yester—"

He saw her through a haze of red. "Do you *know* how frantic I—we've been? We nursed you throughout the night, terrified you would not live to see morning!"

"Oh, Nick, I regret that you assumed—"

"You—" He threw up a hand and shook his finger at her. "You—" What could he say? He could hardly be-rate her for *not* being ill when he'd prayed half the night she wouldn't die.

Surely she had not pretended... Without finishing the thought, he stormed out of the room. Relief was too over-powering to describe, and the fear had not quite let go of him. He wished to God he could saddle a horse and ride out, let the storm rage around him and beat the emotions that racked him down to a manageable level.

Unfortunately Wrecker chose the moment he exited the house to accost him with a question. "How'd the weddin' night go, sar? Ye ain't lookin' too pleased wif her."

Nick punched him right in the mouth, cutting his own knuckles on the wretch's teeth. He shook his injured fist and glared down at the brute. "Get out of my sight. And *stay* there!"

Wrecker scrambled away on all fours. Nick stalked off through the pelting rain to the stables. His temper rarely got the better of him and it troubled him that it did so now. A man who allowed his emotions to rule him was no man at all in his opinion.

Soaking wet and somewhat cooler, he entered the place where he had used to come to escape his father's wrath. The smell of hay, leather and horse brought remembered comfort.

There were only three mares and a carriage team now. The hunters, including his favorite gelding, had either been sold off or had died since he'd left for India. He regretted their loss.

"I'll buy more," he promised himself as he ran his palm over the velvety muzzle of a curious roan who stuck her head out to see who was there.

Too much had changed here, he thought with a sigh. Some of it good. The old man was gone.

"How many years did I waste as a boy, looking for

things to love about that man?'' he asked as he stroked the mare's neck. He had wanted to honor his father as he had his mother, but there had not been much to admire about the man or the public figure.

Nick's actions this morning reminded him all too vividly of the preceding Earl Kendale's behavior. That he had inherited his father's ways was Nick's worst nightmare. He fought it daily, hourly, but knew now that he must redouble his efforts. He must strive to show kindness toward his wife and his servants, and to also use the power of his title to England's best advantage. Above everything, he wanted to be a good and honest man and a truly noble earl, as unlike his father as he could possibly be.

He felt a soft pat on his back and swiftly turned.

Confused, he scanned the low-lit interior of the stables. ''Who's there?''

No one answered. For some reason, he thought of his mother and the values and gentle encouragement she had given him when she was alive. Desperately, he wanted to believe she had imbued him with those qualities that might save him.

''I miss you,'' he muttered to the cold, dark air that surrounded him. Again he felt a touch on his back and whirled.

It was only the mare, seeking more attention. Nick smiled at her and at himself. ''Daft,'' he said to the animal, raking her forelock with his fingers. ''Em's made me daft. I'd best go see what damage I've done and whether I can repair it.''

Slowly he closed the stable doors and trudged through the downpour to the main house. He did not look forward to the task of asking her forgiveness yet again—especially when it might not be forthcoming this time, either—but he could scarcely wait to see if she felt even better after her breakfast.

As it happened, she was sitting up in bed holding court. Dr. Evans and Lofton were cackling like hens at something she had said.

She wore a smile that gleamed as white as the lacy nightrail she wore. Emily's bright golden mass of hair was piled atop her head, but a few curls had escaped to form long question marks over each ear. She looked adorable. And the picture of health. He felt like weeping with relief and crushing her to him as if she were a long-lost child. Or lover.

Even as he looked at her, however, she sneezed.

He frowned. She'd caught cold. "We should have delayed the wedding," he announced. "The dampness yesterday has made you ill after all."

"Don't be a goose," she argued with a sniff, sounding more like the girl he'd once known than she had at any time since their ill-fated reunion.

Deliberately shoving his guilt aside, he forced a smile. "All the same, I hope you will remain abed and take good care. Have you eaten?"

She grinned at the seaman. "Lofty brought me an egg, toast and that wonderful tea that shipped with you. It was wickedly delicious. I hope you have chests full of it."

"We are certainly blessed in that respect," Nick assured her, trying for a conversational tone. "We've a *ship* nearly full of it."

Emily nodded, fixing him with a curious look. "I must say, you've improved yourself since you were here last."

He had. After his sojourn to the stables, he had taken the time to shave, bathe and dress. Not much choice about it, since he'd been dripping wet and his face prickly as a hedgehog.

Nick rubbed his chin. "Shall I keep you company for a while?" he asked, glaring pointedly at the doctor and Lofton. "I'm sure you two have other matters to attend."

They took their leave, as he'd intended. Now that he had her alone, he would say what he had come to say.

Taking a deep, fortifying breath, he faced her. "Emily, please understand that I was extremely concerned. If I was curt with you, I apologize."

"Curt?" she asked with a mirthless laugh. "Beastly is more like it. You need your ears boxed."

"I have said I was sorry. What more would you have me do?" he snapped.

She eyed him from under those softly curled lashes and pursed her lips. The look she offered stirred him so powerfully, he lost track of his thoughts. He wanted to kiss her, to slide his arms around her, to stretch out beside her on that bed. Over her...

"If you truly want to make amends, you may read me poetry," she declared in her most imperious voice, the one she once used when pretending to be an actress upon an improvised stage. *The queen of pretense,* he'd once called her, envying her the ability to lose herself in fantasy. He never could. Life was all too real.

"Yes, I think a poem would do very well," she added with aplomb.

"The devil you say." He hated poetry. "What sort?"

"Byron."

"I loathe Byron and you know it."

She smiled her most evil smile. "Yes, I know. And *I* love him."

Nick knew she was having him on. It made him want to laugh aloud. Instead he grumbled as she would expect him to do. "Since when?"

"Since now."

With a long-suffering sigh, he accepted her punishment with mock reluctance when, in fact, he would have done most anything to remain in the room with her and keep her in this playful mood.

He walked over to the table by the window, picked up the book and took a seat in the chair where he had slept. Only after another prompt from her, did he open it to a selection at random and read.

"And thou art dead, as young and fair
As aught of mortal birth..."

He cleared his throat and looked up at her. "Hardly appropriate." He flipped several pages and began again.

"I had a dream, which was not all a dream
The bright sun was extinguish'd, and the stars
Did wander darkling in the eternal space..."

He shut the book. "I refuse to spout more of this morbid drivel."

She lifted her brows and sniffed. "Try 'She Walks in Beauty Like the Night.'"

His graceless rendering of the poem seemed to satisfy her need as well as any horsewhip might have done, while Nick secretly savored the penance.

They were playing as they used to do. He knew the first moment of real joy in seven years. How he had missed her.

"Thank you, Nicholas," she said brightly. "Now if you would, leave me to my own devices for a while and send me up a novel. Tell me you have something besides what I found in the library."

"I do, and your wish is my command, of course," he

said with no little pique at being dismissed while enjoying her company. His words sounded a bit sharper than intended.

"How accommodating you are, Kendale," she returned with asperity. Though she addressed him quite correctly by his title, she was also sharply reminding him that his father had borne the same name and the attitude Nick was displaying now. A deliberate taunt she had to know would sting.

Though he still could see humor lurking behind her scorn, the scorn itself hit too close to the mark. "I am *not* like my father."

"I pray that is true," she told him solemnly, her voice free of any humor now.

She meant what she said. And she spoke for both of them whether she knew it or not.

Nick wondered if the old man had started out this way, striking out in an occasional bad temper. Mounting vitriolic attacks that grew more and more frequent until they determined who he had been. Very likely, Nick decided.

He all but shuddered with the realization that he could easily become the same sort of man if he allowed it to happen.

His father's upbringing and education were virtually the same as his own. The difference being that his father had not known a friend like Emily Loveyne.

There had been no one like her for the young Ambrose. No one to make light of what seemed weighty matters to a boy on the verge of manhood. No one to poke gentle fun at his self-importance and overweening pride. No one to make him laugh and embrace the day. Nick's mother had despised her husband and no one blamed her, least of all Nick. What a joyless lot, the Hollanders.

He met and held Emily's clear blue gaze. "I would

not be like Father, Em,'' he assured her. ''Do not let me be.''

She gave a slight shake of her head. ''Were you angry because I am not ill, Nicholas?''

''Of course not. You frightened me is all. I went a bit wild.''

Her smile bloomed slowly, like a morning glory opening to the sun. ''Then I really do forgive you. But I warn you, if your temper flies free again, I shall demand you read every last sonnet in the library.''

''Properly noted.'' Nick wished she would pardon him for past sins as readily as for his bad temper. ''That kind heart of yours will be your undoing one day,'' he warned her wryly. While she was in such good humor, he decided to risk all and delve into the topic that troubled them most. ''Em, there is something we should discuss. Are you up to it?''

Her smile died. She shrugged and looked away. ''If you like.''

He hardly knew how to begin, but he had to start somewhere. ''You know I would never have boarded that ship if Father had not forced me to go. I swear to you by all that's holy, he did use force or I would never have gone away.''

She shot him a look of incredulity. Then she dropped her gaze and toyed with the edge of the coverlet, frowning. ''But you stayed away.''

''I had to,'' he replied. ''He threatened to ruin you and your family if I returned and tried to resume our...friendship.''

One corner of her mouth lifted tremulously. ''Friendship?''

''Well, yes, I thought that is what we had,'' Nick replied. "Somehow Father must have learned about the kiss, and assumed—"

"As did everyone in the county," she replied, then continued. "So he tossed you onto a ship for India. I do wonder what he told Dierdre about that."

Nick sighed and rolled his eyes. "We've already established that there was no reason for him to tell her anything. There was no real betrothal, only his wish for one. What more can I say to that?"

She eyed him keenly then, as if to judge his honesty. "Swear to me you never promised to wed her, Nick. Can you swear it?"

He placed his right hand over his heart. "I swear."

She nodded slowly. "All right, I will take that as truth. But you could have written to me and explained your departure easily enough. He would never have known of it."

Nick was taken aback. "But I did write."

"Strange. Your letter never arrived."

She did not believe him about this, Nick saw. Serious doubt clouded the clear blue of her eyes. Her questioning of his word made him feel defensive. How dare she not believe him? "You did not write to *me,*" he accused.

"And where should I have sent the missive, Nick? I had no inkling where you were for years. Only when the earl died did anyone know for certain you were in India. You could have been anywhere at all." She swallowed hard and her breathing grew rapid. Was she going to cry?

This mounting agitation was not a good sign. He was losing ground here. "Just know that I did not leave here voluntarily and I would have returned if I could have done so without putting your family's welfare at risk. Those are the facts, Emily."

She sneezed again. It gave him the perfect excuse to

leave dangerous ground. He had to admit he did not want her asking any more questions about the day he had kissed her. What if she demanded to know whether he had loved her then? No woman would want to hear that, no, he was only a young man caught up in a mad infatuation.

She would not be glad to know that he had assuaged that lust with numerous women since that time and now recognized so-called *love* for what it was. The word was a fabrication invented to prettify what took place between a man and woman.

He wanted her as fiercely as he had then. But the additional feelings he had for Emily were a bit more noble. He cared deeply for her and liked her enormously. Being near her made him happy. But even that admission would not suffice if she asked him outright if he had loved her.

He could lie, he supposed, but he didn't want to. Neither did he intend to admit the truth.

Again she sneezed.

"Listen to yourself," he said. "You *have* caught cold. I'll send Lofty up with more of that tea you like."

He turned to go. If he did not leave the room immediately, he knew he would have to take her in his arms and show her how much he wanted her delectable body. And more. Something ephemeral that he'd only touched briefly. Some thing he could not name that had remained with him for seven long years and warmed him when nothing else could.

Perhaps she represented home to him the way his father and Bournesea never had. There was comfort within Emily's arms that he could find nowhere else. And he had looked.

He could make love to her. He had the right to now. But she would protest. And the scare she had provided last night brought home the possibility that any soul at Bournesea could fall ill with cholera at any instant. He must keep his distance for a while longer until he was sure it was safe, for he'd had more exposure to the disease than anyone else here other than Dr. Evans and the three patients who had it.

Painful as it was for him to accept, regaining Emily's friendship would have to take precedence over seducing her. She might be content enough without a bedmate, but she certainly would be needing a friend in the near future. The Countess of Kendale was unlikely to find any close chums among her new peers, or have any left among her old ones, for that matter.

The poor girl had no inkling yet how much she would need him, even if she no longer wanted him as a man.

Emily hugged a pillow to her breast and relished her conversation with Nick, even the cross words. He had not wanted to leave her, after all. His father had made him go. And he would have returned if possible. Best of all, he swore that he and Dierdre had been in no way attached.

She had not dared ask how he felt about her, for fear of what he might say. He had been worried about her. That bode well, didn't it? She asked herself why on earth he would become so upset if he did not love her.

Of course, his concern might have been that there was another probable case of cholera to deal with, not because it was she who fell sick with it. That sobering thought dampened her euphoria.

He had been contrite about his outburst of temper, so he must care. But then, she argued, Nicholas always had been man enough to admit when he was wrong about a thing. She also knew he would do anything in the world not to be like the old earl. That worry alone might have prompted his apology. Had it also prompted his explanation about why he'd left her?

She released the pillow and tossed it away from her, crossing her arms over her chest and sighing with resignation.

No matter how she tried to twist events to her liking, or how hard she wished something good to come of this, there was the great possibility that Nick did not love her and never had.

Their banter had roused fond memories of how it once had been between them. Before she knew she loved him and thought that he loved her.

He had taught her to ride so that they might gallop the fields of Bournesea together. Where his tutor had failed miserably, she had taught Nick to read music and play the old piano on which she had learned.

Together they had spent many a day sharing such pursuits, and were great friends despite the differences in gender, age and station. Always, he had shown her the greatest respect. In turn, she had shown him little of the awe most people would think his due as heir to the earl.

He often said that he loved how she totally disregarded that. Apparently, not many had done so, even when he was away at school. His friends were few, he had admitted once, and that made her all the more special.

"Perhaps not so special *now*," she muttered, feeling tears threaten. But she had wept enough over this and would not weaken again. Someone had to make pie of this mincemeat and she knew very well it would have to be her.

The door to the armoire creaked and slowly drifted open on its own. Emily stared at it, round-eyed with wonder.

Of course! She should dress and go downstairs. There was no point at all to her lying about feeling sorry for herself. She got up and went to choose something to wear from the wardrobe Nick had put at her disposal.

This entire house felt like a dark, dank mausoleum. The men confined here must sorely need cheering. Even if she was not allowed to associate freely with them, she could give them music and lighten this dreary day.

"An excellent idea, ma'am," she said to Lady Elizabeth, whose presence surrounded Emily in the form of gowns bearing the remembered scent of lilacs.

Emily laughed at herself as she dressed, amused by her fanciful invention. She needed a boon companion and had chosen the most illogical, of course. The countess would do just fine. "Just stay close by," Emily beseeched, "or else I must talk to myself."

Humming under her breath, straining to recall the notes of something other than the hymns she played every Sunday, Emily headed for the music room. If she remembered correctly, she had once seen a piano in there.

Chapter Six

Nicholas wondered if he could have avoided mutiny these past two weeks if Emily had not been at Bournesea. The men, already chafing at the inactivity under quarantine, jumped at her suggestions as if they were mandates from the Queen herself.

Scouring and polishing came naturally to most of them since they had been charged with keeping one ship or another spotless for most of their lives. But who on earth would have thought the sea dogs would take to gardening the way they had? Who would credit how they had scrubbed themselves to a fare-thee-well each morning and arrived, hair slicked down and clothing relatively clean, to hear her Bible reading from her perch on the first floor balcony?

But the music was her crowning touch, Nick thought with a smile. She played beautifully and welcomed the accompaniment of Brian Somer's concertina as the men joined in the singing. The woman constantly amazed him, and he was not the only one so affected. The men adored her.

The first week had been hell, at least for him. Each time he touched Emily, came close enough to inhale her sweet essence, or merely watched her from across a room, he felt drawn to do things he knew she would not welcome. A chaste kiss, perhaps she would tolerate without upset, but Nick knew he would never be able to stop with a kiss.

She had grown too desirable to resist. Knowing that her innocence was his for the taking, his by right, made it even more difficult to set his longing aside than when he'd been a randy young buck who thought himself in love.

Therefore, for the second week of their confinement at Bournesea, he had purposely kept himself as far from her as space would allow. Still, her music found him, its sinuous, haunting curls of temptation beckoning him closer and closer until he found himself caught fast in her spell, his body wild to make her his.

Tomorrow he would be free to leave at last. The quarantine would be over. What a relief that would be to put a full day's journey between them.

She would be eager to take Joshua to her father and visit at the vicarage. Nick planned to go to London to settle matters with his solicitors and also explain to Worthing that he had married Emily and why. The last was no chore to be anticipated with any relish, but it must be done. After that, he would remain in town for a while and give Emily time to settle her father and Josh into the manor permanently if she wished.

Tonight, he had ordered a feast and a celebration to commemorate everyone's good health and success in avoiding an epidemic. No one else had fallen ill with cholera and the three who'd had it were now fully recovered.

At the moment, he needed to speak with Emily to see whether she needed help with last-minute arrangements.

He left his study where he spent most of his time and headed for the ballroom. She was there, as he knew she would be, festooning the place with greenery gathered by the men.

"How grand," he said, observing her handiwork. "I wish you had more flowers to work with, but those in Mother's garden have scarcely budded as yet, despite all your efforts."

She tossed him a casual smile as she twisted a strand of ivy around one of the pedestals holding a pot of gentians. "Yes, roses are what we need," she told him. "I do wish I had some from Father's garden. We have real beauties there now."

"I could send someone for them," he offered.

"No, these will be fine." She stood back and admired the arrangement she had created. "Simple, but elegant. What do you think?"

"Beautiful," he assured her, knowing that not a man in the place would care a jot for flowers when they could look at her. Nick smiled at her appearance now, however. Blond curls rioted from beneath the atrocious mobcap she wore and her gown was the same sad-looking thing she had worn the day she sneaked in the back gate. A streak of soil decorated one side of her face.

She grinned. "I must look rather a mess," she said, wiping her hands on her skirt.

"Charming in your dirt," he replied, wishing he dared tweak her impudent little nose. "Take a few hours to bathe and rest before the gathering, why don't you? I've sent Joshua to collect your father. When they return, I'll entertain them until you come down."

"Thank you, but I shan't be long getting ready. I'm so excited!" she exclaimed, clasping her hands together and whirling around to give the ballroom one final check. "Our last day! Can you believe it?"

"None too soon to suit me," he said with alacrity. "By the way, I've asked Lofty and Simmons to assist you in moving your family's possessions here while I'm gone. Will you need more help than that?"

"Gone?" she questioned, her eyes wide. "Gone where?"

"Town," he replied. "I have business to conduct that has waited too long as it is. Estate affairs, and so forth. Things left undone since I inherited. Political matters, as well."

Emily frowned as she walked over to stand closer. "You'll be quite busy, then. It is the height of the Season, isn't it?"

Nick nodded. There would be social occasions he should not miss if he planned to make any use of his title in the coming years. He would need to establish himself, show them what sort of man he was, and gain friends if he meant to create any influence at all. What good was being a lord if one didn't fulfill the governing duties that went with it?

Emily brushed her hands together as if dusting off her worries. Her chin rose and set with determination. "I shall be ready," she announced.

Before she closed her mouth Nick was shaking his head. "Not this time, my dear."

"Yes, this time," she argued. "Leave me here and I will follow you the moment you leave the gates. No idle threat, Nick."

He threw out his hands in exasperation. "Can you not understand *no* when I say it? You are *not* coming to London!"

"Yes, I am."

"Why, for God's sake, would you want to?"

"Not so much that I want to, exactly, but I must," she declared.

"Oh, and why must you?" He really was interested to know why anyone would voluntarily go if it wasn't absolutely necessary.

He hated large cities in general, London in particular. But then, Emily had never traveled, so she would not know the perils of unclean air and overcrowded conditions. Or the very real threat of being rejected by the Society she thought would welcome her with open arms.

"It's no safe place, Emily," he told her.

She smiled winningly. "You'll take me along for protection, then. If anyone threatens you in the least, I shall beat him about the head and shoulders with my parasol. It's a good sturdy one, too, with a thick, oaken handle." She made two parries and a thrust with her imaginary weapon.

He laughed in spite of himself and shook his head. "Ah, Emily. You are one of a kind." A firm hand was needed here. He sobered and cleared his throat. "But, seriously, you cannot come."

"Facetiously, then, if you insist. But I *will* go to London, either by your side or in your wake." She shrugged and tilted her head to one side, a challenge if he'd ever seen one.

"You vowed to obey me," he reminded her gruffly.

She held up one hand, her fingers crossed. "Not really."

"That is so childish, Emily. You are a grown woman. Try acting like one."

She swept right past him, her dusty skirts brushing his boots as she did. "Very well, but you must excuse me now. I have to pack."

He whirled around to catch her and missed. "Emily, you are *not* coming with me!"

"Behind you, then," he heard her call as she hurried down the hallway to the stairs.

Damnation, the little hellion would drive him mad. But deep inside, he could not deny the hope that began to bud like the roses she tended. Apparently she planned to tend him, too, and inconvenient as it was in this case, he found he liked her proprietary attitude.

Because, if she cared that much, she surely would not make him suffer much longer in the state he was in. Perhaps she would decide to forgive him after all if he played his cards properly.

The worst of her anger seemed to have abated. Just because love did not exist was no good reason to deny themselves the comfort of…companionship. He smiled.

"I'm comin' wi' ye, m'lord," Wrecker said, joining him, both of them looking up the stairs after Emily.

"Fine," Nick said, bracing his hands on his hips. "Why don't we make a damned parade of it? You have a reason, too, I suppose?"

Wrecker didn't quail as many would have done after having suffered Nick's fist in anger once. The man had not mentioned it since, and as far as Nick knew, had not taken a lesson from it, either.

"Ain't none know Lunnon loik me, m'lord," Wrecker told him. "Born and raised in th' stews. Been all over th' city since I was big enow t' grab on to th' boot when a toff's carriage rolled by. Our lady'll need me ta keep 'er safe and show her th' ropes when you ain't by, m'lord."

"Your presumption astounds me," Nick lied. Nothing Wrecker did surprised him at all. The man was either a cagey rascal or a dimwitted cluck. Nick suspected the first, since Wrecker usually said and did exactly what he pleased. "You think I will allow you to guard my wife?"

"Aye. She's a angel fell down off a cloud, she is," Wrecker declared softly, his gaze still on the spot where they'd last seen Emily. "I done 'er wrong, sayin' all them things I said when she first come 'ere. I owe 'er for it."

Nick didn't disagree. He also understood that Wrecker had a reason other than reparation for his lecherous thoughts. The man fairly worshiped Emily now and made no secret of it.

"The captain will be sailing within the week. What of your berth on the *Merry May?*"

The seaman sighed, dragged off his moth-eaten cap with one hand and scratched his stringy hair. "Done wi' ships, I reckon. I got a bit o' coin put by and I'm thinkin' you'll pay me more, eh?"

Nick considered it. It never hurt to have an extra man aboard when traveling. And if Emily did any shopping or went about in the city without Nick, she would need a stout guard, as well as a guide. London could be confusing at best and dangerous at worst, especially for an innocent country miss who had never been there before.

Wrecker would defend Emily with his life, Nick was certain. Though he wasn't much to look at, and not the brightest candle in the chandelier, the captain swore he was the most trustworthy as well as the strongest of the crew.

"Can you shoot?" Nick asked him.

Wrecker grinned. "Aye, but I be better with a blade."

"Four shillings per week?"

"Five. I pulled in three as a rat-catcher at tharteen."

Nick nodded. "Fair enough. Come with me, then. We'll get you outfitted with your livery."

He led the way to the attic rooms where he had stored

the old earl's clothing when he'd appropriated the master suite. There were no other garments at Bournesea that would fit Wrecker, large as he was. And Nick didn't deny that he enjoyed the irony of clothing a lad from the stews of London in his father's expensive woolens.

"Livery, sar?" Wrecker sniggered. "Yer havin' me on, ain't ye?"

"Certainly not. You'll need to look the part of a footman if you go about with the countess, won't you? Might want to wash up a bit, too. All over and with soap," Nick elaborated, looking at him meaningfully. "And have one of the crew give that mane and mustache a trim."

Though Wrecker frowned, he agreed. "Wouldn't do this bit for nobody else," he muttered just loud enough to hear.

"Neither would I," Nick admitted with a dry laugh. "If she were anyone but who she is, she would obey me and remain here where she belongs."

Life could turn out to be so much more difficult for Emily in London than she envisioned. Either he or Wrecker could ensure her physical safety wherever she went, but who would shield her from the contempt she might suffer as a commoner turned countess? Should he warn her of that? Or should he remain silent and hope the slings and arrows would miss their mark?

Nick faced the remote possibility that there could be a scandal over his invalid betrothal contract. But he doubted that would come to pass. Worthing would be no more eager to instigate a sensation than Nick was. It could blacken both their family names. And Worthing, with a marriageable daughter and a socially active wife, had far more to lose in that respect than Nick.

However, the good opinion of those he must serve with

in the House of Lords when he commenced his duties there did matter a great deal to him, Nick admitted.

Respect was one thing he had been determined to gain once he assumed the title. While it was true that anyone who had known his father would believe the man capable of forgery at the very least, they might decide Nick was no better.

Making accusations against his father and seeming to set aside a binding contract of such import might very well cause them to think that.

Emily's regard mattered, as well. She had just begun to relent and perhaps forgive him a little. They might have a chance at a decent life together if she did.

Somehow he would have to persuade Worthing to keep the matter quiet if the man threatened to cause a stir. Nick wished he could isolate Emily against any stray gossip that might occur relating to it. But how was he supposed to do that when he couldn't even keep her out of London?

He could not leave the explanation until Worthing came home to the country when the Season was over. That really would be unforgivable. He owed the man, and also Dierdre, the truth immediately.

That document lying in the desk drawer in his study promised to cause him no end of trouble. He would be glad to rip it to shreds once this matter was settled. Until then, he didn't want to look at it again unless he had to. It represented all of the machinations his father had gone through to control Nick's life. He made a mental note to retrieve the damned thing and place it in his satchel before leaving in the morning. His solicitor would want to examine it.

Wrecker broke into Nick's worried thoughts with an observation. ''Lady Em'll knock 'em off their pins when

they sees 'er in town, won't she! Her and them fancy
gowns.''

Nick clenched his eyes shut and shook his head. Here
he was about to outfit Wrecker so he wouldn't disgrace
them once they arrived in the city, and he hadn't given
so much as a thought to Emily's attire. How could he
allow her, as his new bride and countess, to turn up in
his mother's frocks that were at least ten years out of
fashion and a size too large?

Was he imagining it, or were his problems multiplying
by the hour?

Emily bathed and dressed in record time. Lofton and
Rolly had hauled up buckets of water to fill the copper
tub for her. In less than a quarter hour, she had finished
with that, donned a lavender georgette creation that did
wonders for her complexion, and was working on her
hair. The dampness of it aided her in arranging curls that
would dry just so and stay put where she'd pinned them.
She hoped.

How eager she was for the party tonight. Her father
and Josh would be so proud of her for orchestrating her
first real entertainment.

The men had brought a trunk from the attics at her
insistence. Already, she had filled it with the countess's
clothing that would see her through their time in London.

How fortunate she was that Nick allowed her to make
use of his mother's things. If he only knew how much
courage they gave her. Thank goodness she would look
presentable for him.

''He must be worried I won't measure up to the task,''
she said to the small mirror perched on the dressing table.
Emily forced a smile and raised her brows at her reflection. ''But I shall surprise him.''

One errant curl suddenly tumbled from its pin and settled along the line of her neck. Emily sighed, started to repin it, then decided she liked the effect and left it as it was. "Not quite so severe. Yes, much better. Not so like the prim vicar's daughter now," she said with a laugh. "Lady Elizabeth, are you at it again?"

She jumped up from the small vanity chair and whirled around, arms out as if dancing with a partner. "So, what do you think?"

No one answered, of course, especially not the countess who had been dead these ten long years. But Emily liked to believe if the lady had been present, she would have approved. She certainly would have done more than slide the filmy lavender stole off the side of the bed so that it landed with a plop at Emily's feet.

Executing a very deep curtsy just for practice, Emily scooped up the wisp of fabric and donned it appropriately so that it draped over both arms at the elbow. She was ready to meet anyone alive on equal ground, she thought to herself.

Pride goeth before a fall. The words echoed in her head like a dire warning. Not a caution from the imaginary spirit of the countess, however. No, Emily knew it was her own inner being issuing a reminder. Hadn't she been conditioned to seek humility by a lifetime of listening to her father's sermons? But try as she might, she could find no reason to deny things were going well for her.

They were going exceptionally well, she thought. She would be on her way to London tomorrow with her husband. Though he was not keen on the idea, she was not about to let him go alone. How would they ever come to terms with this marriage of theirs if they were not together? It would take time, especially given the set of problems they faced at the outset. They had time. And she would ensure the togetherness. All would be well eventually.

She had Nick's word that his father had forced him to leave her when he would much rather have stayed. And he'd avowed that the old earl had only made up the tale of a betrothal to Dierdre Worthing so that Emily would be angry with Nick and forget him. Why shouldn't she believe Nick over his father, who was known to be cruel?

What purpose would be served in expecting things to go awry at any moment? None that she could see. Pride could be a good thing, could it not?

Tonight she would not worry about anything other than who she would dance with first while Rolly played fiddle and Somers, the concertina.

With a smile on her face and a lilt in her step, Emily went downstairs, realizing she was a bit early for the celebration.

She needed to stop by Nick's study first to filch a bit of paper from his desk to complete one last task before leaving for London in the morning. The men who would be moving the family and her own things from the vicarage to Bournesea House should have a list of what to bring.

The chore would only take a few moments of her time and might save Father a bit of confusion in the coming week. Then she could focus solely on the party tonight and her trip tomorrow morning.

Chapter Seven

"**W**hat the devil do you think you're doing?" Nicholas demanded. He could not believe his eyes. Not because she was radiant in that gown or because her hair shone like rich gold in the lamplight. No. What she was up to was the thing that shocked him so. How dare she plunder through a man's desk as if she had a perfect right.

The instant he'd walked in and seen her, the betrothal document flashed through his mind. If she had found it there, not knowing it existed, she would never understand. God, how remiss of him not to think of that until now. How stupid not to tell her of it in the beginning.

Emily glanced up, one hand still inside the drawer of his desk. "Looking for paper," she told him, appearing not the least bit guilty about snooping. "I need to make a list."

He stalked over and physically removed her from where she stood, insinuating himself between her and his desk. He slammed the drawer shut. "Then ask for it," he said through gritted teeth. "I do not plunder through your things, do I?"

Emily huffed. "Since I don't *have* any things here to *plunder through,* that seems irrelevant. When I do have

things, you may retaliate if it will make you feel better.
I have no secrets.''

He did. ''I would appreciate your granting me my privacy.''

She narrowed her eyes at him. ''Do *you* have secrets?''

The audacity of the woman! ''If I told you, they would
no longer be secret, now would they?''

Aside from the current document he was loath to explain, Nick could well imagine her in future, discovering
things she had no business knowing. Once he became
embroiled in international matters, her prying could prove
dangerous. Not that Emily would ever discuss such things
out of hand, but it was the principle of the thing. A man
should possess an inner sanctum, shouldn't he? He always had. Anyone who had ever worked for him would
never dream of such a trespass.

Nick opened a drawer to the right and yanked out a
stack of stationery with the family crest embossed.
''There's your paper,'' he said, plunking the sheets in her
outstretched hand.

She accepted, watched him for a moment longer, then
shrugged. ''I shall need a pen.''

Nick impatiently pointed to the small case with
mother-of-pearl inlay that sat on top of the desk blotter.

''May I sit?'' she asked, brows raised in question as
she gestured toward his huge leather chair, ''Or is the
chair off-limits, as well?''

''Do I amuse you, madame?'' he asked, heartily angry
at the way she was so obviously suppressing a smile. Her
eyes sparkled with it.

He pulled out the chair for her anyway. It seemed Emily was destined to invade all corners of his existence, no
matter how sacrosanct. He did not have to like it, but he

might as well get used to it. "Do make yourself comfortable," he snapped with sarcasm.

"Aren't we in a mood," she commented, tossing him a look of weary forbearance. "And here I'd intended to offer you the first dance this evening. You might as well forget that." She selected a pen and carefully unstoppered the inkwell.

Nick propped one hip on the corner of the desk and glared like a hawk, watching her nimble fingers manipulate the writing instruments, trying like the devil not to imagine them manipulating him. The fact that they would not at any time in the near future did nothing whatsoever to improve his disposition. Well, he wouldn't touch her, either. "I never dance," he informed her.

She dipped the pen, raked it on the edge of the bottle and examined the point. "Of course you dance. I taught you myself."

The memory of those lessons rushed in as if she had yanked open a door.

For some reason Nick suddenly found the whole situation absurd. The document was safely concealed. Why was he making such a to-do over this? Had being an only child all his life rendered him terminally possessive of his things? He supposed so.

He had never liked to share. Except with Emily, he recalled. Once he had wished to give her everything her heart desired. He did now, too. Hell, she could have the damned desk, the chair, the pen, the entire study if she wished. A smile escaped before he could catch it.

She was ignoring his reprimand anyway. Nothing frightened this girl—woman, he corrected himself. Not anger, or threats, or even cholera itself seemed to scare her. Em always bounced up, plucky as ever, resilient as a ball of India rubber.

Nick folded his arms across his chest and continued watching while she wrote in fine, slanted letters, the column of whatever it was she fancied done or remembered.

"Is the list for me?" he asked, schooling himself to sound more companionable, less acrimonious. He was not willing to apologize, for he was in the right here, but he no longer wished to keep berating her. Especially when she was giving so little notice of being berated.

She looked up at him from under long amber lashes. "Why, yes, it is for you. A list of books to purchase, actually. Books of *poetry,*" she added, pointedly, raising both brows for emphasis. "I suspect I shall need to lay in a good supply of them for the future. Tell me, how do you feel about Keats?"

Nick grimaced. "Slightly nauseous. He was mad, you know."

"Good for him. Top of the list." She placed a final dot on the paper, laid down the pen and slowly leaned back in his chair, her slender hands lying along the curved arms of it. He watched her fingers flex nimbly, idly stroking the smoothly polished wood. Rhythmically stroking... His breath caught in his throat.

"Are you over your tantrum?" she asked, thankfully distracting him.

He shook off his lecherous thoughts and forced a grin. "Yes. Absolutely. So, shall I get that dance?"

"Of course," she said as she rose from the chair. "And your privacy, too. I regret the intrusion."

Rather than regretful, Nick thought she looked and sounded victorious. Admittedly, he had forfeited this round, but he could be gracious.

"You're forgiven," he said, offering his arm. He smiled down at her sincerely. "Just think, we have had our very first quarrel."

She leveled on him a world-weary look. "Hardly that."

"Our last then," he suggested with an emphatic nod.

Emily laughed. "Hardly that, either. I'd wager on it!"

In mock horror, he stared down at her. "Egad, the vicar's daughter laying a bet? Unheard of!"

The expression on her face stole his breath. It held both fear and hope. "Yet I have placed one of the largest wagers that ever a woman can, haven't I?"

Nick inclined his head, granting the truth in what she said. This marriage of theirs was a gigantic gamble for both of them.

As he walked her to the ballroom, he thought of the betrothal contract again and the wife his father had intended for him. Had it not been for the quarantine and this necessary marriage caused by it, Emily might never have allowed Nick the opportunity to explain why he had left her. She would hate him still. And if he had finally accepted that he could never have Emily, this might be Dierdre Worthing on his arm.

He wondered if it would be wicked beyond all reason to celebrate the occurrence of cholera.

"I haven't told you yet how beautiful you are in lavender, have I?" he asked.

"No, as a matter of fact, you haven't."

Nick saw she was blushing bright pink, pretending to be totally unaffected by the compliment as she shrugged and added, "However, I should think you'd make mention of it if only to counter your wretched behavior."

"You are beautiful in lavender," he said simply, resisting the urge to elaborate.

"Then I suppose I must excuse you from the sonnet readings," she replied, holding up a finger. "This once."

"Thank God that worked," he muttered, heaving a theatrical sigh of relief.

She laughed gaily as he had meant her to. Nick was glad that was the way her father, brother and the entire crew saw them as they entered the ballroom arm in arm.

The temporary image they projected at that moment was exactly how Nick wanted them to be. But he knew this instant of happiness and accord was as evanescent as a bubble of soap.

She was only beginning to trust him, venturing with small, hesitant steps toward the camaraderie they had once enjoyed. They were nowhere near the point they had reached the day he had kissed her, when she had opened her heart to him.

There were so many problems down the road that Emily didn't see yet. She had gambled with the stakes higher than she realized and was compounding her risks by accompanying him to London. Hell, she was compounding his, as well, but to force her to stay here would destroy whatever trust he had gained from her thus far.

The seaman Rolly, struck up a saucy reel on his battered old violin the moment he saw them.

Without a pause, Nick slipped his arms around Emily and began to waltz her in circles across the highly polished floor. He laughed at her surprise and halfhearted protests while the crew cheered him on.

For this evening he would hold her close and forget everything but the music and dancing with his lovely new wife. A man deserved at least one worry-free night on his honeymoon.

Actually, a man deserved considerably more than that, Nick thought wryly, but he knew he would have to be content with a few dances until their marriage was on firmer ground.

Despite the fact that he had to wait to claim her fully, and even in view of the difficulties they might encounter with Emily's being accepted as his countess, Nick felt more optimistic about their life together than he had at any time since the awkward ceremony. They had a fighting chance to make everything work, he thought, so long as they stayed on the same side of the fracas.

"Rolly's beginning to tire, I expect," she commented after they had danced through several tunes. "Shall I play and offer him a rest?"

Reluctantly, Nick led her toward the piano, a huge old grand that had grown sadly out of tune in its disuse before she'd arrived. It could still use a thorough tuning, but no one minded. Emily played so well it was easy to ignore the occasional sour note.

"Do you recall 'Folly of the Rose,' Em?" he leaned close and asked when he had seated her on the piano stool.

She said nothing, so he persisted, "I've not heard it since I came home. We could—"

"No," she said in a clipped voice he'd not heard her use before, even when she was angry. "I've forgotten it," she declared.

Immediately she positioned her fingers and ripped into a rollicking sea ditty that Lofty was overly fond of singing.

Too late Nick remembered the opening words of the song he had encouraged her to play. Words they used to sing together.

Where they once strolled together, she now strolled alone. Rose remained on the vine and her lover was gone. Oh, the folly of loving...

The rest escaped him for the moment, but Nick realized he had made a grievous error in suggesting that selection.

Much to his chagrin, he had been too focused on the memory of walking with Emily across the meadow. Nick had been recalling how they'd walked then, hands clasped and swinging to and fro between them as they sang and made ridiculous faces at one another over the sappy lyrics.

Apparently she had found new meaning in the words even if he had not.

Tomorrow, on the way to London, he would talk to her about it, explain his reason for the faux pas. She didn't appear disposed to discuss anything with him at the moment and he couldn't say that he blamed her.

One step forward, two steps back, Nick reflected. This marriage business was damned hard work.

Morning seeped in, its dampness invading the very stones of Bournesea House. Emily snuggled beneath the covers and briefly wished she did not have to leave the warmth of the bed.

Memories of last evening brought a sleepy, contented smile. Nicholas finally had shown her his true charming self again after hiding as he had behind that facade of gruffness he had acquired abroad.

Emily knew he still wished he could leave her behind, though he was being gracious in his capitulation. She would have to be satisfied with that, she supposed.

Understandable that he would not be enthusiastic about presenting her, daughter of a country vicar, to the aristocracy as his wife. She was not all that eager to be presented.

Nick's kindness was deeply rooted enough that he

would never tell her that he dreaded it, of course, but she was not so simpleminded that she couldn't figure it out for herself. However, she had decided that they might as well meet this challenge head-on at the outset. The longer they waited, the more difficult it would be.

They were married and that was a fact. Nick had stated his intention to reside in London for a good portion of each year. The sooner everyone there accepted that he had her as a wife, the better.

She threw back the covers and hurried through her morning ablutions. Since Lady Elizabeth owned no traveling garments, Emily donned her own sturdy black day gown, thankful that her brother had thought to bring her clothing back with him when he'd gone to fetch their father for last night's celebration. This was the only thing even halfway appropriate for a daylong carriage ride.

She might not make such a grand entrance into the city, but no one would see her other than the servants residing at Nick's house in town.

Quickly, she gathered up her cloak, gloves and reticule and started down to tell Nicholas she was ready to leave.

When Emily reached the doorway, she turned and took one last look around the countess's chamber. ''I wish you were coming with me, my lady,'' she whispered, then smiled at her own silly fears. She was the lady now. The countess. She must remember that above all.

''Good morning,'' Nick greeted her with a curt nod as he continued supervising the placement of their trunks atop the closed coach.

Emily cast a quick wave at Wrecker who was performing the task. Young Sam Herring would be driving and was already in place, attempting to keep the prancing team calm. Another of the men approached, holding the reins of a saddled mare.

"Will you be riding?" Emily asked.

Nick frowned at the mount. "She'll be hitched behind us. Either Wrecker or myself must ride for a few miles along the way. There are locations where an outrider will be needed."

Emily did not need to ask why. She had read about the dangers inherent in travel. Due to lack of employment, many a man had been forced to resort to thievery. Coaches transporting the well-to-do were always fair game for highwaymen.

The mounts tugged at their traces, obviously none too thrilled to be doing their duty on a bleak, foggy day such as this, but ready to have done with it since they were committed. Though her pride would never allow her to show it, she knew exactly how the poor beasts felt.

Nick opened the carriage door and turned to assist her inside, then climbed in behind her. "Still certain you want to go?"

She smiled confidently as she arranged her skirts and situated her reticule on the seat beside her. "Of course!" she said brightly. "I wouldn't miss it for the world."

The coach rocked and creaked as Wrecker moved around on top, securing their luggage. "All set up here, m'lord," he called down.

"Then let's be off." He raised his silver-headed cane and knocked on the ceiling, signaling Sam Herring that they were settled inside and prepared to leave.

Emily put on a smile and clutched the edge of the seat as the carriage lumbered through the gates. "I've not much experience with carriages," she told Nick. None, in fact. She could not recall ever having been inside one. Her father had only a one-horse trap to carry him about the country. "This one seems very grand," she observed, scanning the interior that was outfitted with coach lamps and rich-looking fabric. The smooth leather seat, though tufted, felt slippery beneath and behind her. One short stop and she would surely slide forward into his lap.

"It's quite old and not very well sprung," he noted with a grimace. "Father should have replaced it." He shoved his leather satchel into one corner, then shrugged out of his lightweight cloak and made a show of tugging off his gloves one finger at a time.

He unbuttoned his suit coat as he raised a brow. "Would you mind if I sat beside you so that we can both face forward?"

Emily didn't think they would fit, what with her voluminous skirts. "We could exchange places," she suggested.

"No, the trip will not be a smooth one, apparently, and riding backward might make you feel ill."

"Do you?" she asked quickly. "Feel ill, that is?"

He shook his head and reached across to assist her in gathering her skirts to one side to make room for him. "Not yet, but we wouldn't want to risk it, would we?"

Suddenly and gracefully, despite his great height, Nick moved across the carriage and joined her. "There. Much better," he stated firmly. He lay one long arm along the back of the seat and propped the other along the window ledge so that he could grasp the edge of it.

Emily wriggled, attempting to make herself comfortable, though she felt a bit discombobulated, being this close to him. The spicy scent of his pleasing cologne, a subtle yet enticing male sort of essence, seemed to envelop her. Her heart beat too fast and she could not seem to gather her wits.

"Relax," he advised. "You can't mean to sit on the edge of the seat all the way to London."

"No, no, of course not," she answered, laughing nervously. Where should she put her hands? The one next to him was wedged between her thigh and his, captured there by the weight of her skirts and his thigh-length coat. Through the fabrics and her glove, she could feel the hard muscle of his leg. Her other hand had lost its purchase on the seat and was now fisted uselessly in the folds of her attire.

"Lean back," he suggested when the carriage rocked side to side. "You'll feel more secure anchored against me."

Emily doubted that. Already her head was reeling and not entirely from the motion of the carriage. Still, she did as he asked, feeling very daring and adventurous to willingly place herself in the niche he had created for her.

He had braced his boots against the floorboard and the base of the opposite seat. Emily abandoned her long-held propriety and propped the soles of her own sturdy half boots against the seat edge of the expensive leather cushion. "Yes, better," she agreed, though she wondered how she would maintain this position for the better part of a day.

"We shall stop for luncheon and a rest at Browley," he told her. "The inn there was once an adequate place to dine. I wonder if it has changed over the years."

"I wouldn't know," she replied absently. She had never been over ten miles in any direction from Bournesea village. Today's adventure took on a small element of fear. Fear of the unknown and of her own inadequacy.

With her thumb, she rubbed her wedding ring and thought of Lady Elizabeth who had worn it before her. It had seemed to take on the role of talisman for her somehow without her even realizing it. Through her glove, the little gesture she now made imbued her with the courage to face what she must.

A mile or so later, they reached the main road. Either their way had become smoother or Emily reckoned she had grown used to the motion and Nick's nearness. She abandoned herself to the gentle rocking motion, not much minding the creak of the carriage springs and the wet clacking of the horses' hooves against the muddy road.

"You see?" he said, a smile in his voice. "This is not so bad, is it?"

Emily looked up at him. His strong arm surrounded her. His body radiated heat against hers. His face was mere inches from her own. Her gaze settled on his mouth, then crept slowly up to his eyes. The hooded look of blatant desire in them almost frightened her.

Silly to be afraid, she thought, swallowing hard. This was Nick, her friend, whose arms had held her every bit this closely last evening as they danced. She had not been afraid then, had she?

And their lips had been much closer than this at one time. The memory of their one passionate kiss suffused her thinking then and must have communicated itself to him. His mouth lowered to hers and pressed against it.

The carriage bumped once, jarring them apart. Instead of backing away, Nick cradled her face with his hand and reclaimed her. Emily's mind blanked beneath the on-slaught, her entire body shivering in anticipation as he drew her closer, turning her so that her breasts pressed against the front of his coat.

With her free hand, she reached between them and tugged the unbuttoned coat aside, mindlessly cursing his stiff brocade waistcoat and shirt that lay between them. Her corset bit into her ribs as she twisted her torso for a closer meld.

He burned kisses across her cheek, her brow and then her ear, exposed beneath the simple black hat she wore to services each Sunday to cover her pinned-up curls. She groaned low in her throat, unmindful of the fact that she encouraged what he was doing.

''Emily,'' he whispered, the sound of her name tangled with the fervent caresses of his breath and tongue. She swiftly turned her head so that her mouth caught his and took what she had dreamed of for seven long years.

His hand trailed from her face down her neck, briefly cupped her shoulder, then settled on one breast. Her indrawn breath of surprise only fueled the conflagration. Nick's kiss grew wild and urgent, his hold tighter as she responded in kind to him.

She loved the sounds he made, sounds pulled from deep inside him by the way she made him feel. The ability to move him so drugged her with a heady sense of power she had never thought to know. It begged increasing. Emily slid one hand beneath his vest and caressed the muscles that encased his rapidly beating heart.

On and on he kissed her, driving her to distraction with hands that roamed her body, claimed it without any of the protective hesitancy she recalled in the boy he had been.

Cool air reached her legs as her skirts crept up above her calves. Long, strong fingers smoothed their way past the garters that held her silken hose above her knees. At last, the subtle slide of skin against skin as his hand moved higher, gradually smoothing its way closer, closer still…

''Nicky,'' she breathed against his mouth between kisses.

Suddenly he removed his hand and hastily replaced her skirts. ''What am I thinking?'' he asked, his voice gravelly and full of frustration. ''We can't do this here.''

''W-why not?'' The words had slipped out unbidden.

She knew as well as he how woefully inappropriate this was. "No, no, you're right," she agreed, pushing against his chest to put distance between them so she could think.

His self-deprecating laugh sounded as woeful as she felt. For a brief second he drew her close again, held her rather fiercely, then let her go. "Forgive me, Emily. This was not what I intended."

He grabbed his cane and gave a knock on the roof, a signal to halt, Emily supposed. The carriage began to slow down, then rocked to a stop. "I had better ride outside for a while," he told her with a guilty glance.

Emily said nothing. What was there to say? Embarrassed, she avoided looking at him. With shaking hands, she put her bonnet to rights and retied the bow beneath her chin.

By the time she had finished, Nick had climbed down and closed the door. He didn't even pause to excuse himself and say he would meet her at the inn. He just left her there.

She risked a peek out the window and saw him round the back of the carriage. The saddled mount he had brought along was tied there, so she supposed he would be riding horseback instead of up top with Wrecker and Sam Herring. The carriage felt cavernous without him in it. Cold and uncomfortable to the extreme.

Emily noticed he had forgotten his cloak and knew she should remind him and hand it out. She scooped it up just as Sam Herring snapped the reins and called "Get up!" Too late for that, she thought. They were on their way.

It would probably be hours before they reached the inn. Snuggling herself into a corner, Nick's cloak covering her, she buried her face in the wide collar of the light woolen garment, closed her eyes and breathed in his enticing scent and tried to pass the time with sleep.

Emily came awake to a horrendous jolt that bounced her right off the seat and onto the floor. Horses screamed. The carriage lurched, tossing her this way and that. She grasped for something—anything—to secure herself against the hurtling conveyance.

Herring shouted madly, his high-pitched voice unintelligible except for the tone of fear.

"Nick!" Emily screamed, rattling about like a bean shaken in a jar. She sucked in a breath and held it, too scared to scream again.

The coach pitched sideways, rolled upside down, came right, then rolled again.

Emily scrambled madly, grasping at any and every thing to brace herself against the wild tumbling, but found no purchase. At last, the entire assemblage came to rest with a final bounce. On its side.

"Oh, God!" she exclaimed, afraid to move.

Then she squeaked in her throat, her lips tight against a terrified cry. Wide-eyed, she looked around, hardly able to see in the low light. Though both windows had broken out, only one was upward toward the sky. All she could see was fog.

"Nicky?" she screamed, and burst into tears. Shaking and sobbing wildly, dashing at her face with the back of one forearm, Emily fought hard for control.

Shivering, moving as carefully as she could, she tried to stand and failed. Glass crunched beneath her and the carriage rocked.

Nick would get her out of here, she thought, repeating the thought until he could make it come true.

"Nick! Wrecker! Sam?" she shouted as loudly as she

could. One glance at the broken window above her head revealed no husband, no curious driver or seaman-turned-footman peeping down. Only the heavy fog swirled in, adding moisture to her face already wet with tears of terror. Had all three men been injured?

No, Nick had been riding the mare, hadn't he? She had not actually seen him mount. He could have been on the coach with Wrecker and Sam. She prayed he hadn't been.

It appeared she was on her own. But first, she had to get out of this silk- and leather-lined cage.

Sniffing hard, she took several deep breaths and tried to stand up. The carriage shifted, rocking dangerously like a teeterboard, and her legs buckled beneath her.

What if the thing tipped and began to roll again?

Chapter Eight

Emily remained still for some time, terrified that another shift of the coach might send her crashing to her death.

She brushed a trembling hand over her brow and winced. Unable to locate her reticule which contained a handkerchief, she wiped the trickle of blood away with the back of her glove. There was a cut at the edge of her hairline, probably caused by flying glass when the windows shattered.

Tentatively she checked for other injuries. Bruises began to ache, but no bones seemed broken.

She waited a few moments for someone to come to see about her. By chance, her hand brushed against the small reticule she'd brought with her. She took out her handkerchief, wiped her face and patted her brow. At least her head had stopped bleeding.

She tucked away her handkerchief and looped the drawstring of her reticule around one wrist so she would not lose it again. Nick's leather case was lying in one corner. She picked it up and held it to her chest, resting her chin on the edge. He would need this in London. If they ever reached there, she thought.

How far had they traveled from Bournesea? Too far to

walk back for assistance, she knew that much. And that inn Nick had spoken of must surely be too far away, since it was nowhere near noon. Or was it? She fiddled for her time piece pinned to her lapel. Unfortunately, there wasn't sufficient light to see the hands of it.

She huffed out a breath of frustration, drew in another and shouted at the top of her voice, "Nicholas! Wrecker? Herring? Can you hear me?"

In the stillness that followed, she thought she heard a scrambling in the brush outside.

"Emily!"

It was Nick! "Here!" she called.

Immediately, the outline of his head and shoulders appeared in the window, silhouetted against the meager light. He was prone, looking down at her.

"Are you hurt?" He sounded breathless, as if he had run a long way.

"Only a scratch on my head and a few bumps. Are you all right? What of Wrecker and Sam?" They had surely been thrown off or crushed beneath the coach as it tumbled.

"I haven't found them yet. I've been trying to get to you. Damn this fog! Can't see past the end of your arm."

"Get me out of here," she pleaded.

"In a moment. Listen to me carefully, Em. Don't panic, but you should know the coach is resting on the edge of a precipice," Nick told her. "Very carefully, you must try to stand. No sudden movements, now."

Emily got her feet under her and rose slowly, inches at the time, until she was upright.

She heard Nick release a tortured breath and draw in another. "Come now, grasp my wrist with both hands," he commanded. "At the slightest movement of the carriage, you must freeze."

"Yes," she said with a jerky nod. "Yes, that is what I must do. I can do it." Somehow, his making the decisions for her felt comforting. Strange, when she usually hated for anyone to do such a thing.

"Are you certain you're able, Emily? I will come inside there and lift you out if need be, but since our balance seems precarious, you'd do better to let me lift you out. Are you too afraid?"

"Certainly not!" she declared, frowning up at him. She was scared to death, but not about to admit it.

Gingerly, Emily straightened her legs and stood on tiptoe. She tried to ignore the stiffness and painful bruises she had acquired. The top of her head remained well below the opening of the window.

"I wish I weren't so short," she remarked unnecessarily.

Nick grunted in agreement, then cleared his throat. "This is the difficult part, Em. You must not struggle or try to help when I lift you."

She looked up at him, wishing she could see his features, judge the extent of his fear. "There's a danger we will fall, isn't there?" she cried. "Plummet like rocks thrown down a well!"

"Let's not dwell on that, shall we? Just do as I say."

She swallowed hard, then held up his leather case. "You might want this."

"Leave anything else," he ordered as he took it from her. "Let's get you out of there. Nothing else matters at the moment."

As soon as both her hands closed around his wrist, he began to lift. Soon her feet were dangling. Nick now crouched above the open window and slowly pulled her up. She could hear his labored breathing. Or was that her own?

Her skirts caught on the fragmented glass around the window frame. The coach groaned and she felt as if it slid a few feet beneath them.

"Don't struggle!" he warned. "I'm going to release your hands now if you will bend at the waist and rest your upper half outside the window. You're almost free."

She felt him tug gently but persistently on the folds of her skirts and petticoats until he had them billowed outside, bunched around her waist. Her lower half, bare except for her pantalets, stocking and half boots, remained inside.

"Emily, don't move," he advised. He worked his gloved hand beneath her, obviously feeling for any remnants of the jagged glass. He broke off several and she heard them clink as they dropped back inside.

"When I stand up," he said, his voice tight with apprehension, "I shall lift you out the rest of the way. We must be quick. It might be necessary to leap for it if the coach slips again. Leap that way," he instructed, tossing his case off one side. "Cling to me and I'll try to break your fall. Once you hit the ground, grab anything to anchor yourself. Ready?"

She made a strangled sound of agreement. He grasped her beneath her arms and yanked her free of the window. With that effort, the very earth seemed to shift beneath them.

Nick shouted as he tumbled backward. Emily heard a high-pitched wail of terror and realized it was hers as they landed with a thud and began to slide.

The thunder of the coach crashing downward drowned out any other sound they might have made. Emily realized she had one arm locked around Nick's neck and the other around a spindly tree. Half its roots had been torn out of the ground. She craned her neck to see where they were.

The fog had lifted a bit, but not much. Again her legs were suspended, this time over the rocky edge of the cliff.

"Hold on," Nick ordered in a grated whisper. His arm tightened around her back. "Give me a moment to catch my breath."

Emily pushed her face into the curve of his neck, her nose pressed against his stiff collar and neckcloth, and prayed for them. And for the small, damaged tree that was their anchor.

Nick recovered soon, convinced her to let go of the sapling and began inching his body and hers a few feet up the slope toward better purchase.

"There now," he said finally, rising to a sitting position and assisting her in doing the same. "We should assess our damage," he suggested, his voice tense. "Let me see that scratch of yours."

He leaned close and brushed the hair away from her brow. His hand shook. Suddenly his eyes clenched and his arms enfolded her. "Oh, God," he said, grasping her so tightly she could scarcely breathe.

"It's nothing," she assured him as she clung to him. "Really, I'm all right."

"I know, I know," he said. But for a long time, he held her without gentling his grip at all. Emily smiled, infinitely glad to be alive and in his arms, no matter how she got there.

Eventually he released her. "We must see about the men," he said, looking back up the slope. "Are you up to the climb?"

Emily nodded and stood, balancing carefully so that she wouldn't go rolling back down the way they had come.

"Thank you for saving me," she said sincerely. "I should be dead if not for you."

"Try not to think about it," he advised. "Concentrate on getting up to the road." He spied his case, which had landed nearby, and walked over to pick it up. "We'd best hurry. Take my hand."

Halfway up, they discovered Wrecker lying facedown, unconscious. Nick knelt and rolled the man over to check for injuries. "He's just knocked cold, I think." Nick began chafing Wrecker's face with his hands and calling his name to bring him around.

The giant opened his eyes and squinted up at them. "W-what happened?" He ran a hand through his hair and sucked in a deep breath. "We o'erturned," he growled, answering his own question. His worried gaze flew to Emily, then melted to one of relief.

She patted his shoulder. "Are you injured?"

Wrecker stretched, shaking each arm and leg to see whether they worked. "Banged up, but I'll do," he assured her.

Nick got to his feet and offered Wrecker a hand. "Can you stand?"

"Aye. Naught wrong wi' me but I lost my wind." He grunted as he stood and sucked in several noisy breaths.

"I was riding behind the carriage. Did you see what happened to Herring?" Nick asked, looking around them while Wrecker raked mud and leaves off his clothes.

"Sam flew forward when we hit summat in th' road. Th' carriage tongue snapped clean in two. His hands was wrapped in th' ribbons, puir sod. Likely got drug aways afore he got loose." Wrecker hawked and spat to one side, then shook his head sadly. "*If* he got loose."

Nick was already making his way up to the road. "Assist Lady Emily. I'll go and find him and the team."

"Be careful!" Emily called as she watched him hurry away.

She picked up Nick's leather case and began making her own way through the briars and vines while Wrecker followed, wheezing under the effort.

When they finally reached the road, neither Nick, Herring, nor the horses were anywhere to be seen.

"There 'tis," Wrecker said, pointing to the log lying across the road. "Summat spooked them horses just round that bend in th' road. Rabbit, most like. They reared and took off like a shot. We was already leanin' when we hit that thing."

Emily walked over to examine the obstruction. The branches and foliage of it lay well out of the path. Only the trunk, which had roughly the circumference of one of Wrecker's stout legs, lay crosswise the road.

She walked over to the base of the fallen tree. However, it had not broken naturally, she noticed immediately. The stump of it stood a few yards from the edge of the road, hack marks from an ax clearly apparent on the light-colored greenwood. Someone had deliberately felled this, then dragged it to where it now lay.

Her gaze flew to Wrecker's knowing one before he quickly glanced away to scout the surrounding area. He did not appear to be surprised, and she saw that he already held a pistol in his hand.

"Thieves?" she questioned in a near whisper.

He shrugged, moving closer to her. "Let's us go o'er there, by that rock, ma'am," he suggested, pointing with his free hand. "Least our backs won't be exposed."

Emily wasted no time. Shivers ran down her spine at the thought of robbers nearby, men who would cause a wreck to relieve the passengers of their wealth. It made no sense to her, when she thought about it. "Why didn't they simply hold up the carriage as highwaymen usually do?'' she asked.

Again Wrecker shrugged. ''Don't know. Hope we don't get no chance to ask 'em.''

As it happened, they did not have that chance, for which Emily would be eternally grateful. Nothing else happened until she heard the jingle of harness a half hour later.

Down the road from the direction of London rode Nick on his mare and Herring mounted bareback on one of the team that had broken free and run away. Nick was leading another of the horses. She and Wrecker heaved tandem sighs of relief.

The first thing Nick noted was Wrecker holding a weapon. The footman and Emily were backed up against a huge rock as if to ward off an attack. Wrecker left Emily where she was and came forward to meet Nick as he halted and dismounted.

''Warn't no happenstance, m'lord,'' Wrecker said immediately, looking pointedly at the chopped end of the tree.

''Damnation.'' Nick cursed himself for not checking that before he took off after Herring and the horses. If there had been thieves waiting... He looked around at the sparse cover available.

No one could be hiding nearby unless they were secluded behind one of the low outcroppings of rocks that dotted the landscape. One or two people might conceal themselves, but not a group of mounted highwaymen. There was hardly a place large enough to hide even one horse near the spot where the tree had been placed.

''Well, I suppose whoever planned this decided not to

follow through." He glanced at Wrecker's pistol. "Do stay alert, however."

He went over to Emily and put his arm around her shoulders, guiding her toward the horses. She must be frightened out of her mind. Any other woman of his acquaintance would already have succumbed to hysterics.

"We will ride on to the inn and get you settled," he told her gently. "I'll hire someone to come back here and try to collect our things from the wreck if they can get down there."

She looked up at him, eyes wide and lips trembling. "Someone attempted to kill us," she whispered.

Nick smiled, shook his head and squeezed her closer. "No, no, of course not! The tree across the road was merely meant to force us to stop the carriage. That's all it would have done if something had not stampeded the horses. There would have been plenty of time to stop. The highwaymen would have stepped out of hiding and demanded our money. A simple robbery attempt, that's all it was. The wreck of the carriage must have put them off."

He wondered whether she believed him. It sounded plausible, even if it wasn't true.

Someone had deliberately spooked the horses somehow. Any coach or carriage traveling behind a runaway team and encountering such a large obstruction would certainly overturn.

If it had tumbled end over end on the hard surface of the road instead of rolling side to side down the brush-cushioned slope, the conveyance would have broken apart. And if he had been inside the coach with Emily, they would never have made it out of there without going over that cliff. Neither of them would have survived.

No highwayman with any sense would arrange to halt

a carriage where there was no place to conceal himself until the moment of approach. There were much better places down the road to set up a robbery. But this place, with that curve in the road so that the tree would not be seen until too late to avoid it, was altogether too well thought out to suit Nick.

He hated to consider that the person or persons intent on his demise had followed him from Gujarat, or else had agents here in England. World trade was cutthroat these days, especially when one delved deeply into the politics involved in it.

When he had left India, Nick had resigned his active role in gathering intelligence and keeping the ministry informed of political problems in the countries he visited as a merchant. Obviously, his enemy or enemies either had not received word of his planned retirement in that area, or they held ill will against him for what they might consider spying.

It was spying, of course, consisting of an involved network of local informants he had recruited himself just for the purpose of informing the government, through him, of changes that would affect world trade. He also had ensured that the flow of information would not cease, though he would no longer be the one in charge of reporting it through channels.

The attempt on their lives might have been made by a business competitor. One in particular came to mind. Julius Munford had been the primary suspect in the two attempts on Nick's life before he'd left India. It would not take long to find out whether Munford had followed.

One thing Nick did know: he must find out precisely who wanted to get rid of him and why, and then institute some countermeasures. And he had to do it soon.

He wished he had been able to persuade Emily to remain at Bournesea. However, now that he considered it, she might be safer with him than left there with so little defense and unaware of the danger. Kidnapping was a grave possibility, one he could scarcely stand to think about.

There were few men he trusted here in his own country to offer her any protection, and the ones he felt he could rely on were either about to set sail again, with him at the moment, or waiting in London.

Yes, he decided firmly, Emily probably would be better off by his side despite this latest attempt. Now that he knew to expect trouble, he would be prepared for it.

The inn proved far more comfortable than Emily had expected. The charm of the white-washed, half-timbered exterior also lent itself to the inside where a portly innkeeper greeted them.

Obsequious, yet cheerful, their host bowed and scraped, then scurried up the stairs ahead of them. All the way he nattered on and on, apologizing in advance for the humbleness of the accommodations and promising to make up for it with the evening meal. Apparently, the man's wife boasted French blood somewhere along the line. Emily supposed he'd concluded this somehow aided her culinary skills.

She could not discern whether the inn met Nick's expectations. He still seemed preoccupied by the wreck.

He dismissed the innkeeper the moment they entered the chamber, then addressed her. "Please remain here until I return. Wrecker will be waiting downstairs in the public room with Herring. Lock this door and do not open it until I return."

Nick started to leave, then turned with a further admonishment. "And be certain that it *is* me before you unlock it. A public inn is not the safest place in the world for a woman alone and Wrecker is none to swift on his feet at the moment if you should call for help.''

"Aye, aye, *sir*," she snapped, a bit put out by the sharpness of his tone. After all, he was not the only one affected by the devilish upset.

One hand resting upon the door frame, the other propped on one hip, he summoned an unexpected grin. "Applying for the job of first mate?" he asked.

"Only mate," Emily replied seriously.

He laughed. "Seems you're already hired. I'll see you in a while."

"Take care, Nick, and please hurry back." Emily watched him nod, wishing they had time to discuss all that had happened. When he closed the door, she approached it and turned the key.

There were things he had not yet shared with her about the attempted robbery that caused their wreck. Emily wished he would not try so hard to spare her worry and simply tell her what the problem was.

She also thought they should address what had almost happened between them earlier in the carriage. Though she had not planned to give in to her attraction to Nick quite so soon, Emily had to admit that he had certainly made an excellent case for doing so.

Matters between them had grown more and more congenial to the point where she was quite ready to take the next step in solidifying their marriage. More than ready, if the truth be known. So, apparently, was Nick. Remembering those daring caresses of his made her hum with anticipation.

"First things first," she muttered to herself as she sat down and began to remove her muddy half boots and her stockings.

Though there was no fresh linen with which to wash, she found a half-filled pitcher of water beside the basin on the table. She should clean off the mud as best she could and at least make herself halfway presentable for Nick when he returned.

She retrieved her drawstring reticule from the chair beside Nick's satchel where they had set them when they entered. Stretching the small purse open, Emily fished out her handkerchief. The tiny square consisted of more lace than soft linen. It hadn't helped much in mopping up blood from the scratch on her head and would not do much in the way of cleaning the mud off of her, either.

Perhaps Nick carried a supply of extras in his satchel. She had read somewhere that gentlemen always brought along extra gloves wherever they went, so there were probably handkerchiefs in there, too.

She laid the leather case on its side in the chair and proceeded to figure out how to operate the metal fastener. Men were much more practical than women when choosing accessories, she was thinking as the latch popped open.

Her glance flicked to the door, prompted by the tiny niggle of guilt she knew she would feel if he knew she was plundering through his things. She sighed. It wasn't as if he could walk in and catch her at it. The door was locked. Besides, he would know that she had opened it, anyway, wouldn't he, if she used one of his handkerchiefs?

Shoving aside her overactive conscience—as well as the memory of his anger when he'd caught her at his desk—Emily opened the case wide and began to examine the numerous pockets positioned along the sides. Three pairs of gloves. A comb and brush. An extra neckcloth…

''There,'' she remarked to herself when she located

several folded squares of pristine linen. Slipping one out, she started to close the case when something caught her eye and held it.

A long brown envelope rested on top of a bundled sheaf of other papers. On the front in large letters was written Betrothal Contract.

She sank to her knees before the chair, the wind sucked right out of her sails. *This could not be.*

Maybe it was not what she thought. It could be something Nick was holding for someone else, perhaps one of the men. Couldn't it?

Gingerly, as if the thing contained something dangerous, she lifted the envelope upright and examined the words on it.

She noted that it was not written in Nick's distinctive, slanted handwriting, but in a more upright scrawl and quite large as though to draw attention to what was inside. Well, it had certainly grabbed *her* full attention, she thought with an angry twist of her lips.

With a disgusted sigh, she quickly opened the unsealed flap and drew out the document.

Upon unfolding it, she saw that it was exactly what she feared it was. Proof that Nicholas had lied to her outright. He *had* been betrothed to Dierdre Worthing since his eighteenth birthday, long before he had courted Emily, long before she was even old enough to be courted.

All those years ago when she'd thought they were such good friends, he had never once mentioned his betrothal. And then he had kissed her, pretended love for her and, though he had never proposed, he had certainly left the impression that he was free to do so.

Worst of all, when she had asked him directly before

the wedding if he was engaged to Dierdre, he had sworn there was nothing official. A blatant falsehood. Why?

His lies of omission before he'd left for India, she could understand, though not condone. He had wanted her even though he was not free to offer her marriage. But what purpose did his denial of the betrothal serve when he was about to wed Emily in spite of it? Perhaps it was because he did not want her to know how he had intended to use her, then cast her off when it came time to marry someone else.

Emily realized she had clutched the paper so fiercely the edge of it was quite crumpled. Deliberately, she smoothed it out, wishing she could rip the blasted thing to shreds.

The document in its original intent was worthless now, of course. But it served one purpose: it had dashed all her hopes of eventually establishing a happy marriage with Nicholas.

How could she ever trust his word when he had deliberately lied to her more than once about something this important?

The furor Dierdre's family might raise over this breach of honor could affect them the rest of their lives. Entire fortunes had been lost in lawsuits over such things. Nicholas surely knew that better than she did, yet he had not warned her.

Her imagination began to run wild.

Perhaps Nick had never expected her to reach London.

Chapter Nine

Nick entered the inn midafternoon after assisting the local men he had hired to salvage what they could from the wreck. The carriage itself was a total loss, of course, smashed beyond repair. He refused to think what would have happened had Emily gone over the cliff along with it.

He had retrieved a change of clothing from her battered trunk before having it loaded upon the private coach he had hired to carry them on to London.

Nick debated about whether to stay here the night. Emily might be too upset to travel on. If they did so, it would put them long after dark arriving. Yet, if they did not, it would mean sharing a room at the inn. He would leave it up to her.

"Wrecker, go and tell Herring that he can take the team horse and return to Bournesea. He'll be able to ride if he goes slowly, but with that injured arm, I know he can't drive. I have hired someone to take his place."

"I could drive," Wrecker informed him. "But we might need us a lookout what can shoot."

"Just so," Nick agreed, meeting Wrecker's knowing

gaze. "I will explain later why I did not involve the local constable in this matter. But for now—"

Wrecker interrupted. "Got to do wi' troubles brung wi' ye, ain't it? Never you mind, I'll keep a eye out and a ear open. You see to Lady Em. She took a right good shaking."

Nick clapped Wrecker on the shoulder and nodded. Then he went up the stairs to the room where Emily waited. He hoped she had gotten some rest and was recovered enough to go on.

He knocked on the door and she asked immediately, "Who is there?"

"Nick. Open up."

She did so, stepping aside as he came in. "I brought you clean clothing," he told her, laying her gown and things on the foot of the bed and setting the small slippers beside them. He tossed his own clothes down next to hers and turned, flexing his right arm and shoulder as he asked, "So, how are your aches and pains? I feel as though someone dragged me all the way here by the boots. We had quite a climb down to the carriage to fetch the baggage."

"I am doing well enough, thank you," she said in a clipped voice. She did not meet his eyes. And her fair skin appeared mottled with red as if she had been weeping.

"Are you certain?" he prodded, stepping closer, reaching out to tip up her chin.

Moving away, avoiding his hand, Emily clasped her upper arms and turned so that he could only see her back.

"Something is wrong," he guessed. "What's happened? Did someone come to the room while I was—"

"No, no one."

Then what? he wondered. Was she upset that he had

been gone for several hours? Maybe she was hungry. "We need something to eat. I'll go down and order a meal for us while you dress."

She said nothing.

"Will you be able to travel on today or should I arrange for us to stay the night here?"

"We can go now," she said, her voice curiously devoid of inflection.

"Are you afraid, Emily?"

She shook her head, the movement jerky but emphatic.

Nick studied the stiff line of her back and shoulders. Something definitely was amiss here, but at the moment she did not seem inclined to tell him what it was.

How unlike Emily to be so closemouthed about anything. Little chatterbox that she was, he could count on her letting loose before long, he would wager. And when she did so...

Nick let it be. He let *her* be. He would allow her to freshen herself, then he would feed her a belated luncheon, load her into the hired coach and wait until she grew weary of giving him the silent treatment.

A husband's lot, he mused, not at all unhappy with the idea that he, along with thousands of other husbands, must tolerate these small feminine gambits. They were a fact of married life, so he had heard, and he rather looked forward to experiencing all of them.

Silence suited him very well at the moment anyway. Wouldn't Emily be appalled to know that? He smiled to himself as he went down to order an early tea.

Her usual sunny nature had taken a beating by the morning's events and she was suffering the effects of it now, that was all. There had been nothing for her to do but dwell on it for the better part of the day. When he provided continued reassurance that nothing of the sort would happen again, she would recover soon enough.

Had she not been ready to allow him to make love to her in the carriage? Remembering her sweet willingness, Nick knew he would have no trouble regaining that once they were comfortably established in town and she felt safe again. There would be no more of this marriage-in-name-only foolishness. They would have enough other problems to deal with once they reached London. Thank God he would no longer have to worry about that.

Emily spent the remainder of their journey wondering what she should do next with regard to Nicholas. Her first impulse had been to confront him and demand an explanation. But she already had the explanation, didn't she? Nick had lied to her.

Why he had done so was no mystery. He had told a bald-faced lie for the same reason he had lied by omission seven years earlier. He wanted her. She did not doubt that fact. He might never have loved her or intended to marry her, but he did desire her, both then and now.

She also thought he hated the fact that he desired her as fervently as he did. Why else would he avoid taking what she had readily offered? Emily knew he thought she would hamper his aspirations in London. Perhaps she would. Perhaps he had thought of nothing else since their marriage and now wanted rid of her.

Her second impulse had been to run home to her father and to refuse to see Nicholas ever again. A childish response, she knew, and quickly discarded the idea as impractical and ridiculous. She never ran from a problem. It went against her very nature to do so.

Now she avoided looking directly at him, though he

sat right across from her, apparently quite willing to suffer riding backward all the way to London. Fat lot she cared, Emily thought with a sniff. As if, knowing what she did, she would want his arms around her now. Or ever, she qualified.

Her peripheral vision caught his smile. She ignored it. Fortunately, he did not attempt to force conversation. After a few brief comments about the hired coach—which she agreed was better sprung, though less well-appointed than the other—he had retreated to his own thoughts and left her to hers.

Dark, those thoughts were, too, and grew darker still as daylight waned and the hours passed. The interior grew black as pitch. Emily slid to one side of her seat and braced herself into the corner where she could lean her head against the wall. Her neck felt stiff, her back ached and she dearly wished for a long, hot bath.

She closed her eyes, putting aside any decisions until she could think more clearly.

"We are almost there," Nick said softly, waking her with a gentle shake of her shoulder. She bolted upright, astounded that she had allowed herself to sleep.

The clopping hooves of the mounts echoed off the paving stones, a lonely sound. The hour was late and there surely must be a dearth of traffic on the streets.

The coach halted soon afterward and Emily felt a sudden wave of apprehension wash over her. Like an evil tide, it left all sorts of ugly imaginings in its wake. Would Nick's servants mock her? Would they greatly resent his making the vicar's daughter his countess? Had they all been privy to his betrothal to Dierdre?

Some of these people, she would know, for this is where Nick had sent the staff who had resided at Bournesea. La, what would Mrs. Waxton, the pruny old housekeeper, think of her now? Well, she had never liked Emily in any case. And Rosie Hempstead, the tweenie Emily had played with as a child? What would Rosie say, having to call Emily *my lady?* They wouldn't like it, either of them, nor would any of the others she had greeted as equals every Sunday morning since she could remember. Why had she insisted on coming here?

She groaned at the thought. "I do not wish to do this tonight."

Nick's hand found hers in the darkness. "Don't fret, Em. All will be well. Trust me."

Trust him? Emily almost laughed aloud. She wouldn't trust Nicholas any farther than she could spit. A ladylike thought. She felt like spitting, though.

Instead she squared her shoulders, lifted her chin and worked up her courage. She had faced worse. She was the countess and she would act the part. If anyone did not like it, including the exalted earl who had insisted on a marriage he obviously did not want, they could...they could just...go hang!

Wrecker opened the door, let down the steps and stood back. Nicholas exited first and turned to assist her. Emily gave him her hand and focused her attention on placing her feet where they should go so she would not trip on her skirts and fall into the street. What an ignominious introduction to London that would be. She could see it in the morning papers: Upstart Countess Tours Our Fair City From The Ground Up.

"Welcome to Kendale House," Nick said as he steadied her.

She tugged her hands from his, brushed down her skirts, then straightened her bonnet. As she did all of this, her eyes adjusted to the dim light afforded by the gas

lamps—wonders she had read about, but never seen—
and she saw the house.

It loomed over them, an unwelcoming, imposing gran-
ite monstrosity, an intimidating display of wealth and influence. Bournesea was larger, but did not seem nearly
so forbidding as this place. Whoever had constructed
Kendale House had done so for the primary purpose of
causing the small to feel smaller, Emily decided. And this
was to be home for half their years? She gulped, battling
the urge to flee.

"Come," Nick said with a lightness she would not
have expected. "Time to surprise the household. I should
have sent a man ahead to warn of our arrival. That's what
father used to do. We hadn't one to spare, however, so
we'll make the grand entrance."

"Nick, couldn't we—" she whispered.

"The knocker won't be out. You'll have to use your
knuckles," he said to Wrecker.

This sort of surprise certainly wouldn't endear her to
the servants, Emily knew. She hung back, shaking her
head in refusal. "Wait, Nick. Surely you have keys.
Couldn't we sneak in and retire without waking them?
Everyone will surely be abed at this hour."

"*Sneak* in?" He chuckled as he tucked her hand into
the crook of his arm and urged her toward the steps leading up to enormous double doors. "No, I'm afraid that
would not be acceptable in this instance. Or in *any* instance," he added, as if he thought she might err later
on when he was not around to advise her.

"Just because I entered Bournesea by stealth that once
is no reason to vilify me in advance for possible misdo-
ings in the future," she retorted. "I only thought to save
waking anyone out of a sound sleep tonight."

"Can you imagine how horrified they would be to find

us here in the morning unexpectedly? Besides, it's not yet ten o'clock. They won't keep country hours here," he informed her.

And neither would she in future, she suspected. "If that is your way of reminding me of my provincial background, it was most effective. I am properly cowed."

"You know very well that was not my intention," he argued. "Behave now, and for heaven's sake, smile."

"You want me to *smile?*" The last expression in the world she wished to adopt at the moment.

The sound of Wrecker knocking upon the door reverberated in the stillness around them.

Nick watched him, too, in the anemic light cast by the streetlamp, as he answered her. "Yes, of course you must smile. And you might as well strike the requisite pose."

"Pose?" Emily stiffened, throwing her chin up a notch and raising a brow at his implication that she would have to pretend composure. Never mind that it was true.

"That's the one," he said with a single approving nod. "Even Mother did not do it so well. Looks like you swallowed starch. Steady-on for the gauntlet run."

What the devil was he talking about, *gauntlet run?*

When the doors opened a crack, then swung wide, Emily saw only on an older fellow wearing untidy livery and a look of pure astonishment. "Master Nic... My lord?" he stuttered. "We had not expected...uh, welcome home." He retreated a few steps from the portal so that they could enter.

"Upton. How are you faring these days?" Nick asked, striding inside, one hand locking Emily's in the bend of his elbow so that she had no choice but to match his pace. "How good to be home again. And I have brought my countess to meet you." He looked down at her, "My bride, Lady Emily.'' Then he gestured toward the old man. ''This is Upton, our chief butler.''

''Mr. Upton,'' Emily acknowledged.

The man inclined his head in response, then remembered himself and bowed. ''My lady.''

''Where is everyone?'' Nick looked around the cavernous vestibule as though he expected a full turnout of occupants to leap out from behind the statues and gigantic fern stands and greet them.

''Uh…a m-moment, my lord.'' The old retainer motioned toward another set of doors to his left and their right. ''If you would be so kind…?''

''Of course, Upton. We shall wait in the drawing room while you inform the staff we are here.''

Emily tugged on his arm and said in a low voice, ''Nick, it's not necessary, we could—''

''*Wait* is what we shall do. In there,'' he interrupted firmly. He guided her quickly away from the butler and Wrecker. Once he had ushered her into the drawing room, he quickly struck a lucifer, lit the nearest lamp and then closed the doors.

The room seemed dank and overlarge, its shadows looming. The very presence of the old earl seem to pervade this place, she thought. She rubbed her magic ring, but experienced no comforting warmth this time. Fear always made her cranky.

''You never even apologized for waking the man,'' she accused Nick. ''And you could have explained our late arrival by telling him of the wreck.''

''What happened is none of Upton's affair, and an apology from me is neither expected, nor would it be welcomed,'' he stated, turning away from her as he examined their surroundings.

"Well, it would have been polite, Nick," she said, making a face at him behind his back.

When he looked at her again, his brows were lowered and his lips firm. Then he spoke in a near whisper. "Please remember I am *Kendale* to you, Countess, or *your lord* in the presence of staff. And never, *never* offer a suggestion or argument opposing what I have decided."

He closed his eyes for a moment, then spoke again, his voice gentler this time but no less commanding. "You may, of course, say anything you choose to me in private, but do, in company of others, try to maintain the fiction that I am somewhat in charge, will you?"

Emily realized in that moment that Nicholas might be as uncomfortable as she about assuming a title, even though his was certainly arrived at more expectedly than hers. Could it be that he was actually worried that he might not have the hang of it yet?

There must be thousands of rules she had never even heard of that governed everyday behavior of the nobility. Ridiculous rules she would probably have to learn. How many had Nick forgotten in his seven years away?

All bluff and strut aside, he was nothing like his father, and Nick had not spent many of his adult years preparing to fill an earl's position in Society. The old earl had, for the most part, ignored him until the two had found themselves at cross-purposes.

Be that as it may, it would serve nothing for her to undermine Nick's authority over the household. She could not expect to achieve any right soon, and someone certainly should have some. She curtsied gracefully, proud of herself for not being pettish. "As you wish, my lord."

He rolled his eyes, sighed and pressed his fingers to

his forehead as if it hurt. "Damn me, will this day never end?"

"You have the headache," she observed, concerned about him despite her pique.

He quirked up his mouth in a half smile. "Yes, but it is I who should be asking you that question."

"It's a mere scratch. I didn't bump it."

"Good. I'm certain we shall both feel better once we've had some sleep. And I promise everything else will be fine eventually. You are not to worry."

"I do not intend to." She did not want him to smile or to try to charm her or to give her any assurances of his well-being or her own. Moreover, she had no inclination to put on noble airs with those servants his butler was busy herding up to meet their new mistress. All she wanted at the moment was to have a hot bath and be left alone.

He reached out and touched her arm, trailing his fingers down it until they clutched her hand. "There could be a few problems at first, Em," he warned. "If anyone here should…withhold respect, you are to notify me immediately. I shall deal with it."

"No, you will not," she said, removing her hand from his and clasping hers together in front of her. "You need not solve my problems when I am perfectly capable of doing so myself." She lifted her chin another notch. "And please be so kind as to address me properly, my lord."

Just then, someone—Mr. Upton, she supposed— knocked softly on the door, preventing Nick from arguing about it. Ready or not, it was time to establish her place within the household.

Nick looked almost as worried as she felt. Summoning her courage and trying to forget her current state of dishevelment, Emily joined him at the door as he opened it wide.

Her first thought was that she had never expected so many people would be necessary to maintain a household in London. But of course there would not usually be so many. The Bournesea staff was here.

On closer inspection, she recognized approximately a third of the people. The familiar faces made her smile. The problem was, few of them returned it, and so her tentative expression faded. Obviously, they were not that happy to see her here.

She hoped they were only upset at being rousted out of bed to greet a new mistress, but she much doubted that was the reason.

Nick proceeded to make introductions so rapidly he might as well have spoken Chinese for all the good it did her. She would never remember all their names, she thought, almost panicked at the realization.

What would she do if she had occasion to speak to one of them? And of course, she would in the course of the days or weeks to come. No, the years to come, Emily quickly reminded herself. These people were her servants now, her responsibility as well as her husband's. It was she who would be required to solve their everyday problems, to see that they received proper clothing, performed their duties and kept Nick's two households running smoothly.

He squeezed her elbow and was looking down at her. What had he just asked?

"Would you please choose someone to assist you temporarily, my lady?" Nick repeated.

Assist in doing what? she wondered. Then it occurred to her that she would be expected to have a maid. All ladies had maids, did they not? She tried to recall the woman's name whom Lady Elizabeth had employed.

Quickly Emily scanned the crowd gathered in the foyer, but did not see the face she sought. That woman had been up in years, older than the countess. Perhaps she had been retired or let go. After all, the old earl would have had no use for a lady's maid after Lady Elizabeth died.

Knowing she had to say something, Emily spoke the only name that came to mind, one that had popped into her mind as she had worried about what the staff would think of her now that she was countess. "Rosie? Miss Rosie Hempstead?" Emily bit her lips together as she looked from face to face, searching for the young tweenie she had known well in her youth.

Should she have called Rosie *miss?* Was that acceptable? Well, why not? Everyone deserved respect.

For a moment, she feared Rosie had not come with the others. What would Emily do then? She would choose a stranger before asking for Mrs. Waxton. Emily was fairly certain one did not ask a former housekeeper to lower herself to body servant. Besides, who would return and manage the manor, even if the woman did not quit in a fit of anger.

"Yes…miss…m'lady," croaked Rosie as she squeezed between the taller servants to present herself.

The poor girl, bright red curls all askew, bobbed an off-center curtsy, trying to hide her bare feet beneath the long rumpled robe she wore. Her bright green eyes were wide, her gaze darting from Emily to Nicholas to Wrecker and back again. She chewed both her lips, appearing apprehensive about being singled out.

"Rosie, you will accompany your lady to the countess's suite. Mr. MacFarlin, you shall attend me," Nick ordered Wrecker. "The rest of you are excused. We shall see you in the morning. Thank you for the welcome and good night."

The four of them stood there until everyone else had dispersed. They remained silent, watching while Upton locked the front doors and took his leave of them. He eyed Nick, Emily and Wrecker as if they were here for some nefarious purpose and ought to be locked outside instead of in. Rosie, he treated as if she were quite invisible.

As soon as the old man had gone, Nick turned to Wrecker. "Congratulations on your promotion to valet," he said with a quirk of his mouth.

He addressed Rosie. "I assume you have no objection to serving the countess."

Rosie shook her head, curtsying yet again, this time with slightly more competency. "No, sir—m'lord. None at all."

"Your mother, has she retired now?"

"Passed away, m'lord, some five years ago."

Nick shook his head sadly. "How sorry I am to hear it. Mrs. Hempstead always had a kind word for everyone." He drew a deep breath. "I would have expected you to take over her position at Bournesea."

"No, m'lord, the earl said I was too young for a housekeeper. I'm a 'tween stairs maid like I always was."

"I see. Well, assume your new duties, then. We shall see how it works out."

"Yes, m'lord." Rosie bobbed again, clutching her robe together in front with both hands. "This way, miss—m'lady," she mumbled, backing toward the huge curved staircase until she reached it.

Emily followed, lifting her hem to trudge wearily up the stairs to the second floor, then on to the third. All the while she wondered who was more insecure in their new and unfamiliar stations, her or Rosie. At least they had something in common at the outset. She hoped Rosie knew more about what was expected of her than Emily did or they'd both make hash of it.

"End of the hall," Rosie offered, gesturing down the corridor as they reached the third-floor landing. "Will you be wanting bathwater?"

"You needn't bother. I hate to keep anyone awake long enough to haul it."

Rosie grinned, seeming quite at ease now that they were away from the men. Her carroty hair bobbed wildly as she shook her head. "Oh, no, ma'am! Water comes down right out of a pipe! Can you imagine that?"

Emily could not. "Are you quite serious? How is that possible?"

The maid laughed merrily, then clapped a hand over her mouth. Quickly she looked about, as if she feared someone might have heard and would leap out to punish her.

In a whisper she continued. "We was sorely behind times in the country, miss—ma'am. Here, water's piped in from the roof cistern, big as you please. Not hot, but I can start the fire and heat some of it for you." She sighed loudly with appreciation, obviously still in awe over the wonders of the accommodations in the London house even after a fortnight.

"Isn't it hard to empty?" Emily asked, making idle conversation, glad to have at least one friendly person in the house with her.

Rosie shook her head in answer. "It drains out through another pipe. And wait till you see what else! We've no need to empty chamber pots here, can you feature that?"

Embarrassment colored her cheeks bright pink. "Not that you'd ever had to do such, but—"

"Oh, I've emptied my share," Emily assured her, also whispering as they hurried, side by side like co-conspirators toward the door at the end of the hall. "I have read that they toss…everything out the windows into the street here."

"Not here we don't. There's a convenience that works like the bathing tub. Water runs in, everything else out!" Rosie exclaimed as she flung open the door to the bedroom and virtually skipped her way across it to another door.

Emily remarked on the fact that the countess's bedchamber here was much like the room at Bournesea, only a trifle smaller in size and done up in pale blue. The hangings and drapes were the more formal velvet, not the lighter-weight chintz.

She stepped up to the door through which Rosie had disappeared. Sure enough, there was a large metal tub in the shape of a huge shoe.

"I always wanted to do this," Rosie confessed, as if she were talking to herself. "All I've been allowed to do is clean in here, dust and the like. See, I can catch some in the bucket and warm it over the fire in the bedchamber."

Emily watched the girl eagerly labor over a small lever that apparently opened the pipe. There came a rumbling, creaking noise and a few moments later, water began to stream sluggishly into the tub.

"There now! A flamin' wonder, ain't it!" Rosie announced with a brushing motion of her hands. She pointed to the other convenience. "There's the privy."

Emily nodded, laughing aloud with the maid for no

reason other than pure delight in the modern marvels of city life.

While they waited for the water to flow in and fill the bath, Rosie sat back on her heels and rubbed her palms against the lap of her robe to dry them, looking extremely satisfied with herself.

"So, here we are. You, the new countess. Me, the new lady's maid. You will keep me, won't you? I could use a bit more blunt, if you know what I mean, and I'll do whatever you say."

Emily hardly knew how to react to Rosie's sudden familiarity after the girl had acted so timid downstairs. "We shall see," she said, but smiled encouragingly as she said it.

"So we will," Rosie agreed with an impudent grin. Then she crossed her arms and put on a sly look. "And you can trust me not to add a word to the gossip about you belowstairs."

"'Gossip?'" Emily asked tentatively, not altogether certain she wanted the answer. "But we just arrived. How could anyone possibly have time to gossip about me?"

Rosie looked smug. "Oh, they'll be atwitter soon enough, I warrant, wantin' to know how a vicar's girl tied up with a earl, now won't they? Us from Bournesea know how, of course, but I for one won't be telling."

"Telling what?" Emily demanded. "Just what do you think you know of it?"

Rosie sighed loudly with exasperation and rolled her eyes. "That his fine young lordship was under those skirts of yours long before he took sail. Now he's back and your good ol' da called him to account for it, that's what. I say bully for the vicar. Wish I had me a da like him who could shame a earl into marriage. Then I coulda been a countess."

Emily stared, not quite certain what the girl was implying. "You?"

Rosie grinned and shrugged. "Why not? Even if I didn't plan it all out and had no say in it, I paid as much for the privilege as you did yourself."

"Y-you *slept* with him…uh…Earl Kendale?" Emily stammered, shaken to the core by what she'd just heard.

"Didn't *sleep* exactly," Rosie admitted with a wriggle of her arched red brows and a comical twist of her lips, "but if you mean did I warm his bed, then th' answer's yes." She leaned closer. "And I've got to say, it weren't half the chore I figgered it would be."

Chapter Ten

"Kindly leave me, Rosie," Emily said after she recovered from her stunned silence. "Don't bother heating the water. I find I am too weary to bathe after all."

Though Emily sorely wanted to believe that it was the old earl's bed Rosie had warmed, she knew better. The man had been nigh sixty years of age. The girl would never have spoken of such dalliance with a smile or a fond memory.

No, it was surely Nicholas who had seduced the poor thing and filled her head with stars. Just as he had almost done with Emily. She felt like pounding her head in frustration as she bemoaned the stupidity of young women everywhere.

Rosie reached over and patted her hand, all sympathy. "Ah, Emmy. I mean, m'lady..." She frowned when Emily moved away, unwilling to be touched. "I put a foot wrong didn't I? Shouldn't have told you about me and his lordship."

Emily looked up and realized Rosie had tears in her eyes. "Never mind that," she told the maid. "It is simply late and I am exhausted. Go on to bed now."

"You'll turn me off, won't you?"

"No."

Rosie got up from where she was sitting on the floor and turned off the water. Shoulders slumped and head hanging, she trudged out the door of the bathing room.

Emily wanted to follow to reassure the girl, but she was simply too tired and dispirited. But what had happened was not Rosie's fault. She had been hardly more than a child seven years ago and should not bear any blame for succumbing to Nick's charms. Even though Emily was at least two years older, she had almost fallen into the same trap. The man had no shame and no conscience.

Her compassion suddenly stirred by the little maid's early loss of innocence, Emily called out, "Rosie, I prefer coffee over tea when I awaken. Will you see to it, please?"

The bright smile had returned when Rosie whirled around. "You just ring me the minute you wake, m'lady. I'll be here quicker'n a flea hops a dog."

Emily sighed with relief when the door finally closed and she was at last alone. She rubbed her temples wishing she could erase the pain there. The ache in her heart was worse, but there wasn't much that would alleviate that one.

She had thought Nick's keeping his betrothal a secret hurt, but knowing that he'd had Rosie in his bed, probably at the same time he had been courting Emily, was an even worse betrayal. He had played both Emily and Dierdre as fools, and had not done Rosie any favors, either, in stealing her innocence.

"He was young," she reminded herself. But he wasn't young now and he had still lied about his engagement to Dierdre. Much as she wanted to find some excuse for his wretched behavior, Emily could not think of one.

Now she was married to him and must somehow make the best of it. The future looked worse than dismal at the moment.

She removed her clothing and quickly dipped into the tepid water. It hardly seemed cool at all compared to the iciness that had formed inside her.

When she had scrubbed herself clean, Emily got out of the tub, wrapped a length of toweling around her and walked back into the bedchamber. There, she pulled back the soft blue covers on the high tester bed, dropped the toweling and crawled between the sheets.

Lack of a nightgown didn't matter. Nothing could warm her, she thought. Nothing.

Morning dawned gray and still. No wind or rain, but both seemed imminent, Nick thought to himself as he dressed. It seemed a pall hung over everything.

How he had longed to go to Emily after the household had retired. He wanted to hold her, as much to satisfy himself that she was well as to comfort her. But he had known how exhausted she was and that he would probably have found her asleep. Soon he would approach her alone. Perhaps tonight when she was better rested.

The poor lamb must be incredibly worried about how she would get on here at Kendale House and, indeed, London in general. If last night had been any indication, she might have a rough go of it with the servants. He also knew that any interference on his part would dash any chance she had of establishing any authority either here or at Bournesea.

He rang for Wrecker and sat in a chair beside the window to wait for him. The man would make a laughable valet, but Nick had left his real one back in Gujarat. The man simply could not sail.

A short knock and the door opened. "Aye, m'lord?"

"Come in. We ought to talk about this. Will you be content acting as valet? The pay is better than footman and you'll have a private room."

"Thanks be. Every footman you got snores like thunder. Last night, I might as well've been aboard ship agin there wuz such a bleedin' racket. What do I do for ye then?"

Nick figured he would have to work on Wrecker's brashness, but not now when he needed to secure his help. "Your primary duty will be to guard my wife when I'm not with her. Each morning you'll report to me as you're doing now and I'll tell you what I require."

Wrecker grinned. "Long as you can dress yourself."

Nick laughed. "Not one of your tasks, I assure you. But if you don't serve me as valet, I shall be obliged to hire someone else who does not know the circumstances. I don't like to take strangers into my confidence, you understand."

"Ain't no use in paying some fop to tie your neckcloth when what ye need is a bloke handy with his fists."

"Precisely put. I like the way you cut right to the heart of the matter, Wrecker. By the way, I shall be addressing you either as MacFarlin or by your Christian name. What is it?"

"*Percy*, but even Ma don't call me that. I go by Wrecker, always has. What's wrong with it?"

"Not a thing," Nick assured him. "I simply thought you might prefer something more businesslike to suit your new station."

Wrecker paused and thought about it, worrying his chin with his thumb. Then he sighed. "Guess you're right. MacFarlin will do, then." His shoulders straightened as he assumed a new air of importance.

"I can keep them Hessians shined up for ye. Mebbe tote yer clothes to th' maids downstairs fer cleaning. Anythin' else?" Wrecker asked, shuffling his big frame into a more comfortable position as he stood roughly at attention. He was throwing himself into the spirit of the thing.

Nick smiled up at him. "Don't tup the maids. The staff is off-limits. Agreed?"

Wrecker frowned. "Even that springy-haired chit what tends our lady now?"

"Especially that one," Nick insisted. He relented a little when Wrecker seemed ready to rebel. "Of course, you may court Rosie if she agrees to it, but see that you always treat her with respect."

The grunt of disappointment was almost comical, but Nick ignored it. "At the moment, I'd have you go down and order my and my lady's breakfast served in the morning room. You will eat your meals with Upton and the housekeeper in the upper servants' dining room. Mind your manners and try not to shock them with any gruesome tales of the sea."

"You mean I can't even *eat* with th' lass?" Wrecker almost whined.

"Of course. Rosie is the countess's maid, at least for the present. Unless otherwise occupied with her duties, she should be there for meals."

Wrecker hardly waited to be dismissed. Nick was glad someone looked forward to the day enough to hurry downstairs to meet it.

With a grunt, he rubbed his bristly chin and looked at the scuffed and muddied footwear Wrecker had promised to polish and then promptly forgotten. Resigned to shaving himself and shining his own leather, Nick got on with it.

While buffing his boot, Nick paused to wonder whether Emily might be having similar problems with the maid she had chosen. Rosie was merely a between-stairs maid, trained to housework, not in performing a lady's toilette, styling hair and maintaining a wardrobe.

Worse than that, Emily herself had little knowledge of what needed to be done. Nick worried that he had put his new bride in a very precarious position here. Both women would need some sort of education in what was expected of a countess and what a lady's maid must do to assist her. Nick knew no one he could ask to do that for them, so he supposed he must undertake the lessons himself.

Their instruction would have to wait, however. Before he did anything else after breakfast, he needed to visit the Ministry and give his report. He would have made it three weeks earlier had it not been for the cholera and the resulting quarantine.

Lord Chalmers would have received news of Nick's planned return and must believe him lost at sea by this time. His lordship might regret that had not happened once Nick informed him of the mounting unrest in India. The place was a veritable powder keg waiting for a spark.

Nick sighed. He had a bride way out of her depth in Society's waters, a possible assassin lurking about, and ominous trade issues that could destroy the economy, not to mention his shipping business. Was there no good news to be had?

Nick gave his other boot a quick brushing and dropped it to the floor beside its mate. He felt fatigued by the day already and had not even had his coffee yet.

Emily greeted Nick from her place at the table in the morning room. "Good morning, Kendale," she said brightly, offering him her most brittle smile. "I see you have triumphed over our encounters yesterday. How is your headache?"

He shot her a frown, then turned his attention to the display of food on the sideboard. "My head is fine. And yours?"

"Quite recovered." She watched Nick serve himself a bit of the egg dish that looked none too appetizing and choose a slice of bread to go with it. He paused a moment before taking his seat at the head of the table. Emily wondered if he was worrying about assuming his father's role. His countenance did look troubled.

She had decided upon awakening that she needed to assert herself and to throw off the miasma associated with her hasty marriage and its attending difficulties. Her missish behavior last night shamed her in the light of day. The carriage mishap had unsettled her, that was all. A good night's sleep had put her to rights and she was herself again.

After all, life was what one made of it and she did not intend to live hers at the mercy of unforgiving servants and an untrustworthy husband. She would simply have to turn them all around to her liking.

Had she not managed her father's household since she was hardly more than a child? So Kendale House and Bournesea Manor were run on a much larger scale, with dozens of servants instead of just one, what did that matter? The concerns were the same, and she could handle it.

Had she not overcome that nearly ruinous incident and regained her good reputation among the townfolk? Yes, and she could do that here, as well.

Emily felt confident as she imagined Nick's mother patting her on the back, encouraging her to forge ahead and make a place for herself. Perhaps she would even rally to the extent of reforming that unruly son the woman had left behind.

"I see that you are not a morning person," Emily observed, taking the initiative.

Nick sipped the steaming coffee he had just poured from the silver pot in front of him. After a moment he answered. "And I see that you *are,* more's the pity. Pray, don't be this cheerful every morning or I shall have to drown you in the Thames."

Emily smiled. "Grumble away, then," she said, slathering butter on the toasted muffin she had selected. "I, for one, have plans for the day that do not include you, so you may return to bed if you like."

That got his attention. "And just what is it you're planning, if I may be so bold?"

She took a bite, chewed and swallowed, letting his curiosity build. "I have called a meeting of the staff. We should send the Bournesea people home. Have you any objections?"

He thought about it. "None at all. That makes good sense. Give them today to make ready. Order the coaches hired and brought around at first light tomorrow. That way, they can be home before dark."

"Already arranged. I spoke with Mr. Upton. He promised to send someone to take care of that. I expect word has traveled throughout the house already, but I think I should announce it formally."

He watched her carefully, she noticed. "Shall I attend this assembly?"

"Are *you* returning to Bournesea?" she asked pointedly.

"Of course not. We have only just arrived."

"Then you might wish to take care of your own business while I tend to mind. Go and do…'' She flicked a hand in a dismissive gesture. ''Whatever it is that earls do.''

Nick laughed. Then he drank down the rest of his coffee, tossed his napkin beside his plate and got up.

At first she thought he would simply leave her sitting there without another word, but instead of heading for the door, he marched to her end of the table, leaned down and kissed her fully on the mouth.

Heat engulfed her as his mouth met hers. He tasted of coffee and something sweet that hinted of cloves. His lips and tongue were warm and insistent. The hand that held her chin up caressed her throat. *Heaven.*

Before she was ready for him to, he released her and stood back, his hands resting on his hips. ''You amaze me,'' he said, seeming quite amused. Then he shook a finger as if admonishing her. ''Sometimes you even scare me. Is there anything in the world you will admit you cannot accomplish by yourself?''

Emily slowly shook her head, still entranced by the kiss, wanting more and knowing she should not, hardly hearing what he said to her.

Again he laughed. And then he did leave. If her knees had not turned to mush, she might have stood and run after him. But once the flash of heat inside her cooled, she was infinitely glad she had not.

What he had asked her finally registered. Oh, yes, she would fully admit there was one thing she could not do alone. But that thing was best left undone, given Nick's propensity to do it with other women. She would bet her last farthing Rosie had not been the first, nor would she have been the last.

She suddenly realized that she should be angered by that impudent kiss. Apparently, Nick would say anything, do anything, to get a woman into his bed. He had almost convinced her that she should surrender and forget all he had done. He had the right to expect her to do so, but Emily could not relent just yet. She knew that every time he made love to her, she would wonder who else in their household was enjoying his favors. Even Rosie might, given her past with Nick.

No, he was not to be trusted, and until she knew she could trust him, there could be no true marriage between them.

Upton appeared soon after Nick departed. "The staff is gathered in the hall as you requested, madam."

Emily almost jumped up, then recalled her station. She ignored him as she finished her last bite of jam and bread, washed it down with the remainder of her coffee and wiped her lips with her napkin. She made a point of glancing down at the watch pinned to her shirtwaist, then over at the head butler. "I believe I specified nine o'clock, Mr. Upton."

"So you did, madam," he replied with a haughty lift of his chin. "It is now ten of the hour."

"I am fully aware of the time. You may go and await me with the others."

He turned on his heel without another word. She might have made an enemy there, she thought, but Upton had radiated disapproval from the moment he had gotten over his shock at meeting her last evening.

Come to think of it, he had not shown Nick much in the way of respect, either. Those pinched frowns and that haughtiness of his did not bode well for his future.

The man was the old earl's hire and obviously clung to that particular loyalty. If he could not adjust, he might soon find himself retired.

Emily poured herself another cup of coffee, her third and last, and sipped it slowly. She purposely waited for eleven long minutes before leaving the table to assume her morning duties.

Chapter Eleven

Nick was in no mood to suffer any foolishness when he returned to Kendale House that evening. He only hoped things had gone better there than where he'd spent his day.

His meeting with Lord Chalmers only succeeded in convincing Nick of how useless had been his career of intelligencing for the government. Chalmers and his associates had paid scant attention to Nick's dire warnings on the rumblings of mutiny in India. They'd seemed much more interested in how to solidify and expand English rule. Nor had they wanted to hear anything regarding problems with the Dutch and Italians who were rapidly gaining proprietary footholds in trade areas that were considered British domain.

What the hell had he been doing these past few years but wasting time and energy?

As a result of the wretched conference, Nick had formally resigned his position, naming the man he had trained to assume his duties. Poor Stryker would have to come to his own conclusions about working for politicians with minds attuned only to prestige, money and power. As for Nick, he meant to see what he could do about that from his seat in the House of Lords.

He later visited his solicitors who would begin necessary negotiations for the sale of Kendale Shipping. He would retain two ships only, those of his own private enterprise, to continue the lucrative trade in the West Indies.

God knows, he had enough wealth now that he could sell those, too, but he liked to keep a hand in. Besides, he had built that business on his own, wholly independent of his father's credit and influence. Pride demanded he take it as far as it would go. By relying on trusted representatives he could do that without leaving the country.

When he arrived home, Upton greeted him grumpily at the door, accepting Nick's coat, hat and cane with pointed impatience. "My lord, at last you are here."

"Is something amiss, Upton?" Nick asked, his own tone brusque.

The butler cleared his throat, then smirked. "This morning the countess insisted we embark upon a complete inventory of the entire contents of the dwelling, my lord. Each and every item, down to the salt cellars."

"Her prerogative, I believe," Nick retorted. "She *is* mistress here." Had Emily already set the household on its ear? This accounting would better have waited until the Bournesea people had departed and the remaining staff had settled back into their old routine. However, he had to support her decision, precipitously made or not.

Upton huffed. "There was a complete accounting made only eight months ago. If you will permit me to say so, this exercise seems an unnecessary inconvenience to all and indicates a mistrust of those in your employ. An insult, if you will."

Nick stared him down for a full minute. "Are you contemplating employment elsewhere, Upton?"

The rheumy eyes flew wide. "Absolutely not, sir!"

"Then be advised. My lady has given an order, not made a request to be cleared through me. Follow it."

"Yes, my lord. Consider it done."

And done reluctantly, Nick thought with a carefully concealed sigh. He had no wish to begin the time in London chastising his new bride about household matters. Especially after the day he'd just spent. He needed to compose himself before speaking with her about that or any other thing.

Before he could mount the stairs, however, she appeared out of the study. She had that stubborn chin up and fire flashed in those beautiful blue eyes. The set of her shoulders indicated someone had best be prepared for battle.

"Good afternoon, my lord," she said, greeting him with a somber expression as she closed the door behind her. "Shall I order tea?"

Tea? Upton stood just behind him, taking in the exchange. It was scarcely four o'clock. Rituals were not the same here as in the country, but Emily could not know that if no one had told her.

However he realized he could scarcely advise her of it before a servant, especially one who already seemed determined to think the worst of her. It mattered little to Nick what anyone thought of him, but he did not want his wife diminished in the eyes of her own servants.

"Yes, thank you for remembering my request to have it early," Nick replied, adding a forced smile. "I am quite famished after such a full day. We shall have it in the morning room." He had added the place in the event she might unknowingly choose another. "Something simple, yet hearty, if you please."

She nodded and disappeared down the hallway without even noticing the arm he extended to escort her to the room where they would partake. He almost groaned. A bellpull had hung within her reach and a servant stood not six feet from her. Yet she had headed toward the kitchens to give instructions herself.

He could swear he felt the butler's disdain permeate the room.

Without turning around, Nick advised him, "Say one word and it shall be the last you utter within these walls."

Upton obviously understood, for silence reigned as Nick headed for the morning room to await a premature tea and a visit with Emily that he knew he would not relish.

It occurred to him in the meantime that he might avoid conflict by beginning his instruction with Emily's maid, Rosie, instead of Emily herself. She might find it less embarrassing to accept advice on town customs from someone closer to her.

Emily obviously knew Rosie well since she had chosen her from all the others. It would serve two purposes, their talk. He could list the responsibilities of a lady's maid and see whether Rosie would be appropriate for the position in a long-term capacity. Hopefully, she was bright enough to realize her opportunity and be willing to learn the duties she did not know how to do.

Emily arrived ahead of a maid who was bearing a large silver tray. "Set it here on the table, Polly," Emily instructed, "and you are excused. I shall pour."

Quite proper, Nick thought, pleased until he saw Polly give Emily a broad wink and a wide grin. He glared at the little upstart, troubled by her forwardness and also with Emily's smiling response to it. He said nothing until Polly had gone and closed the door behind her.

"Why did you permit that?" he asked, seating Emily and dragging out a chair for himself so that they sat facing one another.

She looked up, her brows raised in inquiry. "Permit what?"

"Polly has no business winking at you."

"Oh, that," she said with a dismissive flap of her fingers. She lifted the cozy off the Limoges teapot and prepared to pour. "Cook recalled your favorite biscuits when you were a boy and made them for you. Polly was only signaling me that she knew you would be pleased with our choice."

"You discussed biscuits in the kitchen with Cook and Polly?" he asked, attempting to keep his tone light so as not to anger her with what was coming.

"Yes. They are orange-flavored. Try one." She appeared defiant as she passed him the bone china saucer and cup filled with steaming tea. "Sugar?"

Nick shook his head and proceeded carefully with his admonishment. "You must have a care how you go on, Emily. If you do not establish yourself in command here, they will take advantage. Servants do not work well if you treat them as friends and equals."

"A proven fact, I suppose? Have you ever treated one as a friend and equal?"

The little minx. She'd issued an open invitation to a confrontation. "I have, of course, but I was not an earl at the time. As countess, you should—"

"Aha, the voice of experience speaks!" she interrupted, nodding sagely as her lips formed a provocative moue. "Tell me, when were *you* a countess, Kendale? How do you know how I must *go on?*"

He hauled in a deep breath, struggling to unearth his last vestige of patience. "You mistake my intent, Emily. This is not a reprimand. I merely wish to offer you a bit of advice since you have not dealt with a large staff before and I have. Not as an earl, granted, but I have observed—"

"Your father in action," she interrupted, completing his sentence.

He absolutely *hated* when anyone put words in his mouth.

Nick clenched his teeth together in a bid for control. If he lost his temper with her, she would do everything wrong in the future only to spite him, and would therefore damage her own consequence.

He remained silent, reached for his tea and drank most of it with one determined gulp, ignoring the burn to his tongue. Then he carefully helped himself to several rolls of thinly sliced ham and a small wedge of Gruyère.

The challenge in her eyes tempted him more than the orange-scented biscuits, but he resolved to resist both temptations. He wanted a heated exchange of words with Emily even less than he wanted to open the box of memories associated with his early life here in Kendale House. Either one would only put the cap on a thoroughly wretched day. He had another ordeal to face tonight that was likely to serve that purpose.

He removed the linen napkin from his lap and tossed it beside his plate as he rose.

"May I ask where you are going?"

"Out," he replied, and without looking at her, continued. "Henceforth I should like tea at precisely six o'clock, and kindly inform your maid that I would like her to present herself in my study at nine in the morning."

''Rosie? What for?'' She bit off the words. He'd been right. She was spoiling for a fight. ''What *for*, Kendale?''

Nick opened the door and paused, half-turned toward her. She had pushed him to the limit of endurance. ''If it had to do with you, madam, I might give you an explanation.''

''Nevertheless, I will require one!''

But he did not give it. Instead he left immediately, figuring that he might as well have done with the onerous task of speaking with Dierdre's father now instead of later in the evening. His mood wasn't likely to improve by delaying it.

Afterward he would have time to make the acquaintance of his father's old club on St. James. He had a feeling he would shortly need a place to retreat when his temper needed cooling.

By damn! Emily was a strong-headed female. Over the years he'd forgotten how willful and tempestuous she could be at times. Maybe he should have kissed her again. That was about the only thing that guaranteed him the last word.

Unwilling to dwell on kissing Emily when the opportunity had passed so ignominiously, he turned his thoughts back to his evening.

Nick hoped he would also find his old friend Duquesne at the club. Guy would be there if he'd received the message Nick had sent 'round by the footman.

If anything went on in London, Guy Duquesne had ways of finding out about it. The man had contacts here in all strata of society that the best of inquiry agents would envy. Hopefully he would have a suggestion as to whom Nick might hire to investigate the carriage incident. Wrecker would be checking on whether Julius Munford had shipped in any time lately.

In addition to protecting Emily and himself from any further harm and settling the matter of a fake betrothal with Worthing, Nick supposed he would have to make time later tonight to think how he would deal with Emily's almost belligerent defiance.

Something had sparked her ill will since breakfast this morning. And while it could not have been his own doing, he knew he must deal with it when he returned. He needed her cooperation if she was to become accepted, both at home and in public.

Solving the problems of England in the House of Lords seemed a relatively simple challenge in comparison with all the other matters on his plate.

Where the devil had he gone? Emily wondered as she watched Polly collect the remnants of the brief and unsuccessful tea.

She swished aside the stiff bombazine skirts of the countess's elegant gray gown she was wearing and plopped down upon the brocade settee.

If Wrecker would agree to accompany her, she could follow Nick. How unseemly would that be, for a countess to go dashing about after her wayward husband? And what if she should find him in one of those unmentionable places where men went in the evenings? She'd read about them in novels, those wicked, sinful dens in the bowels of London where loose women enticed men away from their fortunes and morals. What would she do then?

She looked out the window that gave such an excellent view of the gardens. But it wasn't yet dark, she thought.

Upton appeared in the doorway and offered her a negligent bow. "My lady, his lordship's cousin has arrived. Are you at home?"

Emily blinked. "Of course, I am at home. You see me sitting here, do you not?"

"Very well. Will you receive him here?"

"Yes, show him in."

Upton stepped to one side and gestured to someone standing in the hall. A handsome young man with longish blond hair and a sleepy-eyed smile entered. "Lady Emily, I doubt you will know me. I am Nicholas's cousin—"

"Mr. Hollander, of course." She smiled in welcome.

"I arrived the day you and Nick were married, but Nick refused me entrance," he said petulantly. "I had to hear of the wedding the following day in the village. Me! Nick's *family*."

Emily hesitated only a moment before answering his accusation. "It was a private ceremony. I do apologize for his seeming rudeness, but there was sickness at Bournesea then, and we did not wish you to risk contagion."

"Sickness?" His sandy brows lowered in consternation and he plucked nervously at his collar. "Of what sort?"

"Nothing to trouble yourself over."

He cleared his throat and his worried gaze darted about for a minute before resting on her again. "Well, one can't be too careful, y'know. Typhoid?" He paled further. "Not diphtheria!"

"No, neither," she assured him. "It's over and done, so let's not speak of it. You also visited Bournesea with your mother when you were a lad, did you not? We were never formally introduced, but I do remember you attending my father's services with Nicholas. I believe you snored throughout."

Quite recovered with the change in topic, he pulled a face, then laughed merrily. "I must have done, for I recall none of what he preached. Probably some long-winded sermon warning the young off keeping late hours. I was wont to do that, you know.''

''Were you?'' Emily pointed to one of the chairs facing the settee. ''Do sit down. Kendale is not here at the moment. Would you care for tea?''

Carrick grimaced. ''No, but I could do with a spot of brandy.'' He turned to the maid, who stood entranced by him. ''Would you mind, Polly? You know where it is.''

Polly put down the tray she was holding and hurried to oblige. Carrick could almost be called beautiful, with dark blond hair, dove-gray eyes, patrician features and a slender, graceful build. He bore no resemblance to Nicholas at all, other than the fact that they were both very attractive men who radiated self-confidence. But this man held no candle to the sheer power and masculinity of her husband, Emily thought.

Emily watched the byplay between Carrick and Polly with interest. They obviously knew one another. ''You must have visited here often in the past. Were you close to your uncle?''

He laid his hat and cane down upon the floor beside the chair and raised his drowsy gaze to hers. ''Lord knows, I tried to befriend him. The man was perfectly horrible to everyone, as you must know. Still, he did receive me whenever I came 'round. I suspect he missed Nick all those years and saw me as a sort of replacement or some such.''

''I'm certain you're wrong,'' Emily said politely, momentarily touched by the hint of sorrow in Carrick's expression. ''His lordship must have liked you. At least he didn't send you away.'' She remembered all too well that the old earl *had* sent Nick away. Or so Nick claimed. As things stood now, she still questioned whether the departure was his or Nick's own idea.

She folded her hands together in her lap and leaned forward the least bit to show interest in her guest. "You live in London, I suppose?"

Carrick's smile widened. "So I do, but I also travel quite a lot. I'm a painter, you see."

"Oh, well, that's grand, isn't it? What do you paint?"

He leaned forward, too, resting his elbows on his knees and seeming eager. "Portraits mostly. That's why I've come, to offer you and Nick a gift, a wedding portrait."

Polly presented him with a snifter of brandy just then, and Carrick spared her an indulgent smile as he took it. "Why, thank you, Polly," he said, his tone as smooth as dark silk.

Emily felt an instant shiver of dislike. She recognized a prelude to seduction when she saw one. Or perhaps it was not a prelude at all. Polly smiled back rather confidently. The thought of a gentleman taking advantage of a female servant rankled, especially on the heels of finding out about the liaison between Nicholas and Rosie.

"That will be all, Polly," Emily said meaningfully, and nodded toward the tea things the maid had set aside to fetch the brandy.

Carrick downed the drink, set the glass on the piecrust table nearby, picked up his hat and cane from the carpet and stood. Emily got up, as well, intending to see him out.

"I will inform Kendale of your offer, Mr. Hollander. Will you visit again when he is home to greet you?"

"Soon," he promised, politely holding out his hand. When she offered hers in return, he raised it to his lips and kissed it, planting his full, firm lips against her skin in a rather prolonged and suggestive way. She could swear she felt his tongue. Suddenly all too aware of the peril in being alone with him, Emily tugged out of his grasp and backed up a step.

He laughed. "Don't be so skittish, cousin. Humor an eccentric." He bent forward as if to impart a secret. "We artists must keep up the ruse that we are rakes and libertines. Otherwise we should be thought horribly ordinary and not worth knowing."

Unwilling to betray her unworldliness or to reveal her distress, Emily simply forced a tight-lipped smile as she clutched her hands together tightly at her waist.

Carrick bowed low. "I take my leave of you, sweet cousin. Do give my regards to the estimable earl when he returns. Tell him I shall immortalize the both of you on canvas at his earliest convenience. Upton has my card."

"Yes. Goodbye," Emily said, wiping the back of her hand on her skirt and feeling assuredly glad to see him go.

She reached for the door to the drawing room and firmly closed it behind him. No more guests today, no matter who they might be.

Unable to sit again when she was so agitated, Emily paced. She must decide now whether she should share her impressions of Carrick with Nicholas when he returned.

Nicholas obviously didn't like Carrick much to begin with. It would not do to cause further hard feelings between the cousins when neither of them had any other close family. Carrick's parents, the old earl's younger brother and his wife, were dead. Nicholas's mother had no family living as far as Emily knew. No one had ever mentioned any.

She concluded that it might behoove her to let the mat-

ter of Carrick's unwarranted familiarity pass and simply
inform Nicholas that he had called and offered them the
gift of a painting. Then she would avoid being around
Carrick unless her husband was also present.

She curled one fist inside the opposing hand and
rubbed away the sensation of the man's mouth against it.
Growing up with as little protection as she'd had did have
certain advantages. She knew precisely how to defend her
own person if need be. However, she had become dedicated to adjusting to her new role in life. That considered,
even *she* knew it would appear uncouth for a countess to
knock the bloody stuffing out of the earl's cousin.

Nicholas kept his hat in hand as he awaited Lord
Worthing in the study of Balmanger House on Solden
Street West. He doubted he would be here long once the
baron discovered why he'd come. It was late for a formal
visit—those usually ending at four and the hour being
now past six—so Worthing would realize this was not a
simple social call.

The door opened and Worthing entered. "Nicholas…or Kendale, I should say now. How good to see you
again. Terrible about your father. So sorry you couldn't
be there for the funeral. Fortunately, our family was able,
so he was properly mourned."

"You have my gratitude, sir," Nick declared solemnly, shaking the man's hand. "I know you were good
friends."

"So we were, all those years in school and after. And
you have all his good traits, I'll wager." He slapped Nick
on the shoulder. "Strength. Good head for business, and
all that. He was proud of you, son. Very proud."

A deliberate lie, but one Nick forgave. He wished it
had been true and Worthing must know that.

The portly little man with florid features and wisps of brown hair combed over his balding pate exhibited all the exuberance of a fish marketer attempting to sell herring about to go bad. Or a father with a daughter gone ripe on the vine.

Nicholas got right to the point. "Sir, I've come about the betrothal contract."

Worthing beamed and said in a conspiratorial tone, "We'll have Dierdre down here as soon as she's through primping. She knows you're here. I sent one of the girls to tell her when Jenkins announced you were here." He waved an arm expansively toward the chairs. "Sit and I'll pour us a sherry."

"That won't be necessary," Nicholas told him, hating to dash the man's congenial mood. "You see, the betrothal contract's fraudulent, sir. My father forged my name."

Worthing fell perfectly still, his smile dying a quick death and his eyes growing hard. "You lie."

"No, sir. I swear to you that I knew nothing of it until I found Father's copy in his desk. I deeply regret what he did and beg your pardon for it."

For several long minutes Worthing glared at him. Nick remained stoic, enduring the tension while the baron came to terms with the truth.

"Nevertheless, you *will* honor it," Worthing ordered.

"No, sir, I cannot."

"You would break Dierdre's heart?"

"I doubt that's an issue, sir. Please do not trouble yourself to persuade me on this. I cannot marry your daughter in any case. I am already wed."

The baron did not appear to be all that surprised. "It has not been announced in the papers. You will quietly annul it, of course. Then we will proceed as planned."

"No, that is not possible."

"It would be wise of you to reconsider, Kendale."

"You ask the impossible. I merely came to inform you if you did not already know, and to assure you that none of this needs be discussed any further. If anyone else heard of the alliance my father concocted on his own, simply explain that your daughter decided to cry off."

Worthing threw out one arm, pointing toward the door. "Get out of my house," he growled.

"Of course," Nick agreed. "And again, I regret the inconvenience my father's action has caused you and your family."

"You will suffer more than regret in the near future, you bastard," Worthing promised in a hard voice laced with hatred. "You are not worthy to bear your father's name or his title. I will personally see to it that no home in England will receive you after this. I shall *ruin* you!"

Nicholas calmly left the study and strode toward the front entrance. The baron's voice rose behind him to echo in the vestibule, "Your father made a promise, a vow you would comply. Since you refuse, we will settle this in court, you and I!"

"That would be unwise," Nicholas warned as he turned, his hand on the door handle. "Think of your daughter and her mother and how such a scandal would affect them."

"You will pay. I swear you will pay," Worthing declared, his fists clenched at his sides.

"Were you not already richer than God, I might have considered doing just that, sir, out of embarrassment for my father's treachery and for Dierdre's sake. But since you have more wealth than the law allows, and on principle—because I am not the cause of this conundrum—I shall not surrender a farthing. That is final."

With that announcement, Nick placed his hat on his head and left the house.

Peculiar, he thought, once he had calmed down and was halfway to St. James, exceedingly peculiar that Worthing had never asked whom Nick had married. Could it be that he had already known? Had the *bonhomie* and the switch to sudden outrage been but an act?

He mentally added another name to the list he was forming of those with reason to wreck the Kendale carriage on its way to London.

Chapter Twelve

Nick approached the bow window of White's. Through it, the club appeared to be sparsely attended this evening, which suited him well. He realized he might have to prove his identity to be allowed inside unless Duquesne had received the message to meet him here and would vouch for him.

On his few surreptitious trips to London during the past seven years, Nick had not frequented public places lest he be recognized and his father notified that he was in the country. His business in London had not necessarily required that much secrecy, but Nick simply had not wished the earl to know he had returned.

Duquesne greeted him the moment he walked in, introduced him to the proprietor and several nobles who were already well into their cups.

The viscount held a place of great affection in the hearts of fellow members, Nick observed. No surprise, for Guilford Bollings, Viscount Duquesne, was an uncommonly genial fellow unless crossed.

To Nick, he had always been Guy, his chum throughout school and university, and a friend who had remained true even after Nick's exile. Guy had even visited him in

India once and had written letters regularly to keep his and Nick's friendship current.

If he had a brother, Nick would want him to be exactly like Guy—loyal, witty, and imminently resourceful. Guy sought all manner of derring-do, both to avoid the idleness of his class and to provide much-needed income. Nick admired him enormously. They had in common the necessity to make their own fortunes despite the fact they were both first sons and titled.

Once they had no audience, Guy nudged him with his elbow. "Man, you look mule-kicked. Wedded bliss that dreadful, is it?"

"How did you know?" Nick asked. "Who told you I was married?"

Duquesne threw back his head and laughed heartily, slapping Nick on the back as he turned him toward a vacant table. "God, you really haven't spent much time here, have you? I swear everyone hires gossip runners who possess the speed of Mercury. Winged feet and all that." He yanked out a chair and sat down, throwing up a hand to signal for drinks.

"So it's all over town?" Nick asked, recalling Worthing's behavior. Now that he thought about it, the man had overacted. He must have thought to stir Nick's guilt and make him more amenable to getting rid of Emily.

Guy nodded. "I heard it over a week ago. Actually I believe the news originated with that pretty cousin of yours, what's his name?"

"Carrick. He must have stayed somewhere near Bournesea after I ran him off. Emily's father might even have told him of the marriage if he asked what was going on. The vicar never mentioned it to me, but I can suppose he would have been eager to announce his daughter's marriage to the local populace."

"Vicar? Zeus, Nick, what *have* you been up to? You thought to keep her a secret? Is she buck-toothed and squinty? Who held the gun to your head? Not the vicar, surely!"

Nick smiled indulgently. Guy would have his fun. "She is beautiful. You wouldn't remember Emily from your visits to—"

"Good God! *That* Emily? The fairy child who used to peek at us from behind the rocks when we swam? Never say it!"

"She did no such thing," Nick argued, trying to contain his mirth.

"Did so, and I cannot help but wonder why she didn't hold out for me. After all, I was the larger...catch."

Nick rolled his eyes. "Will you stop? And when you meet her next, you're not to go on this way or she'll be mortified and I shall have to call you out."

"Lips sealed," Guy promised with a chuckle. "Even though I boast the best equipment, I admit you are a better marksman."

"Thank you," Nick said. "I think. Now will you listen? Emily and I might be in danger and I hope you will assist me in discovering the culprit who means us harm. At least give me the name of someone capable who will look into it."

Guy sobered immediately and straightened from his slouch to give Nick full attention. "Begin at the beginning, man, and don't leave out a thing. What has happened?"

Nick explained first about the quarantine and how he had come to be married to Emily. Then he told Guy about the earlier attempts on his life, the carriage wreck and his suspicions regarding it.

"If anyone hired it done here in London, I can find

out who,'' Guy said with confidence. ''But if he acted alone, or secured help elsewhere, it will take a bit of digging to unearth him.'' He stood abruptly. ''Say goodnight, Nick. I'm off.''

''Will you send word, or shall we meet here again tomorrow?'' Nick asked.

''Here?'' Guy asked with an expression of comic disbelief. ''Why, I *never* come here unless forced. Look around. It's damned dull! Expect me at half past eight tomorrow evening at Kendale House. I can scarcely wait another day to meet the fey little Emily all grown up. The chit should rethink what she's missed by marrying too soon.''

Nick decided to impose further on Guy. ''Could you give me the name of a fashionable modiste? One who would be willing to come to Kendale House?''

''Say no more. Expect her and her entourage to arrive at one o'clock tomorrow.'' He grinned. ''Unless, of course, you were asking for yourself and not for your wife, in which case I would suggest a more clandestine rendezvous.''

''Scoundrel,'' Nick muttered companionably as he grabbed his hat and joined Guy walking out.

''Paragon,'' Guy countered.

They parted outside with a nod of accord and not another word.

Satisfied that he had accomplished all that he possibly could for one day, Nick hailed a passing hack and headed for Kendale House. He had nowhere else in London to go.

He pulled out his pocketwatch and saw that it was only half past nine. Despite that, he was exhausted, sleepy and disgruntled. Unless Emily had made peace with whatever or whomever had turned her combative since he first set out this morning, he hoped for once she had decided to retire early.

Emily waited for Nick in the library, desperately searching for a book that would distract her from the day's events. Nothing thus far, she thought, replacing a boring treatise on battle strategy back in its place on the shelf. The entire place seemed filled with tomes only a man would find interesting.

She gave up, settled herself in a chair before the empty, cold fireplace and closed her eyes.

He would be home soon, surely. Even the most passionate tryst shouldn't take all night. After all, those sorts of women entertained more than one gentleman during an evening, did they not? It wasn't as if he'd had the time to arrange for a mistress since they'd arrived.

She shouldn't know of such things. They were never discussed among the women of her acquaintance. Ha! The women she knew probably waited until she was not around and then let fly with all sorts of conjecture about the vicar's promiscuous daughter.

Emily read about such things, however. Novels of romance and adventure had been available and plentiful in Nolan's Book Emporium. She owned six of them herself. There was little to do in one's leisure time other than read in a village the size of Bournesea. Amazing, the things people would relate in books that they would not dare discuss in the presence of another person.

Not that any of those books contained the actual details as such, but they did lead one to fill in the blank parts with vivid imagination. Oddly enough, she had found more particulars within one of her father's own books that was meant to instruct young men about to be married.

Father would be aghast at her naughty indulgences, but he would forgive her if she ever confessed them. God love him, he was such a sweet, gentle man without a jot of censure within him.

Emily knew she was somewhat spoiled because of that, but at least he had taught by example how to love someone without putting conditions on it. He embodied acceptance of foibles and instant forgiveness. His sermons usually revolved around those themes.

Thoughts of that brought her upright in the chair. Was she wrong to judge Nicholas? He had lied by omission, almost seduced her, certainly seduced poor Rosie. Then he'd lied again.

But he *had* married her to save her good name. He had seen that her brother was tended when he was so ill. And he worried so about spreading the cholera, yet had stayed with his men when he might have left them there and gone elsewhere to reduce his chance of contracting it. There was an innate goodness in Nick, she knew. It would be up to her, as her father's daughter, to unleash that and show him the error of his ways.

"Emily? What on earth are you doing in here? It's cold. Why aren't you upstairs in bed?"

"Nick!"

"Are you unwell? You look pale," he said with sincere concern.

She shook her head, not meeting his eyes. "I'm fine, really. I waited up to tell you that your cousin called soon after you left."

"Carrick?" he demanded gruffly. "What the hell did he want?"

She got up from the chair so she would not have to crane her neck so to look at him. Also because he made her feel too small, like a child being scolded for some unknown transgression. ''To congratulate us, he said. He offered to paint a portrait of you and me. A wedding gift.''

Nick said nothing. He appeared lost in thought. Considering the offer perhaps.

''I'd rather he didn't,'' she quickly admitted.

He frowned down at her. ''Why? Did he say something to offend you?''

Emily considered the question, then answered obliquely, ''I don't care to sit for one. Do you mind? Perhaps Carrick would substitute something else, a painting of flowers, trees or the like.''

Nick appeared to be relieved. ''I'll certainly suggest that if he comes again. In the meantime, I think you might be wise not to receive him unless I am with you. Have Upton relay that you are not at home.''

''But that would be a lie, if I am at home,'' Emily pointed out.

''It doesn't matter, Emily,'' he said with a hint of impatience. ''That is what people say when they are not receiving. It merely means that you are not at home to *him* in particular.''

''A white lie,'' she observed.

''Yes, quite. It's accepted.''

''Not by me,'' she assured him. ''A lie is a lie.''

She watched Nick draw in a deep breath as if he were fortifying himself for something unpleasant. Emily hoped it wasn't an argument. Not when she had only just decided to forgive him so that she could begin his reformation.

His voice was extremely deep and even as he suggested, ''Then have Upton tell Carrick that you are at home but do not wish to entertain him.''

''That would hurt his feelings! I could never do that.''

"For God's sake, don't let the man in the house, Em! That's an order, do you hear? Do *not* let him in! Now go to bed!" With that, he turned on his heel and quit the room before she gathered a breath to answer.

Well! He truly was in a foul mood this evening. She had to wonder what set him off like that. Nick was going to be a hard man to live with for all her patient understanding.

The next morning, Emily rose from her bed before daybreak to see to the departure of the Bournesea servants. When she arrived downstairs, Nicholas was already there.

There were some thirty people to see off to the country and he had gathered them in the gardens by the side entrance. She noted four hired coaches lining up, their teams outfitted with pads on their hooves to keep from waking the neighbors with their clopping when they passed along the street.

Emily went to Nick's side. "Good morning, my lord," she said politely.

"My lady," he replied.

She stood waiting, uncertain what role she must play in this farewell, hoping to take her cue from him.

He spoke for them to the assembly. "The countess and I would like to express our thanks for your forbearance in traveling here to London on short notice and your lack of complaint about doing so." He turned over a large packet to Mrs. Waxton and another to Simms, the butler who served at Bournesea. "We have added a bonus for each of you in your pay this quarter and we are distributing funds early."

A quiet, yet delighted cheer went up from everyone. Nick continued. "In addition, you may consider this next week a holiday because your tasks will likely double

once you arrive at Bournesea Manor. Your presence there
was sorely missed as you will soon see.''

They all laughed softly and exchanged knowing looks.
Emily imagined they fully expected to find Bournesea in
a state of chaos when they arrived. She almost wished
she had left it so in order to show them they were needed.
Everyone should feel needed. She certainly missed feeling that way.

Nick reached for her hand and pulled it through the
crook of his elbow, so they stood arm in arm. ''Lady
Emily and I wish you Godspeed and will join you as
soon as the Season is over.''

Emily smiled and nodded.

She would wager the old earl had never been so generous with them. Many sent her inquisitive looks as if
they were wondering whether these rewards were her doing. Suddenly she was sure Nicholas meant for them to
think that was so. He should know that one could not
buy loyalty. However, done was done and they did seem
happy. Even the usually dour Mrs. Waxton wore an expression that approximated pleasure.

Nicholas squeezed Emily's hand insistently as if he
expected her to say something.

She cleared her throat. ''Safe journey to each of you.
Enjoy your holiday to the fullest and please give my regards to my father and brother when next you see them.''
There were muted utterances of appreciation and assurances that they would. Nick then turned her from the
crowd of servants and ushered her back toward the side
entrance that led through the conservatory.

Behind them, she could hear excited murmurs and the
rustling of bags and baggage as the coaches were loaded.

Nick led her inside where they stood and watched

through the glass wall. "That seemed to go rather well," he remarked.

"You were very generous," she said. "Are you perhaps treating them too well? Like friends and equals?"

"No, as valued employees. There is a difference. There must be a distance, Emily, that is all I was trying to tell you. Are you still angry about that?"

She sighed. "No. I am aware there is much for me to learn. If I put a foot wrong, you should tell me."

"I would rather warn you before you do so. By the way, I have arranged for a dressmaker to outfit you with a new wardrobe. She will be here just after noon with patterns and fabric samples."

"I have an entire wardrobe, Nick. This is an unnecessary expense."

He smiled at her, obviously pleased by her economy. "Mother's clothes become you well, Emily, but they are a decade out of date. You should have new ones. Allow me?"

"If you like," she said, regretting that she must relinquish the comfort and confidence of the countess's clothes. At least she would still have the ring. She turned it on her finger and smiled.

"How is the accounting coming along?" he asked, changing the subject. Or maybe he wasn't changing it at all, only exploring another facet of her ineptitude.

"We shall see," Emily told him, feeling defensive. "You thought me presumptuous to order it," she guessed.

He hesitated a moment too long before saying, "No, not at all. You must do as you think best with the household affairs, but if you have questions or doubts, please come to me—"

"And ask your permission," she said curtly.

"Please stop doing that."

"What?"

"Finishing my sentences."

Yes, she thought, he *was* going to be difficult to live with, but she would persevere. "We should go in. Would you like your interview with Rosie now?"

"I said nine o'clock," he reminded her, then relented, "but now will do just as well, I suppose. There's much to do today and getting that behind me will give me an early start."

Emily nodded and headed for the stairs to find her maid.

"Wait," he ordered, halting her in her tracks. "You should use the bellpull and send someone for her."

"Oh. As you wish," Emily conceded. It simply had not occurred to her, she was so used to doing things for herself.

For a moment there she had almost lied and said she had business to attend abovestairs. Pride was a terrible thing and she'd always possessed too much of it.

She reached for the embroidered, tasseled strip of fabric and gave it an angry jerk. They were close enough to the kitchens to hear the jangle.

One of the tweenies came rushing to the hall, stopped short before Emily and bobbed a curtsy. "Yes, mum?"

"Please fetch Rosie for me, Brigid. Tell her to come to the study posthaste. His lordship wishes a word with her."

When Brigid had scurried away, Emily looked up at Nick and raised a brow. "Satisfied?"

"Yes. Now if you will excuse me?" How polite he was. How cool and formal.

"Certainly," she replied in kind, wishing they could simply talk to each other the way they used to do without considering their words so carefully and picking the responses apart for hidden meanings.

More than anything, she wanted to hear Nick laugh without reserve, to have him tease her and ply her with those heated gazes of intense longing and promise he had offered so long ago.

But Nick was no longer that young man she had known any more than she was a green girl living off wishes and dreams. Still, at odd times she saw glimpses of what she'd believed existed between them then.

Despite his lie about the betrothal to Dierdre, Emily knew in her heart Nick had loved her a little in spite of himself. He *had* left off before he'd dishonored her completely, hadn't he? She must give him credit for that.

Perhaps now and again Nick also yearned for what might have been. It could still *be* if he were not so pigheaded and high-handed. She was perfectly willing to change herself to suit him. He could jolly well change to suit her. That was only fair, she thought.

The first thing he needed to do was to understand that she would not share him under any circumstances. Somehow, she must summon the courage to make this perfectly clear.

His evening on the town last night would be his final foray into debauchery. She had already forgiven him that because he had been denied her bed since they married. Fair was fair. But if he thought he was in for an hour's dalliance with Rosie in the study this morning, he had best think again.

With unhurried steps, she followed him, but remained outside the study door, waiting for Rosie. Whatever he had planned for her maid, Emily meant either to prevent or to witness firsthand. One thing for certain, there would be no further unlawful congress between them. She would see to that.

When Rosie arrived, they went in together.

Nicholas set aside the letters he had been going over and looked up when the door opened. "Good morning, Rosie." His gaze flew to Emily's. "Do you wish something of me?"

She nodded and added a smile for good measure. "Yes. I wish to attend the interview."

"Not necessary," he said pleasantly. "I can handle it."

"I daresay you could. Nevertheless, I shall stay."

He shot her a dark look, just as she had expected he would. "There must be other matters for you to attend. The accounting, for instance?"

She took a seat in the arm chair that faced his desk. "Well in hand, my lord. Not to worry." She made a small flourish with her fingers. "Do proceed."

His glare should have pinned her to the wall or sent her running, but she was used to it now. An earl thing he had adopted from his curmudgeon of a father, only he never carried through with the threat implied in it. She endured it with some amusement now, thoroughly enjoying his discomfiture.

"Very well," he said at last, and turned his attention to Rosie who stood before him like a penitent. "This shan't take long. Rosie, I want to confer with you about your new position as lady's maid."

"Yes, m'lord. I welcome the honor. She's a love to look after." Rosie tossed Emily a fond glance of appreciation.

Nick uttered a wordless sound of disapproval and ran a hand over his face as if he'd lost the ability to speak.

His nostrils flared as he drew in a deep breath and let it out. "Please understand that this is no reflection on your prior performance, Rosie, but I have doubts as to your qualifications."

He threw up a hand to silence Emily when she would have voiced an objection. "Be that as it may, Lady Emily has chosen you, so you must apply yourself with all industry to this. It is critical that she present herself at her best at all times. Her appearance and personal comfort are now your primary responsibility."

"Oh, I know that, sir! I do. May I speak free?" Rosie asked enthusiastically.

"I suspect you will," Nick replied with a sigh of resignation.

"Sophie Turnatter what serves Lady Carstairs could teach me. I could ask her if she would."

"Very enterprising, but I would as soon keep this within our own household. I shall order the *Godey's Magazine* so that you can examine the latest fashions, what is worn with what and so forth. There will be hairstyles in it to copy. Have you ever done hair for anyone?"

"I can tend my own, thank you," Emily interrupted, resisting the urge to pat down her coiffure. "What is wrong with it?"

Nick seemed to realize his defeat and simply shook his head. "Nothing. Nothing at all."

She suspected this whole interview had been contrived on the instant, anyway, to conceal his real intention for having Rosie come here this morning. Emily thought him rather quick to improvise it.

He rose from his chair. "Have you any questions, Rosie?"

"None, m'lord. I'll manage Lady Em just fine, don't you worry none."

Nick addressed Emily then in a tone that brooked no argument. "Leave us for a moment. I have a rather personal matter to discuss."

"No." Emily stayed right where she was. Rosie needed her protection and Nick needed a lesson in husbandly behavior.

He looked ready to explode, though he seemed to understand she would not be moved by any display of temper on his part. "Stay then," he snapped and turned his attention to her maid. "Rosie, I merely wished to ascertain whether Mr. MacFarlin has spoken with you at all."

She grinned, toying with one of the red curls that had escaped her mobcap. "He has."

Nick nodded. "I see. Well, if he causes you any bother, you are to let me know. I will speak to him if his attentions trouble you in any way."

"No trouble so far, m'lord. Percy MacFarlin's a gem of a bloke. Got manners and all."

"Well, then, that's settled. You may go now."

She bobbed an impudent curtsy to Nick, repeated it for Emily, and took her leave of them.

"You don't approve of Wrecker's courting her," Emily observed.

"It's not that I don't approve, but I will not have her tolerating his attentions just because she fears consequences if she turns him away."

"A right good explanation for one who must have instilled those very fears in her seven or eight years ago!" Emily snapped as she leaped to her feet to face him down.

Lord save her, she had not meant to confront Nick

about this, but she could not abide a hypocrite. It disappointed her that he was one.

"Exactly what do you mean by that?" He seemed genuinely puzzled. And angry, standing there with his hands on his hips looking down at her.

"Exactly what you think I mean." In for a penny, in for a pound. She would finish this.

"You believe Rosie and I...? So that's why you wouldn't leave the room," he said. "For your information, I have never—"

"What? Tupped a maid in your service?" she demanded. "Go ahead and tell me that if you dare."

He all but snorted fire. "It is none of your affair whom I have or have not *tupped,* as you so indelicately put it!"

She poked him hard in the chest with one finger. "It certainly *is* my affair if you ever intend to tup me, *my lord!*"

"That doesn't seem all that likely at this point, to be perfectly honest! I'm not altogether certain I still wish to!"

"Then set your mind at rest at once!" she declared, "I do not require it! Nor will I allow it!"

On the verge of tears and violent behavior, Emily took to her heels and fled the study in all haste.

She had made hash of it all, she thought, desperately fighting to regain her composure and not run weeping up the stairs to her room.

Worst of all, she realized that she had not forgiven Nick at all and probably never would. The feelings of anger she thought she had vanquished seemed to have taken on a life of their own.

Chapter Thirteen

Late that afternoon Emily nursed a headache so annoying it deserved a name of its own. Madame LeCroix had hatched it, that was for certain. The prim, birdlike woman and her covey of plump-breasted, chirping assistants had invaded the countess's chamber and molted samples of cloth and pattern books like gaudy, excess feathers. Finally they were gone.

Emily lay on her bed, a cold cloth upon her brow, exhausted and exasperated.

Rosie, who had shown the women out, returned bearing a tray. The scent of strong tea and orange-flavored biscuits promised a bit of relief. Emily sat up.

Behind Rosie came Nicholas, elegant in his town clothes, dressed to go out. Or perhaps he had only just come home. Did it matter? At the moment she cared little what he'd been up to these past few hours. She only wished he would leave again, especially if he meant to continue their last conversation. She only wanted to forget about that.

"I'd not thought the woman would spend the entire day," he commented, sounding a bit vexed. He filched one of the biscuits off her tray and took a bite. "Madame

LeCroix informs me that you chose only a few gowns and but two of those she brought ready-made. According to what she related, you made excellent choices, however—''

''You spoke with her?''

''Of course,'' he admitted freely. He popped the remainder of the biscuit into his mouth as he bent to retrieve a square of silk that had somehow escaped LeCroix's sample case.

Emily watched as he straightened, testing the supple material with those long, strong fingers of his. With an effort, she tore her fascinated gaze away from his hands and fastened it on the tea tray Rosie placed upon her lap.

Beside the cup lay the paper of headache powder she had requested. She dumped it in the tea and stirred, risking another glance at Nick as she did so. ''So, you felt you had to approve them.''

He dismissed Rosie with an inclination of his head. ''The fabrics should prove quite complimentary to your coloring and the styles are perfectly acceptable.'' He smiled at her. ''But you will need more of them if we are to introduce you to Society.''

She sipped the tea, closed her eyes and wished him away. ''Then let's not.''

''We must,'' he insisted, but gently, not in that commanding tone she hated to hear. ''You should understand, Emily, that I plan for us to live here in London for several months out of the year. Whenever the House of Lords sits, I intend to be present. Not this session, for I've missed the beginning, but the next for certain. When we are in town, we shall be expected to attend social functions. I'm told as many matters of government are settled socially as there are officially.''

''You could leave me at Bournesea,'' she suggested.

He cocked his head to signify doubt. "I believe I tried that this time, and with little success."

Emily ignored his sarcasm, giving Nick one more opening to be honest with her. "Having me for a wife could make things difficult for you here. Perhaps you would have done better to honor your commitment to Dierdre Worthing, after all."

The smile on his face froze even as it left his eyes completely. "I was never committed to her in any way, Em. I told you as much."

"So you did." With her eyes and her heart, she willed Nick to tell her the truth, to admit that he had pretended love for her while officially bound to another woman. If only he would beg her pardon and be honest with her, give her some reason she could accept for all his lies, they might begin again, this time on the right footing.

"I only came up to invite you downstairs this evening," he said, adroitly dismissing the subject before Emily could declare that she knew for a fact he was lying to her. Not that she planned to. She wanted the admission to come from him.

He quickly continued, his mood growing lighter by the word. "My old friend, Viscount Duquesne has agreed to come for dinner. Will you be recovered from your fitting by nine, do you think? He really wishes to meet you again."

"Again?" she asked, searching her memory for someone of that name.

"I don't think you actually met, but he does remember you as a child. Guy used to accompany me on school holidays to Bournesea now and again. Big blond fellow, charming, laughs a lot? I believe he attended church with me on occasion."

Emily remembered then. She'd felt jealous of the boy

who had claimed so much of Nick's time when he was there, and then had rebuked herself for begrudging Nick another friend. "Would you please give him my regrets?"

"Come now, Em," Nicholas cajoled. "Guy is my best friend and would like to wish us well together. You will enjoy his company, I promise. He would love to meet you."

At that moment Emily saw the young Nick in his smile, the lad who had captured her heart. This meeting mattered to him, she could see. Further denial rose to her lips, but instead she heard herself saying, "Nine o'clock? Very well."

"Wonderful." His smile widened as he reached out and caressed her shoulder by way of thanks. A slow heat permeated her body as he did so, warning her that she was perilously close to wanting more from him. Rather, she was close to *admitting* that she wanted more. Aloud. The memory of the kisses in the carriage that had led to more invaded her mind and would not go away.

"I'm so glad you will be joining us." Fortunately he put a bit of distance between them just then and prepared to leave her. "Meanwhile, have a good rest. Guy and I have several matters to discuss anyway, so you needn't rush. We will await you in the library at nine or thereabout."

Emily granted him a weak smile and a nod. She did not feel up to entertaining anyone, but she would not shirk the duty. Nick had asked her nicely to do this, and she could not deny that his eagerness to introduce her to a good friend of his was flattering. At least that indicated he was not ashamed of her.

His continued dishonesty about his early engagement to Dierdre bothered Emily more than anything. She supposed she would have to own up to going through his leather case at the inn and finding the document, squarely catching him in the untruth. She knew it would anger him. It would anger her even more to have to introduce the proof, but the air needed to be cleared before they could go on.

She knew he did not love Dierdre Worthing and never had, but it signified a truly dark mark upon Nick's character that he would play both Dierdre and herself false by the same deed and then deny any wrongdoing.

Oh, well, tomorrow would be soon enough to address that. It wasn't as if there was any rush about it.

In addition, Emily didn't much care for Nick's high-handed way with the matter of her wardrobe. He meant well, she knew. It was only that his demand of final say in what she wore made her feel even more inadequate. Though she resented his apparent need to approve her choice of clothing, Emily did grant that his doing so did allay some of her worry.

She must allow that she had never paid much attention to current fashions. There had been little need for that, living immured in a small coastal village all her life. She ought to thank Nick graciously, both for the assurance and the spending, but knew she would not.

Pride again, she thought, heaving a huge sigh. Sometimes it served her well, but usually not. Tonight, she decided, it definitely would.

She meant to put on her best face and one of her new gowns and show Nicholas she was quite capable of entertaining. Emily set aside the tea tray, leaned back upon the pillows and closed her eyes.

Her headache was gone when she awoke several hours later and began to prepare for the evening.

Rosie chattered excitedly as she brushed Emily's hair

to a high gloss. Working with studied confidence, Rosie parted it in the middle, then coiled most of it around Emily's head in a smooth coronet. Three long, wavy lengths of it were tortured with tongs into proper curls that trailed down the left side of Emily's neck. A single silk rose the exact color of her gown completed the coiffure.

"*Voilá!*" Rosie announced, standing away, her arms outstretched in presentation.

Emily laughed. "You do a fine impression of someone pretending to be French! I do wonder who inspired you. Madame, perhaps?"

Rosie giggled. "You look a picture, Lady Em. Stand up and see in the long mirror."

In truth, Rosie had done rather well by her, Emily decided. The low neckline of the rose silk revealed a bit more than she would have liked, but Madame had assured her this gown was quite modest by today's standards. Apparently the tops of women's breasts were always exposed so in the upper circles of society, at least they were during the evening hours.

"Well no one's ever seen these before," she remarked to Rosie as she tried to tug the bodice up an inch or so. The snug fit prevented it and she gave up with a grimace. "I wonder what they'll think."

"Nice bubbies is what," Rosie declared, arms folded across her own generous bosom. "Not so big, but shaped right perfect for all that they's small."

Emily found that quite funny. Never in her life had she discussed body parts with anyone, but Rosie seemed not in the least to shy from it. "What of the waist? I can barely breathe."

"Wasplike," Rosie assured her. "That's all the rage,

Madame says. Looks good, but I wouldn't eat much if I was you.''

''Thank you, Rosie,'' Emily said as she took up her fan and flipped it open, turning side to side in a final gauging of her overall appearance. ''I suppose I'll do.'' She bit her lips to redden them a bit. ''Won't I?''

''That and then some, you'll see.''

A glance at the mantelclock assured Emily she had made the transformation in good time. Ten minutes early, in fact. Wouldn't Nick be surprised?

With a lilt in her step, Emily waved her fan at Rosie and went down to greet Nick and his friend.

She heard voices in the library. What if they had not finished their business, or reminiscing, or whatever? She halted just outside the doorway to judge whether or not she should enter yet.

Nick was speaking. ''I didn't think it necessary to warn Emily.''

''Well, I suppose you know best how she would react to threats,'' came the dulcet tones of the other man.

Her husband chuckled mirthlessly as glass clinked against glass. ''Well, Emily's not your usual nervous Nell. My guess is she would lean more toward outrage than fear.''

A long sigh. ''If she did know, she'd probably want to stay as far away from you as she could get.''

''I doubt it,'' Nick replied. ''Nothing seems to scare her.''

They were talking about her, for goodness' sake, Emily thought with a frisson of apprehension. Fear of *what?* Of Nicholas? That was absurd. He would never harm her or allow anyone else to do so.

She tapped her lips with her fan. Of course, she had, ever so briefly, wondered if he'd had anything to do with the wreck of the carriage. Then she had dismissed that as a ridiculous notion borne of shock and fear. If Nick had wanted her out of the way permanently, he would not have gone to the trouble to save her that day. He had put himself in great danger to do so, too.

Did she dare march in there and ask what this was all about? That certainly was her first inclination, but she restrained herself. What she had overheard sounded rather ominous and might be better discussed later when they were alone.

"Well, let's adjourn to another subject before she arrives," Nick suggested. "We'll meet tomorrow and decide what must be done next. Patterson's coffeehouse?"

"That'll do," the man answered. "Say, one o'clock?"

Emily backed against the wall, fanning herself rapidly, feeling a bit faint. And it wasn't the blasted corset, she decided. What in the world could they be talking about? If she demanded to know now, she would have to admit she'd been eavesdropping. Nick would never forgive her for making such an admission before a friend of his. No, better that she wait until the viscount left.

The huge clock in the foyer chimed the hour, reminding her that she was due in the library. Nick might come looking for her and find her standing outside the door with no legitimate reason for lurking there.

She drew in a deep breath, threw back her shoulders, lifted her chin and went in to join their company.

"There you are." Nick greeted her with a wide, appreciative smile that quickly faltered once he got a good look at her. Was her hair wrong? Had she dressed too formally for a simple dinner with one guest? His barely concealed disapproval cut her to the quick. And stirred her anger.

"Duquesne, my wife, Emily. Emily, do you remember

Guy? He was an occasional visitor at Bournesea when you were just a child.''

"My lord," she acknowledged with a curtsy, and held out her hand.

He took it, bowed over it and brushed it with his lips. "Countess, it is an honor to renew our *almost* acquaintance.''

"Indeed," she replied, marking the deviltry in the gray-blue eyes that seemed to miss nothing. Not her sudden bout of nerves, nor her worry over her appearance, nor the newness of her attire, for he was perusing that with avid and unconcealed interest.

So was Nick. But his gaze had locked on her bosom. He actually stepped between her and the viscount, ostensibly to block the other man's view. "Could I pour you a sherry?"

"No, thank you," she replied stiffly. "You know I am not overly fond of spirits." She glared pointedly at the glass he held in his hand.

"Ah, yes," Lord Guy interjected. "Drink does alter the wits, Nick, and before ours go begging completely, one of us should express our great pleasure at the company of one who is so ravishing. Do allow me," he said, stepping around Nick and executing another short bow. "May I say, you look exquisite, countess?"

"You may," she replied curtly, her eyes never leaving Nick's as she spoke to the viscount. "And I thank you for the compliment, my lord."

"That gown is most…becoming," Nick said in a voice that in no way supported his words, leaving no doubt as to the reason for his displeasure.

She wanted to shout that the dressmaker had been his own confounded idea. Left to her own devices, Emily would have worn one of Lady Elizabeth's dresses, all of which were much more demure. Instead, she offered him a quelling look that dared him to say anything further. He turned away and downed the remainder of his drink in one swallow.

Emily decided to ignore him. He had probably imbibed a bit too much of that sherry and it had made him surly. She must remember to water the stuff down tomorrow to prevent this happening again.

"Please, be seated," she invited, gesturing toward the chairs with her fan. She popped it open as she took her own seat and positioned the fan so that it obstructed the view of her chest. "My husband tells me you have been friends for years," Emily said to their guest, politely initiating a safer topic of conversation.

"True enough," Lord Guy replied. He had the most ingratiating smile and a comfortable way about him that probably set most people at ease immediately. He well might have had that effect on her had she not heard his part of their secretive conversation.

The man knew things she did not. Things that had to do with her. Did she imagine that she saw a flash of sympathy hiding behind his good humor?

He continued. "Nick says the same of you, by the way. I should think a marriage would benefit enormously when grounded in the familiarity of friendship. Be that as it may, I have come to tender my good wishes and congratulate you both. I hope you will be very happy together."

"Thank you, my lord."

The viscount laughed. "Please, call me Guy or Duquesne, if you like. Nick always has, unless he thinks of a more fitting sobriquet. Those are usually not repeatable in mixed company, however. He is a scoundrel, this husband of yours, but I'm certain you've noted that already."

"Ah, an insult!" Nick accused with a grin, seeming to make an effort to regain good humor. "Pistols at dawn to assuage my honor. I insist." His words were laconic as he poured himself yet another brandy.

Guy leaned toward her, his voice low. "The dolt is ever encouraging me to duel. One of these days I shall take him up on it and make you a merry widow."

Emily looked from one to the other, uncertain how to interpret their banter. It was merely banter, she knew, but was not sure whether she was expected to join in or to ignore it. She decided to join and lowered her own voice to a stage whisper. "Is he any good with a pistol? Perhaps you should choose swords. We used to fight with cane shoots and I beat him every time."

Delighted, Guy threw back his head and roared, slapping one knee. "Good show, Nicky, I think you've picked a winner here! Should have known you would never choose some ruffle-headed peahen for a wife."

"Why, thank you, kind sir," Emily said, adding her sauciest smile. She touched the silk rose in her hair. "I am certainly glad I disdained ruffles this evening."

Nick looked exasperated. "I could find a place to put some ruffles, if you had them with you."

Mortified that he would dare refer to her décolletage before another person, Emily felt her face heat and her temper rise anew. She lowered the fan and turned to Lord Guy. "He must cling to the image of me as I was as twelve, sitting in a pew and covered neck to toe in white dimity."

"No, you've quite dashed *that* image altogether," Nick declared, glaring at her exposed skin.

Emily rounded on him then, fairly shaking with fury.

"I am what you have made of me, sir, like it or not!" She rose quickly from her seat and gave him her back. Then she whipped her skirts around and added, "Since you quite obviously do *not* like it, you can jolly well do without it!"

She marched swiftly to the door and almost broke into a run. Fortunately she recalled her manners and turned with a forced smile in place for their guest, "I bid you good evening, Duquesne."

Dead silence reigned behind her as she stalked up the stairs.

To put it mildly, her first social occasion in London had not gone well, she thought with a grimace of disgust. Nick had ruined it for her and she had compounded his error by snapping back.

Embarrassed beyond help, she rushed to her room and locked the door behind her. There would be repercussions, she was certain. She recalled the look on Nick's face as she'd left. He would come to her after Duquesne went home and demand an apology. Maybe she should fear him, after all, as the viscount had suggested she should.

"I am definitely at a loss here," she murmured to herself. A draft from the chimney...or somewhere...cooled her heated cheeks like a soothing balm. She wiped the tears from her face and sniffed. Frantically, she rubbed her ring. A bit of her confidence crept back.

"Foolish girl!" she muttered angrily as her eye caught her reflection in the mirror across the room. "Flaunting your chest does *not* make you a woman, you know. A real woman would demand an apology from *him* for criticizing her in company!"

The mysterious little draft billowed the silken hem of her skirt. Emily took that as a sign she should move events along, rather than simply standing still and waiting for things to happen to her.

She marched over and tugged the bellpull that would bring Rosie to assist her. If she planned to confront her husband after his guest departed the house, then she should meet him in something other than this immodest monstrosity he had bought for her and then publicly disdained. Her old blue merino would do just fine.

She pulled it out of the back of the armoire and gave it a hasty smoothing with the flat of her hand. He wanted the vicar's daughter instead of a proper countess? Well, he should be careful what he wished for.

All of this kowtowing and efforts to please she'd been engaged in since her marriage were wearing exceedingly thin. It was time his lordship met the real Emily Loveyne, the woman she had become during his absence of seven years.

No, she would not allow him to evade her tonight and pretend in the morning that nothing untoward had happened. She would await him in his own chamber and not stir a foot out of it to let him sleep until he begged her pardon for his snide remarks.

When Upton appeared a few moments after Emily left and announced that dinner was served, Nick ordered a tray sent up to her. He knew very well she wouldn't show her face again tonight.

''What I said must have sounded like criticism to her,'' he muttered to Guy.

''Now whatever would make you think such a thing? I wonder!'' Guy's shoulders shook, but he managed to stifle his laughter. ''She was absolutely livid. Nothing timid about your little country mouse, I'll say that for her.''

Nick frowned. "Emily's no *mouse.* And how can you fault her for being reared in the country? It's not as though she had any choice about it."

Guy sobered. "I don't fault her for it, Nick. Do you?"

"My God, no, of course not. If you want the truth, I was this close," he said holding his thumb and forefinger a scant half inch apart, "this near to proposing to her when my father had me hauled away to India."

"You don't say! Well, you never confided that before. Have you mentioned it to *her,* by any chance?"

"She would never believe it. There was a time when she would have believed anything I told her. I fear Emily has become far too cynical and mistrustful in recent years."

"She's no longer a child," Guy pointed out.

"You noticed," Nick replied dryly. No, Emily was not a girl any longer. And something had to be done about their current status as man and wife. Left as it was, they would soon be more distant with one another than they had been when living continents apart. It might even gentle her if he went about it in the right way.

He and Guy had almost reached the dining room when Upton appeared again. "My lord, you asked that the countess be served in her room, but the maid says she is not there."

Nick experienced a sudden rush of apprehension. "Then where is she? Has anyone seen her?"

Upton looked distinctly self-righteous as he cleared his throat and answered. "Yes, my lord. I'm told she has gone to *your* chamber. Apparently, she refused the tray. She's…waiting."

Nick managed to temper his sigh of relief that she hadn't hared off down the street somewhere in a fit of temper. "Thank you, Upton. That will be all."

"Very good, my lord." The butler—apparently disappointed that he had not gotten more of a reaction with his tattling—nodded and left. The man's days here were numbered, Nick thought to himself. He would replace him with Jems.

Nick looked at Duquesne.

Eyes twinkling, apparently enjoying the whole farce, Guy said, "I am almost tempted to actually stay for dinner just to see what you would do." He let loose a full-fledged grin. "But I won't. Go ahead, old fellow, see what she's waiting *for*. I'll meet you tomorrow as planned." He knocked a fist lightly on Nick's shoulder. "Don't summon the cadaver back just to open the door for me. I shall see myself out."

"Thank you, Guy," Nick said absently as he looked up the stairs, wondering what in the world had possessed Emily to enter his bedroom.

Considering their last conversation, Nick felt fairly certain Emily wasn't there with the intention of sharing his bed.

The only reasons he could imagine was that she was waiting to apologize for her behavior or to castigate him for his.

He deserved whatever she decided to fling at him, he supposed. There was no excuse for the things he had said, but seeing her in that dress—rather, having Guy see her in it—had driven rational thought right out of his head. He'd had the strongest urge to take off his coat and wrap her in it.

He had also experienced another, much stronger urge, unfortunately, one impossible for him to act upon at that moment. The fact that he could not had only added fuel to the fire. Even now, Nick didn't quite trust himself to go to her when a bed was that nearby.

Waiting wouldn't solve that problem, however, so he took a deep breath and started up to face the music.

She was standing by the window when he entered. "Emily?"

Turning as if startled, she let the drapery she'd been holding aside drop back to its original position. "Nicholas." She sounded defensive.

"I was told you were waiting for me?" he asked, infinitely glad that she had changed into another gown, this one in no way seductive. Even so, he felt the now familiar surge of desire that occurred whenever he was near her.

"Lord Guy has already gone?"

"Yes, he decided not to stay for dinner, after all."

She bit her bottom lip and refused to meet his eyes. "Because of me," she guessed.

"He was more amused than upset, so you shouldn't worry about it," Nick assured her. "I behaved abominably, Em. The fault is mine, not yours."

Her mouth, already open, snapped shut. She turned away from him before speaking. "You chose the dress yourself."

"So I did," he admitted, moving closer behind her, cupping her shoulders with his palms. How delicate she felt, how small and defenseless. "And I'm afraid you wore it altogether too well. Lovely as you looked in it, I was loath to share the view, even with my closest friend."

Her body trembled beneath his hands. She said nothing.

"Emily, do you understand?"

She nodded.

He smiled to himself. "Do you realize how much I want you? How much I have *always* wanted you?"

She sniffed. "Even when you were betrothed to another woman? Even when you knew you could never offer me marriage?"

Nick released her and dropped his hands to his sides. "How many times must I tell you, there was never a betrothal? I would have asked you to marry me if my father had not interfered."

Instantly she whirled around, her face a study in dismay. "No! No more lies, Nick! I cannot bear it." She swallowed hard and clasped her arms around herself. "I saw the betrothal document."

"Oh, that." He could not imagine where she had found the thing, but it mattered little now. "It is invalid."

"I realize that, now that you and I are married, but it was real enough when first you kissed me and pretended to love me!"

"Not even then," he insisted. "My father forged my name to it, Emily. I never signed it and had no notion that it existed until I found it in my father's desk when I returned."

She didn't believe a word of it, he could see. Lips pressed tightly together, she studied his eyes as if trying to find the lie.

"I swear it on Mother's soul, Emily. I never signed the thing. I never would have done so and Father knew that."

After a long moment fraught with tension, she finally asked, "Whatever could he hope to gain by doing such a thing?"

Nick took her hand and led her to the chair beside the fireplace. She didn't resist his touch and he thought that was a good sign. Perhaps she was beginning to credit he was telling her the truth.

Once she was seated, he sat on the ottoman facing her,

still holding her hand in his. "He must have believed I would honor it rather than expose what he had done and cause a scandal."

"Would you have married her if I had not forced you into wedding me?"

Nick had to laugh. "Forced me? As I recall, it was I who did the insisting." Clearly she was not amused, so he added, "I wanted to marry you, Emily. I am glad things happened as they did and that you are my wife. I only wish…"

"Wish what?" she asked in a whisper.

Nick leaned forward and captured her mouth, willing himself not to hurry her, exulting in the heady rush of need that enveloped him, trying to gauge whether she felt it, too.

When their lips parted, he cupped her face in his hands and looked deeply into her eyes. "That you were really mine."

Chapter Fourteen

Emily struggled against her instinct to welcome Nick into her arms, to claim him against all odds and make him hers at last. Good sense warned her that he would use passion to distract her. There were so many things between them that she still did not understand. Things he did not want her to understand, apparently.

His apology had thrown her off guard, probably as he had meant it to do. There she was, all prepared to demand it of him and he had calmly laid it at her feet without her asking. She remembered all too well that Nicholas was the master of the unexpected.

Thank goodness he had stopped with one kiss and given her an instant to think this through.

She grasped his wrists and removed his hands from her face. ''No,'' she told him firmly. Her breath seemed to be restricted, coming in small gasps, a result of his kissing her, she knew. ''We must talk. I came here to…talk, not…I came to talk.''

When he drew back, she took another moment to recover, then explained. ''Nick, I overheard you and Duquesne speaking in the library.''

He scowled, obviously not thrilled that she had eavesdropped. ''And?''

She took a deep breath and watched him closely to judge whether he would withhold the truth. ''He said I should beware of you. Though I know you might prefer anyone else as your countess, Nick, I cannot believe you would ever harm me.''

''Good God, no!'' he exclaimed. ''I'm aghast you'd even entertain such thoughts. I would move heaven and earth to protect you, Emily, and you know it!''

She shrugged. He probably would. But she was by no means certain of it. She also noted he had not responded to her remark that anyone would make a better countess than she. ''Then tell me what Duquesne meant. Why should I be afraid?''

Nick issued a protracted sigh and shifted on the ottoman, stretching his long legs out to one side so that his right hip rested against her knees. She examined his face in profile, his strong features set in a worried frown. ''Someone intentionally wrecked our carriage,'' he admitted.

''Well, I *know* that,'' she declared. ''Anyone with eyes could see that tree had been cut instead of falling of old age into our path. A highwayman placed it in order to stop the carriage and rob us. Then he became frightened or changed his mind and ran away. You told me this yourself.''

He shook his head. ''I didn't want to worry you. There's a good chance it was no highwayman, Em.''

''You think not? Then who…?'' She reached out and grasped his forearm.

''There were two attempts on my life before I left India. At the time, I marked the incidents up to business rivalry. Such things are not that unusual in that part of the world where the law is more difficult to enforce. However, it's entirely possible that the threat has followed me here."

"That's why Duquesne said what he did? Because I might be in danger when I'm near you, is that it?"

"The carriage wreck, a case in point."

"Do you have any idea who might be responsible? Who would benefit?" she asked.

He placed his hand over hers, rubbing the back of it with his thumb, a gesture of reassurance, she thought. "Well, there are a few I could name who might think they would. Guy is helping me investigate. There could very well be a risk involved in your being with me if anyone makes another attempt."

"But *you*, Nick! What of you? Let us return to Bournesea at once where we know everyone! It's not safe for you to remain here where there are so many strangers."

"To tell the truth, I think it will matter little where I am if this person is determined to do me in."

Emily turned her hand over so that she grasped his. "But what can we do, Nick? We have to *do* something! We can't simply sit around waiting for someone to try again."

His smile warmed her straight through. "So you do care for me still?"

"Of course I care! Why ever would you believe that I don't care?"

His smile mocked her as he stroked her fingers in a blatantly suggestive manner. "Why ever would I think that you do? You obviously think me a cad and a bounder, a profligate liar and a seducer of innocents. And who knows what else—"

"Do hush!" she interrupted with a huff, and promptly pinched him hard on the wrist to halt his taunting.

"Ouch!"

"Keep your mind on the business at hand, will you? We must devise some plan to apprehend this scoundrel who wishes to harm you, Nick. It won't do, you know."

He leaned forward and kissed her ferociously, taking her quite by surprise and with a great deal of fervor. Lights flashed behind her eyes and she felt faint. So wonderfully faint.

Next she knew he was on his knees before her, drawing her close to him. Emily felt his chest hard against her breasts, one hand threaded through the hair at her nape, the other tightly clutching the waist curve of her corset.

She felt at once imprisoned and liberated, her senses drugged and yet as alive as they had ever been, zinging with Nick's very essence from every quarter. The manly scent of bay rum, the luscious taste of brandy. The glorious feel of his insistent body pressing against hers. His growl of desire that reverberated within their kiss. She wanted it never to end, never to allow her rational thought again, for she would be obliged to cease this...

Suddenly he released her and moved back. "Emily?"

"Hmm?" she hummed, eyes half-closed, still caught up in the tantalizing spell he'd wrought.

His hands cradled her neck. "Look at me, Em."

She tried to focus on him as she licked her bottom lip, savoring the taste he had left there.

He blinked hard and looked away for a second. "Please, do not do that again unless..."

"What?" she whispered on a shallow, uneven breath.

Giving her a gentle shake, he explained, "You know that I want you. But each time I look into your eyes, I see doubt. I will not continue with this unless you will promise that I have your complete trust."

"Blackmail," she accused softly, the languor he'd inspired lingering in all the recesses of her body. "You're a bad man, Nicholas. Truly bad."

He smiled tenderly, her Nick of old, the one who had teased and coaxed, wooed and won, loved and left. Or had he loved? He'd never said as much, she reminded herself. The daze he had inspired began to disperse more with each second she spent without their lips or bodies touching.

"I could be," he told her. "I could make you mine tonight, right now, take advantage of these unfamiliar feelings of yours, which you do not yet understand—"

"Not so unfamiliar," she announced.

"There's been someone else?" he demanded, frowning.

She gave him such a shove, he landed on his backside, well away from her. "You *are* a bounder to ask such a dreadful thing! Of course, there's been no one else!"

Despite his ungainly position on the carpet, he grinned. "I thought not." He got up from the floor and sat on the ottoman again, observing her closely. "But you gave me a moment's pause there, I must admit."

Emily narrowed her eyes and stared back. "And I suppose you'd have me believe there has been no one else for you in all that time?"

He looked away. "Certainly no one who mattered, rest assured."

"No one who *mattered?*" Emily sprang up from the chair and began to pace, her arms folded protectively in front of herself. "And to think, I almost became another in your lengthy parade of willing wantons!"

"But I did not allow it, did I?" he pointed out. "I stopped kissing you to show you that I had no intention of coercing you into anything you did not wish with all your heart to do. I remained in control for the both of us.

There's your proof that I hold no evil intent, nor do I leap into bed with a woman at the slightest provocation the way you think I must.''

"The *slightest?* Hardly any provocation at all, was it? That's proof only that you were not as genuinely affected as I was. Your so-called control is not so flattering, Nick, I promise you.''

To her chagrin, he laughed. Hard. Though he never did enough of that these days, she was not glad he did it now.

"You want me? Come here,'' he invited, spreading his arms to welcome her. "See how genuinely affected I really am.''

She flung out her hands in a gesture of total frustration. "No!''

"What am I to do with you?'' he asked, not for the first time since their unfortunate reunion. He shook his head ruefully, still smiling. "Contrary little widgeon. You haven't changed one iota.''

"But I have,'' she insisted.

"You are more beautiful than ever, that I will grant you. Come, let's begin again. Grant me your trust. With a bit of faith on your part, nothing prevents us making ours a true and lasting marriage.''

She held her ground. "Nothing but the fact that you blithely sailed away without a fare-thee-well. Nothing but seven years apart with no word of explanation.''

And, Emily thought with a greater surge of anger, there was his misuse of Rosie, but she would not mention that again. He might decide to turn the girl off to avoid another brangle about her, and Rosie did not deserve that.

Nick's arms fell by his side. "What do you mean, no explanation? You know very well Father forced me to go. I told you so.'' He expelled an impatient huff.

''What's the use? You're determined not to believe or trust or forgive, no matter what I do or say, aren't you!''

Emily couldn't look on his disappointment, or she feared she might forgive him, right then and there, no matter what he had done. She half believed him about the fraudulent betrothal. Could he be telling her the truth about why he had left her? Or was she grasping at his excuses with the greedy hands of a woman who wanted him more than life itself?

She had to think clearly and could not accomplish that while in the same room with the man.

With that in mind, she strode past him to the door and opened it. ''We're both overwrought,'' she told him. ''If you don't mind, I think we should continue this another time when a calmer mood's upon us.''

''Suppose I *do* mind?'' he snapped. ''Suppose I want you *now!*''

Emily leveled him with a look of disdain fostered by her indomitable pride. ''Then use some of that control you're so bloody proud of.'' She slammed the door and hurried away before he could reply.

Only after she reached her room, did she remember the danger Nick was in and that they must find some way to resolve that problem. She might be ready to wring his neck herself, but she would die if anyone else did him any harm.

The man made logic an impossibility, and she imagined he would have the same effect on her sleep tonight.

And he wondered what *he* was going to do with *her?*

So much for the noble effort to gain her trust, Nick thought with a delayed grimace. He had meant it as a very temporary gesture, that would hopefully last only seconds, minutes at most, while she decided he was telling her the truth.

But *no*. There she went, flouncing off down the hallway in all her righteous fury, leaving him with utter frustration. Not to mention an aching arousal. Women!

He thought seriously about putting a fist through the wall. That was all he needed, broken knuckles.

Why the devil hadn't he gone ahead and made love to her when he'd had the chance? She would have let him, was more than ready for him. He raked a hand through his hair, then tore off his neckcloth and slung it across the room.

The truth was, he had to have more of Emily than just her passion when the time came. Desire had always been more than sufficient where other women were concerned—and there had been a number of them in his effort to forget her when his letters went unanswered—but with Emily, he wanted love and complete trust along with it.

She had loved him once, believed in him, too. He needed her laughter, her optimism and the camaraderie that they'd had between them then. They'd had moments of it since he came back. Fleeting, but enough to prove it wasn't hopeless. Surely it would be possible to recapture that one way or another. Some of her feelings for him remained.

She didn't want to see him dead. That was something at least.

His gaze jerked to the door when it opened, but it was not Emily returning. "Is there a problem, Wrecker?" he asked.

The new valet raised a bushy brow and eyed him up and down, obviously amused by the state Nick was in. "Looks like there might be. Saw m'lady wagging down the hall with her nose in the air. Make her mad at a inconvenient time, did ye?''

Nick shrugged out of his jacket and unbuttoned his waistcoat, letting them fall where they would. ''Never mind that. How goes the inquiry into Julius Munford's whereabouts? Any news from the docks?''

''He's in London right enough. The *Aphrodite* put in 'bout a month ago.'' Wrecker pursed his lips and noted the clothing on the floor, but he didn't move to pick it up. One job at a time seemed to be his limit, Nick thought wearily, and acting an inquiry agent must be a great deal more interesting to Wrecker than the offices of valet.

''Did you find out his direction?''

Wrecker assumed an air of importance and looked powerfully pleased with himself. ''Wouldn't be worth my salt if I didn't, now would I? A house on Lanette Street. Kept a woman there when he was here last year, but he's got rid of her, so they say. He's laying low, but did ask around about ye soon after he docked. I think he's yer man.''

''Excellent work,'' Nick praised, feeling somewhat better now with one problem possibly near solution. ''First thing tomorrow, I'll arrange for a runner to keep an eye on him. You'll be needed here from now on.''

Wrecker grunted his agreement, then added, ''If you don't want nothing else of me this evenin', I'm going down fer my supper.''

Nick smiled. ''You do that. Send someone up with mine while you're about it. And tell Rosie to make certain Lady Emily has hers, as well.''

Wrecker left, impudently grumbling about the hoity-toity who ''wuz too high and mighty to take a meal at a table downstairs like they wuz supposed to do.''

Fortunately the man had other assets because he certainly was proving quite hopeless as a servant, Nick thought.

All of a sudden he felt hungry and optimistic and no longer disheartened by his argument with Emily. He made up his mind to turn it to his advantage and to enjoy the wooing of her confidence. After all, anything easily had was never properly appreciated, was it?

Apparently she would take some convincing that he was not only content, but happy to have her as his wife. Given the way he had behaved since their wedding, no wonder she had a problem believing it.

It should be safe enough to take her out for a short jaunt now and then if Wrecker accompanied them. After all, if Julius Munford was out to kill him, it was highly unlikely the man would attack Nick openly on a city street.

Even in India, Munford had gone to great lengths twice to arrange a demise for Nick that would appear to be accidental. That was the primary reason Nick suspected him of planning the carriage incident.

There had never been enough solid proof to haul him in. In fact, the man could not be located afterward, even if there had been proof. But Munford had issued public threats against Nick beforehand.

They had been in competition for years. Nick had won that new clipper ship of his when Munford foolishly gambled it away. After a refusal to sell it back, Munford had stated the intent to kill him. It stood to reason it was him behind all of this.

But tomorrow Munford would be safely under surveillance. It was only a matter of time before he was caught in the act of arranging another incident that would never have a chance to come to fruition.

* * *

The following morning Nick was waiting for Emily when she arrived in the morning room for breakfast. He stood and smiled a greeting as she entered, ignoring her frown. "How lovely you look today, my dear," he commented as one of the footmen held her chair for her to sit.

She muttered perfunctory thanks. Whether that was for his compliment or the footman's execution of his duty, Nick could not tell. No matter, he thought, as he waited for her to ingest her coffee.

"Would you care to ride with me this afternoon?" he asked pleasantly. "The fresh air would do you good, I think, and the weather today is perfect."

"No, thank you. I do not ride."

"Of course you do. I taught you myself and you were a natural as I recall. If you're out of practice, we shall find you a very gentle mare to start out. I can borrow one from—"

"I do not *ride*," she insisted with an impatient wriggle, smoothing her serviette more firmly over her lap.

"Ah, you haven't a riding habit yet. I'd forgotten. The open carriage, then, around two this afternoon. I know you have a gown appropriate for that."

She glared, first at the footman in attendance, who obeyed her unspoken command to disappear and close the door behind him. Then Nick had his turn under scrutiny. "Why are you doing this?"

"Doing what?" He sipped his coffee and looked at her over the rim of his cup.

"Acting as though nothing happened between us last night," she accused in a low voice. Emily was ever direct in her approach to matters. He quite liked that she was.

"Because nothing of any consequence *did* happen," he reminded her as he rested his elbows on the table and clasped his hands together under his chin. But something would soon, if he had anything to say about it.

"I had only thought you might like to take some air," he assured her.

"When going out endangers your life?" she asked, her expression prim as that of a schoolmistress. "I think not."

"Very public places such as the park would provide little opportunity for an attack, Emily," he said sensibly. But what if she was afraid? What if it turned out that she had good cause? He would never forgive himself if she were harmed on his account. So he conceded. "Perhaps you're right."

"Of course, I'm right."

"By the way, we received a belated invitation this morning to a musical evening with the Earl and Countess of Hammersley which is scheduled for tonight. Short notice, of course, and the countess apologized for that. They've only just heard we're in town and didn't wish us to feel excluded. I hope you don't mind that I've accepted for us."

Sheer panic gripped her. Nick watched as her expression froze.

"It will be safe, I promise," he assured her. "They live just down the street. Michael is an old friend of mine and his wife, Julia, is a lovely person. This will be a good introduction into Society for you. For me, as well, since I'm practically new to all this myself. Not quite so overwhelming as a full-dress ball, though there will be those to endure in future, no getting around it."

The fingers gripping her fork were white-knuckled and she appeared quite speechless.

He went on, busying himself buttering a slice of toast, allowing her time to adjust to the idea.

"The music should be extraordinary. Julia is quite the patroness, so I hear, and a wonderful musician in her own right. Guy will be there, I'm certain, for he's inordinately fond of music. He, Michael and I attended school together. The three of us set London on its ear when we got away to come here. I expect the entire city will welcome the fact that we've settled into adulthood at last."

She released the deep breath she'd taken. "No doubt."

His stream of mundane conversation had given her sufficient time to come to terms with what he was suggesting, and it hadn't taken long at all, Nick noted with pride. Emily Loveyne Hollander never allowed anything to get the better of her. What spirit she had, he thought with admiration.

Nick pushed away from the table and rose. "If you'll excuse me, I have some business to attend for the next few hours."

"Of course," she said, her gaze lowered to her plate.

He walked the length of the table, tipped up her chin with one finger and smiled down at her. "We'll forego the ride in the park for the time being, but I do want to show you London one day soon."

"Very well," she agreed, then shook her head slightly. "However, about tonight..."

"The blue silk," he suggested, then, with a self-deprecating grin. "No extra ruffles. I'll contain my wretched jealousy as best I can and share your beauty."

She actually smiled back at him, but he warned himself it could be but a nervous reaction on her part.

"I shall see you later." He left the morning room before she could change her mind.

Instead of ordering the carriage around, Nick went through the conservatory and out the back way through the gardens. It was only a half hour's jaunt to Guy's house in Ainsley Square. Gentlemen rarely walked to make visits, but he needed the exercise and time to think. Besides that, the fewer people who were aware of where he went, the better.

His business with Guy would not wait until their pre-arranged appointment at the coffeehouse. Nick wanted to hire a shadow for Julius Munford immediately. Hopefully this would take only an hour or so to complete.

Afterward he would stop by and have a word with Hammersley. Tonight could be crucial to Emily's acceptance and Nick would need all the assistance possible to effect it.

He worried that Emily would not find and secure her place among his peers immediately, if ever. Some were inveterate snobs and viewed anyone outside the topmost echelons as common interlopers. Anything he could do to ease the way for Emily must be done now, today.

Hammersley's evening of entertainment would have a limited list of guests and provide an excellent opportunity to introduce his wife without overwhelming her. Or them, Nick thought with an ironic smile.

Hands in his pockets, his boots eating up the distance along the alley that backed the gardens in Mayfair, he reconsidered the wisdom of bringing Emily out this quickly after her arrival in London. He devoutly hoped things went as he planned.

For her own sake, he did not want to see her shunned and unhappy. However, he would be lying if he pretended that his own ambitions would not also be affected by his wife's acceptance or lack of it.

That might be selfish, but there it was. He was a lord, and respect within the House of Lords was vitally important to him. Emily was more important to him, of course, but there was no reason they should not both be better served by adapting to what they must.

Though he was not all that familiar himself with London Society, there was one every bit as strict set up in British-ruled India. A number of those now living here had once served abroad, so he already had a few friends within the charmed circle.

Emily had met none of them other than Guy. Oh, and the Worthings, he remembered with a grimace. God forbid his and Emily's paths should cross theirs anytime in the near future.

If only he and Emily had already solved the intimate problems associated with their marriage, he might be able to offer her more direction in how to get on with the nobles she would meet. As things now stood, she would see any suggestions he made as criticism and that would only drive the wedge between them deeper than ever.

Even as he considered that, Nick had already begun making a mental list of things she must and must not do and say. That was the easy task. Figuring out how to present Emily with that tally would be the true challenge.

Chapter Fifteen

They were going to hate her, all of them, Emily just knew it. Every last one would smirk and laugh up their sleeve at the country bumpkin come to town. Admitting that aloud to anyone never crossed her mind.

To Rosie, who busily constructed the most outlandish pile of curls on top of Emily's head, she presented an air of confidence that surprised even herself. While the maid chattered mindlessly about the advantages of discreetly applied lip rouge and rice powder, Emily sat with a frozen smile, her eyes trained unseeing on the mirror before her.

Nick, who had come by her chamber earlier to issue his diatribe on rules of behavior, she simply ignored. Did he truly think she would pick her teeth in public or something equally rude? Fie on him. Her manners had surpassed his by the time she was nine and she had told him so in no uncertain terms.

A vicar's daughter had etiquette fed to her along with her porridge even before she learned to walk and talk. But it wasn't her manners she worried about in this instance.

"My father was the younger son of a baron," she muttered, more as a reminder to herself than to inform Rosie.

"That a fact? Well, them persnickety folk tonight won't have a patch on you, will they! And yer mam?"

"A distant cousin of his. She trained to be a governess, but she and Father wed before she took a position."

Rosie tugged one long curl and watched it spring into place along Emily's neck. "See there? If any body knows the ins and outs of what highborn muckety-mucks is supposed ta do, it'd be one of them governess ladies. They *teach* it, now don't they?"

And Mother had taught her. She'd had twelve years of lessons. Emily felt a real smile warm her. "Thank you, Rosie. I honestly can't think what I would do without you."

"Take a sight longer gettin' yer clothes on, I expect." She removed the protective muslin cape from Emily's shoulders and stood back a few feet, hands on her hips, head cocked to one side. "There now, we done a right proper job of it. If you don't set the toffs' heads turnin' wi' admiration, I don't know what's what!"

Emily smiled back, then transferred her gaze from Rosie's mirrored reflection to her own. She had to admit the girl had a knack for styling hair.

The sapphire necklace and earrings complemented the new blue silk gown to perfection. Nick had brought the jewels earlier. She had asked if they were Lady Elizabeth's. Nick had smiled and said they were not his mother's, that they were hers.

She knew, however, that they must have belonged to the countess. Nick had no reason to purchase jewels for her and had not really had time to shop for any since they'd arrived. Besides, they matched her wedding ring perfectly, they had to be part of the set. Touching them gave her added self-assurance.

She hadn't questioned him any more about it. She suspected he had chosen these particular ones to ensure that she wore the blue gown that matched them.

Emily felt a pang of sadness as she touched the largest stone that rested in the hollow of her throat. Would the countess truly have minded Vicar Loveyne's daughter wearing these if she had lived to witness Nick's marriage? The cold metal setting warmed against her skin as if in answer. *No, of course not.*

"I will take excellent care not to lose any of it," she declared softly. Not the jewels or the countess's son. Emily felt as if her ladyship somehow knew of the role Emily had assumed and now entrusted her with everything the countess had treasured.

There were no ghosts, of course. Spirits went to heaven when the bodies no longer held them. Her father said so, and a vicar would know if anyone would. But some essence of the countess must have remained behind and, whether real or imagined, Emily was glad of that.

"I wish you could come with me tonight," she whispered as she ran a trembling finger over the facets of the fiery sapphire.

"Me, at a social do? Law, that'd be a sight, wouldn't it!" Rosie exclaimed with a merry laugh. "Now you'd best go meet his lordship downstairs. He said eight o'clock and it's a bit past that." She pointed to the clock on the mantel.

Emily stood and allowed Rosie to tug at the hem of her skirt so that it hid the froth of lace that edged her petticoat. The neckline of the blue silk was not quite as daring as that of the gown she'd worn when Duquesne had visited. She prayed Nick would approve of how she looked in it. If he didn't, then he had best keep his opinion to himself, she thought with a huff.

She pulled on her long gloves and Rosie handed her the ivory fan. A gossamer shawl completed the costume that transformed the simple country miss into the countess she was supposed to be now. Emily squared her shoulders and donned the attitude to match her ensemble.

No one, most of all Nicholas, must detect the slightest inkling of her fear. She would brave this night out if it killed her.

She swept out of her room and made her way carefully down the wide, curved staircase. Nick looked up, watching her descend, his eyes signaling his pride in her and lending her more confidence than she had felt thus far.

He reached for her hand and assisted her on the last two treads. "My, what a vision you are. Remind me to increase Rosie's wages."

Emily felt herself blush at both his compliment and his close inspection. After a few moments of trying to decide whether he could not tear his gaze away because he really liked the way she looked, or if he was searching for flaws, she grew distinctly uncomfortable. "Will we be late?" she asked.

Her question seemed to break his concentration. "No, not at all. In truth, it will take us hardly less time to get there than it will to get in and out of the carriage. We could walk it more swiftly than ride, but that's not allowed," he said in an amused and conspiratorial voice.

He nodded at the ubiquitous Upton, who responded by opening the front door, and they were off to their first public occasion together as man and wife.

A scant hour later Nick observed Emily as she mingled with the Hammersleys' other guests after the serving of refreshments.

The huge room, bared of all its furniture except for a long and elaborate buffet and the chairs placed along the walls, left plenty of space for those in attendance to circulate. Next door was the ballroom, similar to the one at Kendale House. There, Nick noticed, several dozens of chairs were set in lines for the audience. A temporary dais had been placed at one end to approximate a stage of sorts for the musicale.

"She's faring better than I thought she would," said a voice directly behind him. "Actually she doesn't look too shabby."

Nick turned. "Carrick, I'd not thought to see you here."

His cousin smiled, one blond brow cocked slyly. "I'm the toast of the town, hadn't you heard? Lady Julia has agreed—once I mentioned my connection to you, of course—to allow me to paint Lord Hammersley."

"You had no right to presume upon my friendship with them," Nick said through gritted teeth.

Carrick blithely waved off the reprimand. "Well, I did come by to gain your permission, but you weren't at home." He leaned closer and admonished Nick, "You never contacted me as you promised you would when you refused me entrance at Bournesea. What was that all about, anyway? Your wife mentioned someone was ill at the time?"

Nick wasn't about to tell him there was cholera. It would be like Carrick to report him and there were laws about coming ashore in England with a contagious disease. "It is true we had a bout of sickness there. It would have endangered your health to enter."

"The coughing sickness?" Carrick asked, his face paling. "Or worse than that? Not influenza!"

"What do you care? It hasn't affected you, has it?" Nick snapped. "But to return to our former topic, which you are so adroitly trying to avoid, what makes you think I will endorse your employment by Lady Julia if she asks me about you? I've never known you to do an honest day's work in your life. If I had reported all the minor thefts you performed at Bournesea when we were lads, Father would have hanged you on the premises. I warn you—"

Carrick sniffed. "Oh, come now, Nicky. We aren't children any longer. An artist must take his opportunities wherever he finds them. The Hammersleys won't be disappointed. I'm quite good at what I do. You must come by my studio and be reassured. Friday evening would be an excellent time."

He tucked a printed card in Nick's breast pocket, serious now, his expression indicating that he had something more important on his mind than showing off his painting skills. "Around ten, shall we say?"

"No, I have plans for the evening," Nick replied.

The gray eyes narrowed and Carrick's lips thinned as he spoke, betraying his concealed anger. "We have business to discuss, Kendale, and I am still your heir."

"Hopefully a temporary condition." Nick observed his cousin closely to see how he regarded the possibility of a child supplanting him.

To Carrick's credit, he shrugged it off. "I have considered that." He tapped Nick gently on the arm with his fist and forced a smile. "Fatherhood would make you age before your time, y'know. Gad, you already have wrinkles I should love to paint, old man." He inclined his head in Emily's direction. "More to the point, I would give my eyeteeth to paint your wife."

"You stay away from her or you'll find yourself in the hold of a ship bound for a place you've never even heard of."

Carrick's eyes rounded in mock fear. "I'm terrified."

Nick pinned him with a glare. "If you are not, you should be."

With his smile still in place, Carrick nodded. "I shall see you again soon, cousin."

He drifted away, quickly attaching himself to one of the ladies who seemed enormously flattered by the attention.

Useless fop. Nick shook his head and sighed. There had never been anything but dissension between him and Carrick that had carried over from that of their fathers. If the ne'er-do-well had changed at all in the past seven years, Nick would be much surprised. Still, he supposed he must allow him the benefit of the doubt. That is, so long as the wretch never approached Emily again.

Impatient with the unpleasant interruption, Nick searched for her. Much to his relief, she hadn't moved far from where he'd last seen her, and she still appeared to be at ease.

Lady Julia, at her own suggestion when Nick had spoken with them earlier, gave off the impression this evening that she and Emily were friends of long-standing.

Guy had arrived and hailed Emily effusively, complimenting her as if he had known her forever, adding to her consequence.

The ruse appeared to be working. Everyone greeted her pleasantly, at any rate, and there were no frowns or quizzical looks at the newest member among them.

"She's charming, your Emily," Hammersley observed

as he approached Nick and handed him a glass of wine. "Even the redoubtable Lady Fitzwaren appears less dour than usual in her presence. Look at that, would you? I had no idea the old crone knew how to smile. Perhaps we here in town needed the breath of fresh air your lady provides. Julia is quite taken with her, you know."

"Good. Emily will need friends," Nick replied. "I can't tell you how gratified I am by what you and Julia have accomplished tonight."

"Not us, my friend. You have that wife of yours to commend. Considering your worries this afternoon, I must admit I thought it would take more doing."

Michael scanned the room as if looking for someone, and changed the topic of their conversation. "There are only a few more guests due and then we can be seated. The ensemble Julia has hired are most accomplished."

"Will she be playing for us tonight?" Nick asked. On one of his brief business trips to London, Michael had invited him here for an evening. "She has such an extraordinary talent."

"Thank you on her behalf," his friend answered, smiling with pride. "Perhaps you might suggest her participation. When I do so, she balks, thinking I am prejudiced about her unique abilities. You know how it's frowned upon, a lady exhibiting willingness to show off her talent. One has to beg, so do me a favor and *beg,* will you?"

"Gladly," Nick promised, then thought he might broach the subject of Carrick. "Michael, speaking of talent—"

Hammersley interrupted, his attention focused on the doorway. "Ah, here are our latecomers now. Excuse me while I go and do the pretty."

Nick's heart dropped. The recent arrivals stood arm in arm, awaiting welcome. Dierdre and her father. Too late he regretted that he had made no mention of his contre-temps with the Worthings to Michael and Julia.

He should have known this run of good luck was due a turnaround. Hoping to take the brunt of the Worthings' antipathy and to protect Emily's sensibilities as best he could, he strode across the room to join her.

This meeting could prove disastrous, a scandal to rival them all, one that would surely undo Emily's efforts to win any friends here.

As it happened, Worthing and Dierdre did not approach immediately. They made a quick round of the room, speaking to everyone else, shooting Emily and him the occasional dark look. Emily seemed blissfully unaware of the undercurrent of animosity radiating from them as she continued her conversation with Lady Fitzwaren.

Nick wanted to warn her in the event she had not yet seen or recognized the Worthings. They were working their way closer.

Just as the baron's fiery gaze connected with Nick's, Duquesne intercepted the older man and all but dragged him aside. In Guy's spirited attempt at distraction, Nick heard some questioning reference to market investments. That should keep him occupied for a while.

However, no one knew to waylay the daughter, and Dierdre was making a beeline for Emily.

"Why, Emily Loveyne, how marvelous to see you! Imagine our meeting here, of all places!"

Lady Fitzwaren cleared her throat noisily, then corrected Dierdre. "That's the Countess of Kendale you are addressing, y'know. Mind your manners."

Emily smiled at Lady Fitzwaren and returned Dierdre's greeting. "Miss Worthing. Yes, this is a surprise."

Indeed, Nick thought, trying not to let his apprehension

show. Her smile firmly in place, Dierdre acknowledged him with a fleeting glance. "Kendale."

"Miss Worthing," he replied, wondering whether he dared hope Dierdre had been as in the dark about their fake betrothal as he had for all those years. About as likely as snow in the Sahara.

Dierdre tapped Emily on the wrist with her fan and declared rather loudly, "Lord Vintley must be distraught at your decision. But I daresay you've done a great deal better for yourself than hiring on as his governess!"

Emily smiled sweetly. "I daresay I have. Perhaps there is some other *unwed* lady you know who would be interested in the position you suggested to me?"

Old Lady Fitzwaren coughed to cover a laugh.

Nick envisioned two short fuses attached to either side of a keg of gunpowder. And sparks were beginning to fly.

Michael's hand landed on Nick's shoulder. "What do you say we begin to round up this crowd and herd them in for the program? I expect our musicians are champing at the bit by now. If Julia provided them spirits, we might have to sober them up before they can play."

"Certainly. Excuse us, if you will." Using the pretext Michael had conveniently provided, Nick took Emily's arm and firmly escorted her away from Dierdre Worthing and the anticipatory attention of Lady Fitzwaren.

Their path crossed with Julia's and Nick recalled Michael's suggestion. "My lady, I pray you'll do us the honor of performing this evening."

There were several exclamations of agreement from people standing nearby. However, one of those rather stridently overrode the others. Dierdre had come from behind and boldly looped her arm through Emily's. "Oh, but here is a new *voice* we truly must hear! Tell us, do you know anything secular at all, Emily?''

Nick could feel Emily tense, but she sounded as calm as a day in May when she answered. ''Why, yes, but I would not presume—''

''But you must, my dear!'' Dierdre insisted, withdrawing her arm and patting Emily's shoulder.

''Of course, you must,'' chimed the old Lady Fitzwaren. ''I, for one, would welcome something fresh in the way of entertainment. We'll hear you, too, Julia. That is why we came, after all.'' The dowager turned her bead-like eyes on Nick. ''Well, Kendale, won't you prevail upon your bride to entertain us?''

He looked down at Emily, fully intending a rescue, but she was smiling winningly at the older woman as she answered. ''If you require it, madam, then I should be most honored.''

So it was settled with a chorus of encouragement from all save Dierdre Worthing, who remained quiet and somewhat smug that she had brought off her little scheme.

Nick knew Emily could sing well. But that wasn't the point. He hated to see her trapped into doing so before a crowd of people who would prove a damn sight more critical than her father's congregation or a rowdy bunch of seamen. However, there was nothing he could do now but offer her what support he could.

''Will you be all right?'' he whispered as they were taking their seats.

''Of course I shall,'' she assured him, daintily adjusting her gloves.

They gave Julia their attention as she took the floor and introduced the musicians. Apparently the group performing were to appear at the Holcomb Concert Hall at the end of the week. Nick only half attended as they began to play since he was so worried about Emily's state of mind. She could pretend with the best of them, but he felt she must be roiling inside with apprehension. This was a trial by fire, no doubt about it.

After two instrumentals and resulting applause, Julia returned to the dais and announced, "To our great delight, Lady Emily, Countess of Kendale, has agreed to honor us with the ballad 'A Day Upon the Moors,' written by Sir Joseph Trenton. I shall accompany her on the pianoforte." She smiled and held out a welcoming hand toward Emily.

Nick stood when she did and escorted her to the front of the room to join their hostess. That duty accomplished, there was little to do but to take a seat and see what would happen.

Much to his amazement, Emily seemed perfectly at ease, her white-gloved hands folded primly at her waist, her untroubled gaze meeting that of a number of people in her audience as she waited for Julia to take her place before the keys.

The melodic prelude wove its way around the cavernous ballroom. Then, on a clear note that began in perfect tune with the one Julia struck, Emily began her song.

As soon as he recovered from his astonishment, he glanced around him. Every eye in the room was on her, gazing in awestruck wonder. She sang like a veritable angel, her voice clear and true, her own eyes closed as though savoring the heartfelt tragedy described in the words, their pathos enhanced by the minor notes the composer had employed and Emily and Julia's poignant rendition.

Tears leaked down the cheeks of Lady Fitzwaren. Nick thought he might weep, too, out of sheer relief. No one under the sun could find fault with Emily's accomplishment here. How could he ever have doubted her?

She was used to this, he realized. He wondered how many times in recent years her father must have called upon her to sing solo at his services. Nick had rarely heard her sing alone before.

He didn't know why it should surprise him. At every challenge presented thus far, she had excelled. Except that she could not muster any trust for her husband.

And did you trust her? The voice of conscience echoed inside his head. No, he had not. He had expected her to fail at every turn. Somehow, his father's ingrained notion that she would never make him a proper wife must have lodged somewhere inside Nick's own brain. He needed kicking.

As the last melancholy notes of the song trailed off into the breathless silence within the chamber, Nick vowed to himself and to Emily that he would place full faith in her from here on. She was no longer a girl, but a woman with capabilities he had not been giving her credit for having.

When fervent applause erupted, and people began to stand, he added his own sincere accolade. She was wonderful and he meant to tell her so as soon as humanly possible.

When she modestly declined an encore, he rose quickly and went to escort her back to their chairs. The remainder of the program, he barely heard at all, so engrossed was he in deciding just how to go about making up to Emily for his lack of confidence in her.

At last the entertainment drew to a close and conversation began to buzz around the room.

Everyone would spend at least an hour discussing the

program and how much they enjoyed it. Then the guests would begin to say good-night and depart.

He wished he and Emily could leave immediately, but he would never prevent her hearing all the compliments she was certain to receive. Even now, guests were surrounding her for just that purpose. He was saving his praise for later, when they were alone.

He saw Dierdre whisper something in Emily's ear. Emily gave a succinct nod and immediately accompanied Dierdre toward the doorway. He knew they must be headed for the retiring room, one of the bedchambers Julia would have set aside for the ladies to make repairs to their toilette and such. Not good, those two being alone. God only knew what Dierdre would say to her.

There was nothing for it but to trust Emily to handle the awkward situation on her own. Here was a real test of what he had promised to do, have confidence in her. She could manage, he told himself. In spite of that, his mind's eye pictured Dierdre Worthing dashing down the stairs in a few moments with half her hair yanked out.

Suppose he followed them and they had only gone upstairs for obvious purposes?

He bided his time, circulating among the guests and accepting their kind words about his wife.

Baron Worthing came close enough to speak only once during that time, only to give Nick the cut direct. Though the intentional slight was obvious to everyone around them, no one commented and it drew only a few curious looks. That old device had been employed so often during the past century, it had lost most of its effect.

Nick kept an eye on the doorway where Emily and Dierdre had disappeared. All he could do was hope for the best.

Guy suddenly appeared at his elbow, his expression

indicating that he had observed the goings-on with some interest. He was the only person in the room, other than Worthing himself, who knew of the potential disaster brewing.

"Smile, Nicky," he said. "After all, what is the worst that could happen?"

Nick released a sigh. "Having met my wife as you did last evening, need you ask?" Then he shook his head. "Trust comes hard, but I must believe she will handle herself with decorum."

Guy laughed. "I suppose you must. Care to wager on the outcome?"

"I already have," Nick replied.

Emily accompanied Dierdre Worthing to the retiring room to avoid a public confrontation she knew would embarrass their hosts. At least that was the primary reason. She had to admit she was also bursting with curiosity. There was a fire in Dierdre Worthing's eyes that belied the purred invitation she had offered.

And Emily knew very well that Dierdre had attempted to embarrass her royally with that suggestion that she sing.

Though the Worthings remained in London most of the time, especially since Dierdre had her Seasons, they did own the relatively small manor house not six miles from the church where Emily's father tended his flock.

The family had become part of the congregation generations ago by invitation of one of Nick's ancestors. The names of many Worthing births, marriages and deaths were recorded in the church registry. Emily and her father never visited the Worthings socially, of course, but she had gone with him in his duty as vicar to visit the sick on their estate and to offer comfort to their bereaved.

Dierdre had come to see her once, about two months ago before leaving for London, offering to suggest her for the position as governess to Vintley's children. Now Emily could easily guess why Dierdre had gone to such trouble to see her employed. Vintley lived nowhere near Bournesea. Nick had been on his way home at the time and Dierdre had wanted to make certain Emily's friendship with him had no chance of continuing.

Gloating had seemed to be Dierdre's favorite pastime while enduring her brief spells of country life. Emily had to wonder what she would do now for entertainment.

As soon as they arrived, Dierdre promptly dismissed the maid on duty in the ladies' chamber. She then stood aside to allow Emily to enter first, closed the door behind them and now stood against it as if to prevent her escape.

She was as lovely as ever, Emily noted, if one disregarded the sneer. Her pale yellow, expertly coifed tresses swept back from a perfect oval face. Her eyes were a trifle small, but she apparently had enhanced them a bit with kohl so that they appeared larger. Her nose had a slight upward tilt at the end, ensuring a permanent appearance of haughtiness, certainly in keeping with the rest of her attitude. Her body, squeezed to a fare-thee-well in the middle, protruded lasciviously above the satin neckline of her pink-and-white lace bodice.

She certainly didn't need that additional reddening she had put on her cheeks since she already glowed with barely restrained fury. Perhaps the song had not yielded the expected results.

"The chamber pot's behind that screen," Emily announced with a smile as she gestured toward the corner. "Or do you really have something important to tell me?"

"Indeed I have. Nicholas wants rid of you."

"Does he now? He hasn't mentioned it. He confided this to you, I suppose?"

Dierdre clenched her teeth and pulled in a deep breath. She let it out slowly in an obvious attempt to control her temper. Emily recognized the little exercise, one she often employed herself.

"Nicholas spoke with my father," Dierdre informed her. "His regret is absolute and he has promised to mend matters to our satisfaction." A fake smile bared her teeth. "Surely you realize that mending will not consist of a monetary reparation, for the Worthings do not need more wealth. You must ask yourself, how else would he make things right?"

All of the snide remarks about Emily's clothing, her provinciality, her inability to attract suitors, that Dierdre had offered over the years now echoed in Emily's head.

It was difficult to muster any sympathy now, especially considering her current mission to cause trouble. And yet, it wasn't hard to imagine how it must feel to believe you were betrothed for so many years and then to discover it was but a deception.

"Look, Dierdre, I know that our marriage provides you good reason to—"

"He wants *rid* of you," Dierdre repeated, her voice low and grating. "You've managed to trap him, Emily Loveyne, but he won't stand for it. Not for long." She forced a hateful smile. "He will find a way out of your snare, you mark my words. If I were you, I should be very afraid."

Emily did experience a small niggling of fear that there might be a grain of truth in what Dierdre was saying. Nicholas definitely was not happy with things as they were. He obviously worried—no, almost obsessed—about her inability to carry off the role of countess. And the few times they had come close to making their marriage real, he had deliberately made her angry.

Did he plan to keep her a virgin and eventually cite her refusal to consummate the marriage as cause for an annulment? No, too far-fetched, she decided. But how else would he be *rid of her?* Divorce was certainly out of the question for a man of his standing. It would ruin him completely, and he could not remarry anyway unless she died, so what would be the point of that? Dierdre was merely attempting to cause problems.

"Thank you for the warning," Emily said, keeping her tone conversational. "Though misguided, I am certain it is given in a spirit of helpfulness. You may consider your friendly duty accomplished."

Dierdre's cat smile stretched wider and her kohl-rimmed gaze was keen. "Disbelieve me, then, but you soon will see. You already know you are not his kind."

Emily looked her up and down and made an honest observation. "Neither are you, I think."

Before Dierdre could reply, someone tried the door and she had to move aside. Lady Julia pushed it open and looked in. "Is everything all right?"

Emily closed the distance between them and hurried past both Dierdre and her hostess to await them in the hallway. "We were just leaving," she declared as they followed her out.

"Are you certain nothing is amiss?" their hostess persisted, looking worriedly from one to the other.

Dierdre answered, "Nothing at all. Emily and I were simply caught up in renewing our old acquaintance."

"And apparently nothing about it has changed," Emily added.

Chapter Sixteen

Nick blew out a breath of relief when Emily and Dierdre returned to the ballroom with Julia. He quickly approached Emily and leaned close to speak so that no one could overhear. "What happened upstairs?"

She looked back at him, a strange expression on her face. "What would you expect when ladies absent themselves from a gathering. Must I elaborate?"

Nick stifled a scoff. "Dierdre has just signaled her father and they are leaving rather abruptly. Would you care to explain that?" he asked, keeping his voice low and his face expressionless.

"A megrim, perhaps. It is almost time for everyone to go, is it not?"

"Surely she said something to you," he insisted.

"That I should be afraid," Emily announced, seeming unconcerned.

"Of what? Of *her*?"

Emily shrugged. He noticed that she plied her fan with unnecessary exuberance, given the temperature of the room.

When she stubbornly refused to speak more or to look at him again, Nick gave up for the moment. Obviously she wasn't about to enlarge on what had taken place, at least not here.

"Later I will hear everything," he said aloud, and turned his attention to the room at large.

"Depend on it," she replied, abruptly snapping her fan shut.

She did smile, but if she moved a muscle to do anything else during the final quarter hour of their visit, he could not detect it. Still as a statue, she stood.

Of course, she'd had a lifetime of practice forcing her energy into abeyance, he recalled. Her father's sermons, while not exactly boring, certainly were lengthy enough to satisfy the most pious in the pews.

Over the years she must have worked out some sort of trance state that mimicked rapt attention. Imagining that made him want to smile. Such a thing was so Emily-like.

At last Michael and Julia thanked everyone for coming, then led the way out of the room.

He took Emily's hand and placed it in the crook of his arm. She still would not meet his eyes, making him wonder what she had either done or endured to disconcert her so. Instead of asking again, he remained silent and led her down to the front entrance. As it happened, they were among the last to leave.

Nick admitted he could not have asked more of Emily tonight. Unless she and Dierdre Worthing had quarreled, the entire evening had proved quite successful. Even if they had, to their credit, both had done so discreetly.

Once seated in the carriage, he complimented her. "I was extremely proud of you tonight. You were wonderful."

"How kind of you to say so," she replied. "That makes me wonder just how apprehensive you really were."

"Are you offended?" he asked pleasantly. "Perhaps you should be. I admit I feared you might find yourself at a loss with some of the guests. The elders especially, are such elitists."

"No one asked how blue was my blood, though there were two I think might have liked the opportunity to see some of it." She sounded snippy, probably with sound reason.

"Dierdre and her father," he said. No question.

"Yes." Emily looked him squarely in the eye. "She assures me that you want out of our marriage. That you have said you regret it and mean to rectify your error by some means. What means, Nick?"

He sat up straight. "That is patently absurd! I have never said such a thing to anyone, much less to Dierdre or Worthing."

She matched his glare. "No more lies, no more games, Nick. Tell me what you plan to do."

He glanced out the window. They were almost home. "We will continue this discussion. First, go up and change into something that allows you to breathe. Meet me in the library in half an hour. You and I will settle this once and for all."

"Why the library?" she snapped. "Do you need brandy for fortification?"

He turned his head slowly and pursed his lips for a moment before he replied, "Because the next time we meet in a bedchamber, I promise you it will not be for the purpose of conversation."

Emily remained silent as Nick assisted her down from the carriage and ushered her up the steps to the front door. The clock struck twelve as they entered.

"Will you require anything else tonight, my lord?"

Upton asked as he closed the door and locked it behind them.

"Nothing," Nick said over his shoulder. "See that everyone retires immediately, would you? Good night, Upton."

As they reached the stairway, Emily glanced back at the old fellow and saw his wrinkled features twisted into semblance of a grin. It made her shiver.

"Are you cold?" Nick asked softly.

"A little," she admitted.

"I shall light a fire for us."

"Thank you," she replied, hating the formality with which they spoke to one another, wondering if that would become a pattern in the years to follow. If, indeed, there *were* years to follow.

They parted company when they reached the third-floor landing. "Half an hour," he reminded her as he left her at her door.

Apparently Rosie had dozed off in one of the chairs in the corner of the bedroom while awaiting Emily's return. Emily gently shook her shoulder.

The maid bolted upright and almost fell. "Gor! A fright you gave me!"

"Sorry," Emily said. "Why don't you go on to bed, Rosie. I can manage for myself."

"No, no, I'm awake." Her words slurred as if she had been tippling. She swayed a bit as she stood.

"You seem a trifle unsteady. Are you quite all right, Rosie?"

"Sleepy's all," Rosie said, rubbing her eyes.

"Then undo my hooks and unlace me. After that, I won't need you," Emily told her.

"Oh, no, ma'am, I can—"

"Do as I say."

"Aha, more plans for the evenin', I see. You don't need me hanging about, then, do you?" Rosie said with a wicked grin. "Well, I'll be out of here quicker'n you can snap your fingers."

"Just get on with it," Emily said impatiently as she removed the necklace and dropped it to the dressing table. She started to take the pins from her hair, but decided to leave it as it was since she was meeting Nick later.

Rosie soon freed her of the constricting garments that fastened at her back. It took no more persuading to get the maid to retire.

Confident that no one would remain below to see her when she went down, Emily donned her lawn nightrail and wrapper, firmly knotting the sash at her waist and making certain she was as modestly covered as if she were leaving the house.

Once she was ready to go below again, she wondered what she would do for the next twenty minutes, since she didn't relish awaiting Nick alone in the library.

She was so tired and her eyes felt scratchy. For lack of anything else to do, she turned off her lamp and lay down in the darkness, reflecting on all that had happened tonight.

Dierdre's words haunted her. For the second time now Emily had heard that she should be afraid. First she had overheard Duquesne declare she should, and now Dierdre said the same thing without offering a precise explanation.

No matter what they said, Emily refused to believe she should fear Nick. If he wanted shed of her so badly, why had he not allowed her to perish in the carriage? It would have been so easy to do. One shove, the entire conveyance, with her inside it, would have plunged over the precipice and he would have been free of her forever. But he had risked himself to save her.

Or had he felt he had to do so? Had he suddenly realized he might have been blamed, seeing that he was not in there with her at the time, but had chosen to ride instead? Perhaps it dawned on him how it would look to everyone if his wife was killed while he remained safely on the road. The wicked little voice inside her head insisted she consider the possibility.

"No, it's not true," she muttered, and turned her face into the pillow. Nick might not love her, but he would never consider murder. He did not have it in him.

But you don't know him now, do you? He isn't who he was at twenty-one. Neither was she.

"He's still Nicholas," she insisted vehemently. "*My* Nick."

Given all the excitement and that it was several hours past her usual bedtime, she was truly exhausted. Easy to see how she could let her imagination run wild. But she mustn't.

Her eyes drifted shut as she lay there, determined to discontinue that vein of thought. She had no reason to be afraid of her husband. None.

Vaguely, Emily feared she might doze off, but knew the clock striking the quarter hour would rouse her and she would still have five minutes to arrive in the library at the prescribed time. She wouldn't go to sleep, but would only rest her eyes.

Nick paced the carpet and muttered epithets to himself as he waited. And waited. He glanced again at the decanter of brandy. Tempted, he cursed again. After her comment about his needing spirits to get through this discussion, he would die before he touched the bottle.

Given how difficult the evening must have been for Emily, he supposed she thought she had the right to torture him a bit for submitting her to it as he had. Perhaps she did, but, damn it, he hated to be kept waiting.

Nick pulled out his watch yet again and checked it against the clock. Thirty minutes was long enough for anyone to change clothes. Another quarter hour, quite sufficient to sulk. Without another moment's pause, Nick strode toward the open doorway and headed for the stairs. If she refused to meet him here on neutral ground, then, by God, he would risk the distraction of the bedchamber.

He had just reached the second-floor landing when he heard a muted scream.

"Emily!" he shouted, hoping it was not her. Perhaps it was only one of the maids frightened by a mouse. Nevertheless, he bounded up the next flight, his heart in his throat.

Smoke seeped from the crack beneath her door. Desperately, he tried the door. Locked! He launched himself against the panel, but the stout oak held. "Em, can you reach the door? The key?" he yelled.

"No!" she screamed. "Nick, help me!"

He dashed to his own chamber, then through it to the connecting dressing room. That key was in her door, but on the wrong side. She'd been locked in. His hands shaking with haste, Nick twisted the key and shoved open the door.

In the light of the blaze that was left, he saw Emily frantically batting the heavy draperies with a small woolen throw rug. She coughed violently with each attempt to smother the flames, but her efforts were inefficient.

"Move!" he shouted as he snatched the rug from her.

''I'll do this. Sound an alarm for those sleeping upstairs in case it spreads. Hurry!''

Satisfied she would obey, he continued what she had begun and soon conquered the last of the fire. Smoke filled the room, choking him. He yanked down the charred fabric, stamped on it until it was completely out, then threw open both windows.

In the distance, through the open doors of the dressing room and his own chamber, he heard the frightened squeals and excitement of the speedy household evacuation.

Using what was left of the small rug, he fanned as much smoke as possible out the windows. He hauled water in a vase and poured it on the smoldering fabric and the rug. Several times, he retreated into his own room to breathe relatively fresh air. He feared to leave for longer than a moment or two in the event the fire rekindled.

As soon as the air had cleared enough to see, Nick noted the cut-glass lamp on its side on the floor. The flammable liquid had spilled out and the flame had caught fire to the draperies. He crouched down and examined it. The lamp was from his own bedside table.

Nick glanced over at the door to the hallway. The inside keyhole was empty of its key. If someone had opened the door only enough to reach inside, they could have removed that key and locked the door from the outside. The dressing room had been locked on his side of the door. Emily had had no way out.

He stood and went to the dressing room door. At the distance from either doorway, with only the moonlight from the windows, even with the lighted oil lamp someone held, it would be difficult to tell whether one or two people were on the bed, only that it was occupied.

Someone had tried to kill Emily. Or else, had attempted to kill them both, thinking they were sleeping together.

"M'lord?" Wrecker's voice boomed from the hallway. "Where ye at?"

"In here," Nick called.

"God a'mighty!" Wrecker exclaimed, coughing as he surveyed the damage. "You all right, sir?"

"Yes," Nick said, brushing past Wrecker as he entered Emily's room. "You stay here. Make certain this doesn't catch up again. Where's Lady Em?"

"She's on the front steps. Sent one of the men for the fire wagons."

"And you left her there?" Nick demanded in disbelief.

Wrecker shrugged. "She ain't in no danger. She's surrounded by our folk about six deep."

"One of whom set this fire!" Nick announced. "You are in charge here until you hear from me. I'm taking her somewhere safe."

Emily was exactly where Wrecker said she would be, issuing orders and attempting to instill calm among the servants. Her nightrail, wrapper and face were blackened with smoke. Her hair, the curling tendrils that weren't plastered to her head with dampness, flew every which way. Her hairpins had given up their task and one dangled ineffectively over one ear. She looked like a dirty street urchin.

Nick didn't care who was watching. He simply shoved his way through the crowd and clasped her in his arms, enormously relieved she had lived through this. She was soaking wet all over.

He whispered against her ear, "God, that was close. You were so brave. Smart, too, dousing yourself first with water. You're not hurt, are you?"

"No," she rasped. "I'm fine."

He felt her wilt against him, as if she'd only been waiting to relinquish her command. Still holding her, he spoke over her head to one of the footmen. "Joe, saddle one of the coach horses and bring it around. Make it fast."

Emily reared back her head and asked, "Why? You're not leaving?"

"*We* are leaving," he declared. "I won't have you stay in this house a moment longer."

He looked to Rosie who was hovering nearby. "Go inside. Bring her a cloak. Anyone's cloak that doesn't smell of smoke."

"The fire?" Emily asked.

"Out," he assured her, "but it's no longer safe for us to remain here."

When she would have asked more questions, he shushed her by pressing her face against his chest and caressing her head, gently raking out the useless pins and smoothing her tousled hair as if she were a child in need of comfort. "Everything will be fine, Em. You're not to worry."

Nick did not release her until Rosie brought the cloak he'd requested. He wrapped Emily in it and held her close again until Joe brought the horse.

"Where will we go?" she asked the moment Joe had lifted her up to sit in the shelter of Nick's arms.

"I'll tell you as soon as we're out of earshot. No one here needs to know how to find us." With that pronouncement, he kicked the horse into a gallop and headed for Duquesne's. It was less than a mile away, but he took the long way 'round to make certain they were not followed.

"Do not expect much in the way of amenities," Nick

warned Emily as he dismounted and assisted her down from the broad-backed coach horse. "Guy lives a rather frugal existence."

"Fine," Emily said, sounding a bit breathless.

"What is it? Are you all right? Sure you weren't hurt?"

"No injuries," she answered with a short half laugh. "You've been squeezing the breath out of me."

"Sorry," he growled, loosening his hold and taking her hand instead. "Come, let's see whether Guy's home. He might have gone out after he left Hammersley's."

Nick raised the heavy knocker and let it drop. It clacked loudly in the still night air. He repeated the act.

A few moments later the door opened a crack and a wizened old face peeked out. The lamp he held threw his features into a deathlike mask. Nick smiled. "Good to see you, Bodkins."

The door opened wide and the wrinkled butler stepped back. "Lord Nicholas. Come in, please." As if Nick visited every day.

"Is Lord Guy here?"

"He has gone up to bed, m'lord. Wait in there, please," he gestured formally toward the front parlor. "I shall announce you are here."

"Thank you, Bodkins," Nick replied kindly. He ushered Emily toward the room Bodkins had indicated but did not enter it. It was pitch-dark, so they remained in the doorway, waiting. Nick slid his arm around her shoulders, drawing her close.

Before the old butler had reached the third tread on the stairs, Guy came bounding down, dressed in shirt-sleeves, his vest hanging open. He was in his stockinged feet. "I heard knocking. Who was it, Boddy?"

"The Earl of Kendale and a lady, m'lord," Bodkins croaked.

Guy, his shock apparent, quickly scanned the cavernous foyer until he spotted them in the near dark. "Good God, man! Boddy, give me that light!" He took it and approached Nick and Emily.

"We came to beg a room for the night," Nick explained. "There was a fire at Kendale House." Then he lowered his voice, knowing that old Bodkins couldn't hear him when he did so. "No accident. Emily was almost…" But he couldn't say it. And he shouldn't, he realized, not in front of her. She must be near collapse as it was, and she probably didn't even realize yet how close she had come to death.

Guy took charge. "Bodkins, grab a candle, lock the front door and go to bed now. I'll handle what needs doing."

"Of course, m'lord," the old man answered. "Have a pleasant evening, m'lady, m'lords."

A pleasant evening. Nick almost laughed. It was two o'clock in the morning. Poor Bodkins had gone past his prime, poor old fellow, but he was loyalty personified.

"Come with me out to the kitchen," Guy said. "You'll want to clean up." He addressed Emily, "I regret there are no maids in service, my dear. Will you manage?"

"Of course," she assured him.

Of course she would. When had she not? She had grown used to managing without anyone's assistance in the past few years. With the vicar in his dotage, her brother too young at first, then gone off on that cursed voyage. Nick hated that he'd not been there for her when she needed him.

He now felt the aftereffects of almost losing her tonight—light-headedness, his thoughts flying in every direction, a weakening in his limbs and a sickness in his gut. Not unlike what he had experienced the day of the carriage wreck, only magnified.

How had he not realized then how much he still loved her? He had closed himself off from feeling much of anything but determination and had dedicated all his efforts toward building a fortune, independent of his father's business. Perhaps somewhere deep inside had remained a small hope that someday he would return to Bournesea, defy the old man and claim Emily.

Now that he had her, he had wasted their time together by allowing the past to come between them.

They arrived in the kitchens. Guy set down the lamp and found several more on a shelf. "There are rain barrels outside the door there," he said. "Why don't you start a fire, Nick? Then we'll haul in some water for bathing. There's a tub."

Frugal indeed. Other than expressing regret that there were no maids to attend Emily, Guy had made no apologies or excuses for his lack of servants. Apparently he had none other than Bodkins, who was too old to find employment anywhere else.

Nick embraced Emily and kissed the top of her smoke-scented hair, then walked her to a nearby bench set against the wall. "Sit down here and rest while we prepare your bath."

From now on, he would put Emily first in his life, Nick promised himself. Her happiness must come before any plans he had for himself. There would be no more attempts to integrate her into life here in the city, no more molding her into the countess he had thought his peers expected.

He had one more task to complete here in London

tomorrow evening that would hopefully eliminate any threat to their safety. After he made that visit to Julius Munford they would return to Bournesea where Emily could feel at home.

Emily hugged the cloak around herself as they climbed the stairs. Underneath it she wore only the soft nightshirt Guy had brought down to the kitchens to clothe her after her bath. Her own nightrail and wrapper were ruined, tattered and speckled by sparks that might have burned her alive if she hadn't drenched herself with water first. Delayed thoughts of it made her shudder.

Nick had on a pair of trousers and a shirt he had borrowed from Guy.

That man would make some woman a fine husband, she thought to herself as she watched him climb the stairs before them, lighting their way. He was charming and certainly self-sufficient. And, apparently, an excellent friend to have.

His grand old house could use a feminine touch. The wallpaper peeled here and there, the sparse furnishings were of excellent quality though covered with a fine layer of dust and the fabrics somewhat faded. There were no paintings on the walls and few rugs upon the unwaxed floors. She suspected Guy or one of his predecessors must have lost much of the family fortune along the way. Yet not a trace of bitterness marred his good humor or affected his gallantry.

"The two of you won't mind sharing a room, will you?" he asked as they reached the third floor and started down the hallway. "There is only one."

Emily stifled a gasp. There must be fifty bedchambers in a house this size. What did he mean, only one? Then she realized the others must be unfurnished.

"One will be quite sufficient," she heard herself announce.

Nick squeezed her shoulder in unnecessary thanks, she thought. How else could she have put Guy at ease? She could hardly demand that he and Nick share Guy's chamber. If he had only one extra room for sleeping, then they would simply have to make do.

At the moment she cared very little where she slept or with whom. Given their exhaustion, it was highly unlikely there would be a confrontation of any kind between herself and Nicholas. It took two to argue or to engage in any other kind of intercourse, and tonight, she did not intend to be one of them.

She quickly banished the quiver of apprehension as they entered a spacious chamber containing an enormous four-poster and all the other amenities one might expect in the home of a noble lord. It rivaled any at Bournesea or Kendale House.

"How lovely," she commented.

"Thank you," Guy said simply. He set the lamp down upon the bedside table, lighted the candle beside it and took it with him as he made to leave. "I'll say goodnight, then. Pleasant dreams." With that, departed and closed the door behind him.

A fire burned low in the fireplace, some of the logs now reduced to embers. She saw the massive desk in one corner, outfitted with writing instruments, a bottle of spirits and a glass. "Nick, this is *his* room."

"Yes."

She sighed. "We cannot put him out this way. Go and call him back. We'll sleep somewhere else."

"No, Emily. We shall sleep here."

"But—"

"Accept his gracious offer," he advised.

Emily knew he was right. "He's a good man, isn't he? Kind," she said. "What happened to him?"

"His wealth, you mean? The earl gave most of it away about ten years ago before Guy realized the old fellow had begun to suffer dementia. The rest, including what Guy has acquired from his own enterprises, has gone to support his father and those who constantly look after him on a small estate in the north. The earl's physically well, but quite mad now. Guy refuses to lock him away."

"Oh, how sad." Emily wiped at her tears and sniffed. "I love him for that."

Nick smiled down at her and took the cloak from her shoulders to lay it on the chest at the foot of the bed. "So do I. Therefore, we must not insult him by refusing his generosity tonight. You understand?"

She nodded emphatically.

He walked over to the desk, unstoppered the bottle of spirits and poured himself a dollop. "I hope you don't object. If ever there was a time for a nip of brandy, I think it is tonight."

Emily watched the working of muscles in his neck, the way the glass rested against his lower lip, the way his long-lashed eyes, the very color of the liquid he drank, closed in appreciation. He lowered the glass and exhaled roughly.

"Might I?" she asked hesitantly. If liquor numbed the senses, she definitely needed it. Hers had a keen edge tonight that she seldom, if ever, had experienced.

Nick poured a bit more, sauntered over and held out the glass, his gaze daring as she lifted it and sipped. Twice. Three times, until the brandy was almost gone. She made a face and handed it back to him while the liquid burned a path down her throat, settled in her stomach and slowly spread to encompass her limbs.

"Come, let's go to bed now," he said gently, his eyes holding hers as he tossed off the last of the liquor and placed the glass on the bedside table. "Which side do you prefer?"

"I...I don't know. I suppose it doesn't matter." She had never shared a bed with anyone before in her life. Her own, at home, had been hardly wide enough to accommodate one. Now she would be lying beside Nicholas for the very first time.

Perhaps brushing against him accidentally during the night. Touching inadvertently. The errant thought sent a new streak of heat right through her that rivaled that of the brandy. Unbidden, came the sudden memory of Nick's kisses, his hands upon her in the carriage before the wreck. She rubbed her arms briskly to dispel the tingling feeling.

Nick's defenses seemed to be as worn down as her own. His very stance was different, so casual and unassuming. Yet he looked as confident and powerful as he ever had, perhaps even more so without that aura of formality she hated so much. She couldn't quite pinpoint the change in him or exactly when she had noticed it, but there definitely was one.

Her gaze traveled up and down his body. Would he be sleeping in these clothes? She devoutly hoped he would. Otherwise...

He had turned back the covers and was shrugging out of his shirt. Emily's breath caught in her throat. Not since he was a boy had she seen his naked chest. There were mounds of muscle there and in his upper arms that had not been evident then. And smooth, dark hair. Lots of it. For the life of her, she could not look away. Her hands fairly ached to touch him there.

"Em?" he questioned, breaking her trance as he

reached to hang the shirt on the back of the chair to the desk. "You needn't worry, you know."

Ha! *Needn't worry?* "No, no! I'm not...not worried at all."

"Good. Get into bed. I'll douse the lamp before I finish undressing."

"Finish?" *Undressing?* She quickly crawled up on the mattress and slid under the covers, pulling them up to her neck.

He turned the screw that lowered the wick and extinguished the flame. The room darkened considerably, but Emily's eyes quickly adjusted. He stood silhouetted against the firelight and the dark outline of his body seemed much larger than when she had been able to see his features.

His hands went to his waist to unbutton the opening of his borrowed trousers. He pushed them down and stepped out of them, then folded them. Briefly, she saw him in profile as he laid the garment across her cloak on the chest at the foot of the bed.

He was clearly in an aroused state. Upright. She knew what that meant. And she *was* worried now. The very sight of him stirred hot feelings within her that a woman such as she should not be having. She would like to blame it on the brandy, but knew that would be dishonest.

True, they were married and she had decided to allow him to consummate their union when the time was right. But she knew very well she should not exhibit any eagerness. What did that say about her morals?

Would he be horrified to know how desperately she wanted him? His kisses had caught her off guard in the carriage that day and tripped a complete surrender of inhibitions. She had not even suspected she possessed such feelings.

Tonight that few moments in the carriage seemed to pale by comparison. She burned for him in that place that bore no mention in civilized conversation.

Insatiably curious, she had read as much as she could manage to find on conjugal interactions between husband and wife. And, of course, her father had that book to help him counsel gentlemen in marital matters. Since she was fairly certain no one ever counseled women in such things, Emily had felt perfectly justified in appropriating the information.

According to all instructions, the wife should accept the husband's attentions without complaint, but he should not expect her to actively participate. Emily wondered, somewhat despairingly, how difficult it would be to remain unaffected by what he would do.

The mattress dipped as Nick sat on it, lifted the covers and swung his long legs under them. Heat seemed to emanate from him in waves and to encompass her completely.

A fine sheen of moisture broke out on her brow and she brushed it away with a trembling hand. She heard his huge sigh as he relaxed against the large pillow, one arm beneath his head. Maybe he would simply fall asleep.

Emily was uncertain whether she wanted him to do that, or to get it over with. They had to do it sometime and he was obviously ready. It might as well be tonight. Very well, she *wanted* it to be tonight, she admitted with a small huff of resignation. Now, as a matter of fact.

"You *can,* if you wish to," she told him in a whisper.

"Hmm? Can what?" he asked as innocently as if he didn't know.

Perhaps he really didn't know. There was no reason his mind should be attuned to what she was thinking.

Though he must have been dwelling on similar thoughts, judging by the state of his body.

Nick rolled to his side, facing her. There remained a space between them wide enough for another person to sleep. She wanted to close the distance, but did not dare.

The arm that had rested on his pillow extended just above her head. She felt his fingers smooth her hair back from her brow, a feathery touch that sent tingles all through her.

"It will soon be morning, but may I kiss you good-night?" he asked softly.

Emily released the breath she'd been holding. "If you like."

"I would," he said, a smile in his voice.

Slowly he leaned toward her until his mouth reached hers. The light caress, lips brushing lips, did not appease in any way.

She moved her head a bit to establish a more satisfying pressure, but he drew back, eluding her. Without thinking how it might seem to him, she raised one hand to his neck and urged him to apply himself.

His immediate response almost frightened her. Before she knew what had happened, his body was flush against her own and his mouth devoured hers as if he were starving and she, his only sustenance.

Desire was the one truth between them she could fully trust and it would not be denied.

Chapter Seventeen

The intensity of his need for Emily shook Nick to his core. He hated wanting this desperately, this profoundly, yet he relished it all the same. He crushed her to him as if he might never have the chance again. Twice now, he'd nearly lost her and the very thought of it almost destroyed his reason.

Go slowly, gently, he told himself as he battled the beast within, the one intent on branding her his without any further delay.

"Nick," she whispered against his lips, and the rush of desire was too much. Her fingers slid through his hair, gripping, urging another kiss when the last was not yet finished.

He tugged at the nightshirt, wanting it off her, wanting nothing that belonged to another to touch her.

How silken was her skin beneath his hands, how hot and smooth and soft. And *his*. Her breasts were so firm, budded for him in their eagerness to be touched, tasted, treasured.

He drew his mouth from hers and trailed kisses down her neck, his lips open to trace the sensitive curve that led to her shoulder, then back across the swell of her chest. And there, ah, there, the sweetness of her almost unmanned him in the instant he took her in his mouth.

She shuddered, and her sound of pleasure shot through him like a shard, slicing away any thought of slowing to ensure her needs matched his. Surely they did, how could they not? Never in his life had he abandoned all finesse and rushed a woman so, but he could not pause, much less stop himself.

At last he held her skin to skin, the sweet friction more than he could bear, wrenching a groan from him he could not suppress. *Too fast, too much, too soon.*

He loosened his hold on her for a moment, clenching his eyes, his fists and his teeth, grasping at some vestige of civility that might contain the wildness she inspired in him. He propped on one elbow, ran a hand over his face, then looked at her.

She held up her arms in welcome and Nick's valiant effort nearly crumbled. He inhaled a deep breath and let it out, his eyes closed against the vision that lay before him. He started counting slowly to ten. He made it to five.

"Now, Nicky," she murmured. "Please."

He covered her immediately, though he had gained enough control that he braced himself on his arms. Looking down into her eyes, he saw her desire, a living, breathing entity within her as strong and demanding as his own. He was as humbled as he was relieved.

He knew he should speak, tell her how he loved her, how beautiful she was, but there were no words powerful enough to say these things, so he kissed her again. He lowered his mouth to hers as gently as he could manage and ravished her thoroughly while his body sought even more.

Her legs parted beneath him and he lay between them,

pressing himself against her, seeking her heat, her full acceptance, her heart.

She shifted, opened more and he surged forward into her, meeting a resistance he could not ignore. He had known she was innocent, had never doubted it, yet in his eagerness to make her his, had almost forgotten.

"Please," she repeated, so softly he could hardly hear it. "Do not stop."

Nick brushed her brow with his lips, her eyelids, feeling the tickle of her lashes against his mouth. "Soon," he whispered. "Soon now."

He braced on one elbow, struggling for control as he caressed her face, touched the rapid pulse at her neck with his tongue, trailing it down to the dusky rose of her nipples and around each one. The wordless murmurs of her response fueled his exploration.

Lower he kissed, sliding his body down the length of hers until his mouth rested in the slight hollow between her hips. He nuzzled the edge of her golden curls there with his breath, then moved to graze his teeth along one hip bone, then the other. She stirred restlessly, her hands fisted in the covers.

Would she protest? he wondered, but not for long. His mind flew into the delicious fog of passion.

The scent of her, the soft down that would soon welcome all he would offer drew him inexorably closer and closer still. He kissed her, ravishing her there as surely as he had her mouth. She cried out, moving against him, pleading until he felt the tremors of her release begin. Smoothly he moved over her and entered her again, this time with a surety of welcome neither of them could doubt.

Now her body offered little protest as he slid inside her with a swift and steady thrust. He thought he might die of the pleasure then and there. "Emily," he gasped, just to hear her name, to reassure himself it was truly her in his arms. It was not enough. "I love you," he added, as effortless and sincere a declaration as he had ever made. "I didn't know before."

"Yes," she answered, a mere breath of a word. And she arched against him, seeking more than he was giving.

Nick wanted to laugh. The demanding little chit would not allow him to savor this. Once he began to move, he knew he would be lost, unable to prolong this by will alone. And she was not helping.

He began slowly, knowing she must adjust, learn how. But she would have none of his hard-won consideration. He gave himself up to the rhythm she set, thrusting faster and faster, feeling the tension mount higher and higher until she came apart in his arms with a joyous cry. Nick joined her, reveling in a completion so keen and intense, he thought—hoped—it would never cease.

When the room stopped spinning, he realized he was crushing her into the mattress with his weight. With tremendous effort, he lifted himself away from her and lay down at her side. He snuggled her close against him, burying his face in the tangled curls beside her left ear. She smelled of sandalwood soap, a scent he was fairly sure he could never again associate with a man. He would gift Guy with something else to use, and perhaps a rose scent to offer any future houseguests.

Next time Emily would smell of flowers, he supposed. Each time with Emily would be unique, special, so satisfying as to be otherworldly. Maybe she was a witch, he thought with a smile. He was certainly bewitched, no doubt about that.

"Did you mean that?" she asked hesitantly.

"Oh, my sweet lady, I put my very heart into it," he

assured her with a half laugh. "Why? Did it seem less than you expected?"

She laughed, too. "Not *that*. When you said you loved me, were you serious?"

He brushed his hand over her cheek and cupped it, kissing her lightly on the lips. "I have never said those words to a woman before. Of course I meant it."

She released a sigh and closed her eyes. "We never had our talk in the library. You know, to settle matters between us."

Nick reached down and pulled up the coverlet, tucking it around her. "I would say we have fairly well settled them now, wouldn't you?"

He watched her smile, her eyes still closed. "For the moment. Could we settle matters again in a little while, do you think?"

"A greedy wife, just what I need," he teased. He felt light enough to float up to the ceiling. Happy enough to die smiling.

"Do you think I'm wanton?" she asked. He felt her tense.

"Oh, absolutely," he assured her.

She nibbled on her fingernail for a second, a habit he'd not seen her employ since she was eight or so. Then she moved her hand and clicked her tongue against her teeth. "You know I wasn't supposed to undress."

"You didn't. I did it for you," he reminded her. "Who told you that you weren't supposed to?"

She sighed. "I read it in a book. Well, the book was not for ladies, as you might well imagine. It did advise that a gentleman was only to, uh, lift the lady's nightrail. And he should remain clothed."

Nick stifled a laugh and slid his palm up her midriff to cup one small breast. "Sounds dreadfully tedious. Like sampling lemon ices through a cheesecloth. Difficult to get the full effect, I should think."

She giggled. "Yes, but we did it all wrong, you know. According to that book."

He slid his arm beneath her and rolled her on top of him. "Then I expect we'd better find that book of yours and get this right one of these days. Tell me, do you recall any particular exercises we might implement until we locate these rules?"

She melted atop him like a hot, soft blanket of silk and nipped him gently on the chin. "Not a one comes to mind. I guess we shall have to muddle along as best we can in the meantime."

"I have an idea," he growled as he lifted her hips and settled her in place.

She smiled down at him, a lazy look of both contentment and anticipation in her sky-blue eyes, her golden curls draping around her neck and tumbling down to tickle his chest. Her exquisite breasts flush against him. "I am so glad you came home, Nicky. I missed you."

He felt his eyes mist and a sweet aching in the vicinity of his heart. "You *are* my home, Emily. And I should have been here all along."

The next morning, Emily awoke alone in Duquesne's bedchamber. In a way, she was glad Nick was not there. After such a night, she knew she must look an absolute fright. She hugged the pillow to her, burying her smiling face in it. He loved her.

She relived every moment of their first night as lovers, recalling in minute detail the touch of his hands, his mouth and the wondrous sensation of him inside of her, becoming a part of her body as he had always been a part of her soul.

The scent of him still clung to her and his words echoed in her mind. Words she had longed to hear for what seemed all of her life. She remembered the expression of absolute awe he wore when their bodies joined for the first time.

A wave of need encompassed her, just remembering it all, and she suddenly wished above all to share it. She wanted him here more than anything now. Savoring was one thing, but experiencing the joy again would be much better. She must tell him of that when he returned.

At last Nick was hers.

Even in the harsh light of day, she still believed his words of love. He had convinced her beyond all doubt that he loved her just the way she was. Emily had wanted to tell him that she felt the same and that her feelings for him probably ran even deeper than his for her, but they had fallen asleep before she could find the proper words.

He had put it so poetically, she thought, especially for a man who hated poetry. That only made it more meaningful. Nicky, who could be gruff, his wit acerbic, his compliments double-edged, had doled out romance as if he had invented it himself and saved it all for her alone.

She laughed and rolled to her back, arms outflung as if to embrace the world. She needed to phrase her own avowal of love for him just so. Surely he knew already how much she cared, but the words should be profound enough that he would always remember them, as she would remember his.

What if he returned and found her like this? Would he mind seeing her this tousled, her skin reddened by the heat from last night's fire and portions of it aggravated by the arousing abrasiveness of Nick's evening beard? Well, he might, she thought. But she should tidy up a bit in the event that was what was expected of her. This was no honeymoon, after all. They were guests in his friend's house. She pushed herself out of bed and strolled naked over to the ornate washstand where sat the large pitcher of water and matching bowl.

Her movements unhurried, she bathed herself with the linen cloth she found there. But when she would have dressed to meet the day, Emily remembered she had nothing to wear other than the nightshirt Guy had loaned her after her bath in the kitchen. Would he mind if she borrowed something else until Nick could fetch her a dress?

She shamelessly plundered Duquesne's wardrobe, locating a pair of twill trousers, a fine lawn shirt and a pair of black stockings. Delighted to think what Nick would say when he saw her in such attire, she began to fashion herself a rather outlandish costume for his amusement.

Fortunately, Guy had a narrow waist and hips. His trousers almost fit her except for the length. She cuffed the hems underneath and the stiffness of the fabric held them in place.

The unstarched shirt reached nearly to her knees, but was soft enough that it did not bunch much around her hips when tucked inside the breeches. She found a pair of sleeve garters and gathered up the excess length hanging down her arms.

Feeling rather jaunty, she pulled on a striped waistcoat and buttoned it up to cover her breasts. Insignificant as they were, they had been fairly evident through the thin lawn of the white shirt. She looked in the mirror and laughed again. Nick would love this.

"Medusa," she commented to her reflection as she tugged on the flyaway curls that formed a halo 'round her head. She attacked her hair with Guy's brush and smoothed it as best she could. "No pins," she grumbled. "A shoelace!" she exclaimed as she rifled through a drawer. Once she had tied her locks in a queue, she surveyed the overall effect of her getup and grinned.

She swaggered this way and that, momentarily regretting the lack of shoes. Guy had a shelf replete with boots and shoes, but his feet were twice the size of hers. It hardly mattered, Emily decided. It wasn't as if she was going anywhere. She would wait for Nick here.

He would collapse in paroxysms of laughter the moment he saw her, she thought. How she loved to see him laugh, the way his eyes crinkled at the corners and that elusive dimple in his left cheek winked at her. She'd seen him laugh too little since he had come home. There had been a time when she had known just how to banish his serious side.

Perhaps he would enjoy divesting her of her male disguise and discovering her feminine charms beneath it. Would a man find that erotic? The memory of his lovemaking, as varied as it was enthralling, filled her again with eager anticipation. She could hardly wait.

But wait, she did. An hour passed, then another, and he did not return. Emily began to worry that he had gone out somewhere, perhaps to discover who had set the fire at Kendale House. What if that enemy he'd spoken of found him first and made a further attempt on his life?

She paced and wrung her hands until she could stand it no longer. Guy might know where he had gone. Or she might even find Nick below with Guy and in no peril at all.

The way she was dressed, she shouldn't set foot out of the room, but she had to do something. He couldn't expect her to remain here all day not knowing where he was or if he was in danger.

Emily straightened the waistcoat and buttoned the top

button of the shirt. In any case, no one was likely to see her besides Nick, Guy and his ancient butler.

She left the room immediately before modesty changed her mind.

The stairs felt cold beneath her stockinged feet. Without the traction of slippers, she had to step carefully so as not to slip and fall.

As she neared the bottom step, she heard voices emanating from the morning room where Guy's servant had asked Nick and her to wait the night before. The words were indistinct, but she could tell from the tone that one of the speakers was Nick. A huge wave of relief swept over her.

The door stood half-open into the room. Emily wondered if she should go in, now that she was here, or return to the bedchamber and wait for him? If it was only Guy in there with him, she would join them, she decided. But on the off chance that someone else was present, it might not be prudent to let them see her got up the way she was.

Even though this reminded her of the evening she had eavesdropped on Nick and Guy and caused her a moment's guilt, she still tiptoed closer and peeked through the crack where the door was hinged.

"This is neither the time nor the place for this, Munford," Nick was saying.

Emily stepped back and flattened herself against the wall of the foyer, unobserved. *Zounds!* It was *Munford,* that competitor Nick had mentioned, the one he thought had tried twice to kill him in India. And he had found Nick here!

Careful not to make a sound, she positioned one eye against the crack and peeped again. Guy was in there and so was another fellow, both standing near Nick. Munford stood alone, in profile, a large and imposing man.

"I'm glad I found you both in one place," Munford declared. "I apprehended this inept dolt trailing me this morning," he said, pointing angrily to the stranger Emily didn't recognize, "and he admitted Duquesne hired him on your behalf, Kendale. You've been having me followed."

Nick nodded. "Because you've been asking about me since the day you docked. You threatened my life, Munford."

Munford took a step closer to Nick. "And you know why. Let's get on with this, Kendale," the man said, his voice bitter. "I don't have any more time to waste."

To Emily's horror, he reached inside his coat.

Without time to plan, Emily slammed the half-open door against the wall and launched herself inside the room with a shout to wake the dead. She landed against Munford with the full weight of her body, knocking him clean off his feet. His head clunked against the edge of the marble-topped table and he crumpled to the floor in a heap.

"Emily?" Nick shouted, running to her.

She scrambled to her feet, pointing. "Watch out! He has a gun!"

Guy was already crouching to inspect the one lying unconscious. He slipped a hand just inside Munford's coat, drew out a bulging envelope, then stood and held it out to Nick.

The other fellow probed the lump on her victim's head and felt his pulse. "He's knocked out, that's all."

Nick accepted the packet from Guy. "It appears to be money."

Emily bit her lips together and clung to Nick's arm. "I—I thought he was about to shoot you."

They were all frowning at her.

"He said to *finish* this," she explained. "And I thought…" Her voice trailed off and she simply stared at them, wide-eyed, willing him to reassure her she had done the right thing.

"What the devil are you wearing?" Nick asked, his narrowed gaze raking her as if she were standing there naked.

She shrugged. "What does *that* matter? I could have come down in Duquesne's nightshirt, you know! Why is Munford here if not to finish what he'd begun?"

Guy spoke up. "He arrived prepared to purchase back the ship Nick won from him last year. An exorbitant amount was mentioned. I assume that packet contains it."

Emily looked from him to Nick and braced her hands on her hips. They weren't going to make her the villain in this. "You said he almost murdered you on two occasions, Nick. What else was I to think when I saw the two of you standing there? When he said what he said?"

Nick sighed. "Believe me, I asked about that. Munford just vowed he was in Boston when those events took place. Said he could prove it."

"And you believed him?" Emily demanded with a disbelieving roll of her eyes. "Bogus proof, I would wager. Or he could have been lying to put you off your guard until he could draw his gun and shoot." She nodded toward the man still kneeling beside Munford. "You there, see if he has a pistol."

"We had better get her out of here before he comes around," Guy suggested, eyeing her attire with a poorly hidden grin, "and also be thinking of an explanation. She could be a mad younger brother, perhaps? An underfed footman who tipples in the mornings?''

Nick grasped Emily's elbow, almost lifting her off her feet as he ushered her out of the room. ''Go upstairs and stay there!''

She dug in her heels and slid several feet on the marble floor. ''No!''

''Do not argue with me, Emily,'' he said through gritted teeth. ''And never, *never* do anything so foolish again, do you hear? Suppose he *had* been reaching for a pistol.''

''My lord!'' called Duquesne's hireling in a loud voice. ''The girl was right. He does have a loaded revolver. A Navy Colt, by the look of it.''

Immediately Nick dropped her arm and reentered the room. ''The devil you say!''

Guy stood watching, his brows lowered in a frown. ''Well, I'll be damned. I should have checked further. Maybe that *was* the payment he had in mind, Nick.''

Emily crossed her arms over her chest and raised her chin. ''There, you see?''

''Tie him up and take him into custody, Barrett,'' Guy ordered. ''I'll summon a hack to fetch you both to the station house. We shall see what the magistrate has to say about all this. Munford can offer his proof to *him* and see how it stands up.''

Nick said nothing. He merely pinned Emily with a glare and pointed up the stairs.

''You are quite welcome,'' she snapped. Nevertheless, she marched to the staircase, head held high, satisfied she had done her duty as a wife. ''When you get over your embarrassment, you may thank me.''

A half hour later Nick watched through the front window as Barrett loaded Julius Munford—conscious now and protesting vehemently—into the hack.

"Barrett will take care of him. Have another brandy?" Guy asked, holding the decanter over Nick's snifter. They sat in the same half-furnished room where Emily had attacked Munford.

"Hell, yes. I'm still shaking," Nick replied. "She could have been killed." He huffed, took a healthy sip of his brandy, then gestured toward the stairs with his glass. "And what in God's name was she doing wearing *your* clothes?"

Guy shook his head despairingly. "Outrageous," he declared in heartfelt agreement. "I swear you're going to have to do something about her, Nick. Hide her away in the country, perhaps."

Nick frowned at the suggestion. "Hardly fair. She doesn't behave that way all the time."

Guy scoffed. "Well, no, I suppose not, but you never know what to expect from her, apparently. Who knows how dreadfully she might embarrass you before someone who really counts!"

The criticism caused Nick to bridle. "She was only doing what she thought she must to save us—save me, anyway—and I resent your implication! Emily proved she can hold her own in any situation just last evening."

"Um," Guy grunted noncommittally.

"It's true!" Nick insisted. "You should have seen her. As a matter of fact, I have never before known a woman of such courage. Emily is simply—"

"Unpredictable," Guy finished dryly. "Not *to the manor born*, you might say. By all rights, she ought to have fainted dead away, thinking Munford was drawing a pistol. Any sane woman would."

"How dare you question her sanity!" Nick lunged forward and grabbed Guy's shirtfront, yanking him up on his toes.

The fool had the temerity to laugh in Nick's face. He patted the hand Nick had fisted at his neck. "Whoa, Kendale. I'm only playing devil's advocate here. Can't you see what a treasure you have in Emily?"

"Of course I can see it!" Nick exclaimed. He realized then that Guy had only sought to point that out. He dropped him back on his feet. "All right." Roughly he brushed smooth the handful of shirt he had bunched up at Guy's throat. "Then I suppose I won't kill you."

"Profoundly grateful, I'm sure. Why don't you go and make up your little quarrel with your wife now," Guy suggested.

"I should follow Barrett and Munford down to the station."

"Not necessary just yet. I'll go. You'll be called in when his case is presented."

Nick nodded and sighed. "Looks as though I'll be spending more time in court than in the House, what with my case against Munford and Worthing's case against me."

"Oh, I haven't had the chance to tell you. I had a conversation with the good baron at Michael's. He won't pursue it."

Not terribly surprised, but relieved, Nick guessed why. "Ah, he reconsidered the scandal, I suppose."

Guy shrugged and set his empty glass down on the window sill. "Well, that, too. But it seems Dierdre has made quite a name for herself in your absence. I simply pointed out that no man in his right mind would blame you for crying off any connection to a woman who has thrown up her skirts for every available male above the rank of baronet."

"She didn't!" Nick exclaimed.

Guy nodded. "She did. Everyone but yours truly, of course." He wrinkled his nose. "Though one would think good looks counted for something, my lack of blunt saved me from her clutches. But that's neither here nor there. As for the matter at hand, you and Emily are welcome to stay as long as you like, but I've little food in the house and I think the danger is over. Bodkins has Thursdays off to visit his sister, so you'll have the place to yourselves until I return." He winked. "I'll be away all day."

"Thank you. For everything," Nick added sincerely, feeling a bit foolish and contrite over his loss of temper, but knowing Guy would expect no apology. "We should be getting home so I can assess the damage of the fire. I hope to heaven Emily's wardrobe is sound. Where is her cloak?"

Guy grinned, shaking his head as if still amazed by Emily's appearance. "On the hook just inside the hall. You're in such a hurry, shall I saddle your horse?"

"No," Nick answered with a grin. "I'll do it. Later."

"Don't be gruff with her, Nick," Guy said kindly. "Her heart's in the right place. The girl loves you. Judging by the way I once saw her look at you when we were lads, I imagine she always has."

"I know that," Nick assured him. "I was an idiot not to realize it sooner."

"Well, I shall say goodbye, then, Idiot," Guy said with a snappy salute.

"Goodbye, Advocate. I shall tell her you took her part."

Nick smiled and shook his head as Guy left the house. He wondered if Emily knew she had won yet another heart for her collection.

The staff of Kendale House had gathered around her last night as if she were their queen bee. Wrecker and Rosie doted on her. The people of Bournesea would welcome her gladly when she returned there with him in two weeks. And her husband adored her in spite of his exasperation.

Nick wanted to tell her again how much he cared and how much he valued her concern for him. Even more than that, he needed to hold her in his arms and show her. Immediately.

And all of a sudden, as if he had called for her, there she was.

Chapter Eighteen

"They have all gone," she said from the doorway. "I was watching from the window upstairs."

Nick turned. She still wore Guy's clothes.

She blushed and looked to one side, avoiding his gaze. "I'm not sorry."

"Neither am I," Nick said. "Come here."

He met her halfway and put his arms around her, holding her tightly against him. "I thank you. And I love you," he said sincerely. "But you look damned provocative in those trousers."

She snuggled even closer. "Then I shall steal them and wear them always."

Nick chuckled as he kissed the top of her head and leaned back so he could see her face. "Oh, no, you won't! And I would have your promise that you will never do anything so rash again as to attack anyone for any reason."

"Even you?" she teased.

"Other than me," he qualified with a laugh, then grew serious again. "Do you promise?"

"I do. Unless, of course—"

He pressed a kiss on her lips to silence her. "At no time."

"Oh, very well." She kissed him back, a long, slow mating of mouths that had him randy and more than ready to borrow Guy's bed again.

He shifted his lower body against her. "Shall we go upstairs?"

"I've just come from there," she answered, her voice whispery and urgent against his mouth. "It is such a long, long trip."

He backed to the divan and sat down, pulling her across his lap. "Then we should rest here and fortify ourselves until we're able to travel that far," he assured her between kisses.

She nipped lightly at his lower lip and ran her fingers over the buttons of his waistcoat. "Is this *fortification* you speak of anything at all like *settling matters?*"

"Synonymous," he declared with a breathless chuckle. "Absolutely synonymous."

Nick had just pushed the shirt off Emily's shoulders when he heard a noise in the foyer. "Blast him, Guy's returned," he whispered.

They laughed like naughty children as she scrambled off his lap and began doing up her buttons. Nick hurried to secure his own, then raked his hands through his hair and assumed a dignified air.

Emily sucked in a deep breath to hold back her laughter and tucked her stray curls behind her ears. Together they faced the doorway.

"Well, well. Look at the little countess! What a lovely cartoon for the dailies this would make."

Nick stepped in front of Emily. "What the hell are you doing here, Carrick?" But the pistol trained on his heart made the answer fairly evident. He would never have thought Carrick had it in him.

The smile was almost familial. "I'm here to claim the title, of course. Uncle Ambrose wanted me to have it, you know. Only he died before you did, the old curmudgeon. I must admit that was my fault."

"You killed him," Nick guessed.

"No. Actually, I was waiting to hear of your fate before putting that plan into motion. Illness waits for no man, however, and he kicked up his toes before I was ready. I only meant that I should have been more careful who I hired to get rid of you in India. You truly are a hardy devil, Nick. You managed to squeeze by with your hide intact and make it home again. Since I paid in advance, that cost me dearly, I'll have you know." He shrugged. "But you'll pay for it."

"So *you* hired that done." Nick took a step, moving closer.

Carrick nodded. "Stay where you are. Or don't. It matters very little to me *when* I shoot you. And your chum, Duquesne, will take the blame for it, poor sod. I suppose we should get on with this before he returns."

He rubbed his thumb suggestively over the hammer of the cocked weapon. He was relishing this, Nick thought. Not only was the man greedy, he would actually enjoy killing. And Nick's wasn't the only life he would take. Emily, who might be carrying an heir, also stood between Carrick and what he was determined to have.

"How did you find us?" Nick inquired, playing for time. He had to figure out some way to disarm Carrick or they were done for.

"Simple. Hammersley and I had a congenial chat while I was sketching him for his portrait early this morning. He spoke so fondly of you and how you had main-

tained your life-long friendships with him and with Duquesne. I thought you might have flown to Hammersley's
last evening after my little bonfire."

Nick wanted to strangle him then and there. "How the
hell did you get into Kendale House?"

"My old friend Upton, of course. After my visit with
Hammersley, I concluded you must have come here.
Everyone knows Duquesne's all but impoverished and
keeps only that ancient butler on staff. I watched the
house, waiting for you to exit. Imagine my delight when
everyone in residence left but you two! This almost
seems fated, doesn't it?" He waved the gun casually.

The distance between them was about six feet. Nick
reckoned even a bad shot could hardly miss at that distance.

"A pity you won't live long to enjoy the title," Emily
commented wryly, sounding surprisingly unaffected by
the thought of dying. "You'll be doing us a favor actually. A quick death might be a blessing." She stepped
around Nick.

He wanted to shove her back behind him, but was
afraid to make any sudden moves. Carrick could shoot
them at any time and get off several shots in rapid suc-
cession. He was wielding a revolver that held five or six
shots.

"Remember your promise to me, Em," he said in a
low voice, hoping to remind her that she had promised
him she would never try another foolhardy risk such as
she had taken with Munford. "A promise is sacred."

"I know, dear," she assured him. "We swore not to
say anything to anyone in London about the sickness, but
I want to tell him anyway if he's going to shoot us. Let
him dread an ugly death as we have done. Unless he has
the courage to shoot himself."

Carrick looked confused. "What the devil are you prating on about? If you're planning some sort of trick, it won't work."

"Trick?" Emily said, shaking her head slowly as she released a huff. "I only wish it were. *Abrasia Rosa* is deadly, a most contagious plague. I swear I never thought to see such as I witnessed at Bournesea in the weeks past. And now..." She sniffled loudly. "Even Lord Duquesne rushed out of here when we told him. Brave as he is, the man was terrified. He's probably gone for his physician."

"At Bournesea you had this?" Carrick demanded.

Nick could see the fright take hold. His cousin had always dreaded sickness of any kind and took on any symptoms displayed by those around him who were afflicted.

Emily was aware of it. Nick recalled telling her of it at Bournesea. Whatever she had in mind now was purchasing them time if nothing else.

"How is it I've never heard of this disease?" Carrick asked.

Nick improvised. "Because the discovery of it is so recent, and *was* peculiar to the inner provinces of India. But I'm afraid that isn't true any longer." He had Carrick's full attention now, so he continued. "When I realized several of the men were down with it on the voyage, we tried to contain it, you see. That's why I couldn't let you inside the gates at Bournesea. We were quarantined."

Emily shook her head despairingly. "We were too optimistic in lifting it, I'm sad to say. However, I'm *not* sorry you are afflicted, as well, since you mean us harm. Strange, they say Abrasia rarely takes hold so soon! You only had contact with me, really, and that just two days ago. And yet..." She pointed to him and shrugged.

Carrick laughed aloud, but it sounded forced. His voice was unnaturally loud when he spoke. "Good effort, I'll grant you that. You had me on there for a moment. But you see, I know our noble Nick here would never risk spreading a contagion. If you weren't completely well of whatever it was, he would never have unlocked those gates, much less come to town."

"True, but after a fortnight in seclusion, we thought surely we'd been spared. However," she said as she reached up to her collar and pulled it down to expose her neck and upper chest. "See this? We only noticed late last night as I was bathing after the fire. The initial sign. You have it creeping up your own neck, though yours doesn't look quite as red as mine. Earlier stage, I expect."

"What?" He ran a finger beneath his collar and felt around the inside of it.

Emily nodded. "Itchy, isn't it? Wait until you experience the rapid heartbeats that follow, the mounting confusion, and finally...well, one simply comes undone and...it's all over. At least I needn't dread that now." She lifted her shoulders, held out her hands in a futile gesture and looked at Nick with a perfectly straight face. Then she continued. "It is a hard thing to watch happen." She shuddered violently.

Carrick had blanched and was squinting at her neck and chest, which she had left exposed. A very prominent red rash splotched the creaminess of her skin.

Nick touched his now clean-shaven chin, knowing exactly what had caused her so-called *plague*.

With his free hand Carrick yanked off his neckcloth and undid his collar. "Clasp your hands over your head and come here," he ordered, his voice shaking as he motioned with the weapon. "See if it's the same."

"No!" Nick almost shouted the word, but it was too late. Emily had already danced out of his reach and Carrick held the cocked pistol aimed straight at Nick's midsection.

Arms stretched upward, hands locked together, Emily peered closely at Carrick's collar, the pistol only inches from her head, though still pointed directly at Nick.

She was going to try something. But what could she do? Get herself shot, that was what. Nick debated whether to charge Carrick now and take a bullet himself, on the chance Emily could get away. But Carrick was not limited to one shot. And Emily would never run out of here and leave him, especially if he'd been wounded or killed. Nick held steady, watching for his chance. If Carrick would only lower the gun.

"Oh, dear," Emily moaned dramatically. "Oh, Nick, *look* at this!"

Carrick's gun hand trembled dangerously. "W-what?" His wide-eyed gaze flew to Emily, then straight back to Nick. "You stay where you are!"

Emily darted Nick a meaningful look and mouthed the word "Duck."

Nick's heart almost stopped. "Wait!" He held up his hands in a calming motion. "Easy, Carrick. Look I know this disease can make you do things you ordinarily wouldn't consider. If you surrender the pistol, we can try to get help for you. Once you're well—"

"No!" Carrick cried, shaking, his voice hoarse with fear. One hand rubbed frantically at his throat.

Suddenly, Emily brought her clasped hands down on Carrick's gun arm, forcing it downward. His shot went wild as she raised one knee. Carrick screamed and Nick lunged simultaneously.

All three of them landed in a tangle. Carrick struggled,

keening, one hand between his legs where Em's knee had
struck and the other flailing the useless pistol about. He'd
never had the chance to cock the damn thing again, thank
God. Nick pinned Carrick's wrist to the floor and jerked
the gun from his hand.

"Get off," he ordered Emily. "I have him."

Emily rolled to one side, well away from Carrick, and
bounced lithely to her stockinged feet. She pranced over
to the draperies and tore off one of the cords that held
them back. "Here," she said as she tossed it over.
"You'll have to tie him. My hands are still shaking and
my wrist hurts like blue blazes."

Nick trussed up Carrick with the drapery cord and tied
his feet together with the man's neckcloth. He hurriedly
checked for hidden weapons, then left him lying where
he was.

He approached Emily, who understandably looked
rather shaken. "Let me see your hand."

She nodded and presented the one she had injured.

After feeling the small bones and moving it gently, he
cradled it in his palm. "Your wrist is intact, but something is broken. You broke your promise to me and threw
yourself directly in harm's way," he said softly. "How
old was that promise? Moments?"

"I had my fingers crossed," she admitted, offering that
little one-shouldered shrug she always employed when
guilt plagued her. "Mischief just seems to follow me
wherever I go."

He laughed softly and tweaked her nose. "You *are*
mischief! What a dull life I've led these past few years
without you."

"I'll certainly try to be more circumspect in future,"
she avowed, blue eyes twinkling.

"Of course you will."

* * *

Emily worried that Nick might pardon his cousin's perfidy in the interest of avoiding a scandal, but he promised he would ensure the man never troubled them again. He had locked Carrick, still bound, inside the empty pantry off Guy's kitchen. Then they had saddled Nick's mount and ridden the short distance back to Kendale House. There, he left her with a promise to return as soon as possible after concluding his business with the police.

She now languished in the room where Nick had spent part of his childhood. It was a large, airy chamber with a smaller and more modest version of the bed in the smoke-damaged master chamber.

Clad only in her shift after her bath, she tried to sit still while Rosie buzzed around her, fussing over the fact that a bit of Emily's hair had been singed the night before and had to be cut. Scissors snipped here and there until Rosie seemed satisfied with the results. Obviously that was not all that troubled the maid. "Out with it, Rosie. You are bursting to ask me something, I can tell."

"Do you want one of the old gowns to wear?"

"That is not what is on your mind," Emily admonished.

"They was still packed in the trunk that come from the carriage wreck. I aired 'em out."

"Rosie?"

"Ye'll turn me off if I tell ye."

"No, I won't."

"Mr. MacFarlin asked if I'll walk out with him," Rosie admitted with a worried look.

"I've no objection at all."

Rosie huffed and crossed her arms over her chest. One foot tapped nervously. "He's wantin' to marry me, if ye must know. His lordship won't like it."

Emily bit her lips together. Rosie might be right. "I...I suppose I could speak to him, if you like," she offered, not altogether certain she was up to broaching the subject with Nick. "Just because you and he were once intimate, I should hope he wouldn't prevent—"

Rosie's clapped her hands over her reddened cheeks. "Blimey, ye know about me and Percy? How in the world? We was so careful!"

"Not you and Wrecker. I meant you and Nick. His *lordship.*"

Rosie was already shaking her head, her eyes widened so the whites showed all around. "Me and Lord Nick? We *never!* Who told you such a wicked lie?"

Emily jumped to her feet and rounded on Rosie, shaking a finger under her nose. "You told me. You confessed it that first night!"

"No, no, no," Rosie groaned. "Not *him.* Lord Ambrose, his da! The old sport never showed no good side unless he was naked, but he cut a right smart figger in bed, he did. He was the one!"

Emily whirled around, covering her mouth with one hand to keep from sobbing with relief. That would hardly be appropriate. When she thought she could speak calmly, she turned again and faced the maid. "Then why would you think my husband would not sanction your marriage to Mr. MacFarlin?"

Rosie blinked, then shrugged. "Why, most lords think staffers marrying in the same house causes all sorts a troubles. It ain't usually allowed."

"Not marrying might cause more trouble," Emily guessed, voicing her thoughts. "I think he will agree."

"Oh, thank ye, Lady Em! You'll speak to him on our account, then?"

"Definitely. As soon as may be," Emily said, holding

out her hands to Rosie. "I wish you all happiness, Rosie. Do you love him?"

Green eyes brightened with tears. "Oh, Lady, my Percy's a fine man, he is. Ain't no bloke ever been so nice. He fetched me flowers from the garden out back. And he give me this," she said excitedly, reaching in her pocket to withdraw a simple silver ring with two hearts engraved on it.

"How lovely," Emily said, hugging Rosie on an impulse. She knew it wasn't proper, but she couldn't help recalling the cheery little red-haired girl who had once been simply her friend.

They were both in tears and laughing. Rosie finally stepped back and reached out to touch Emily's face. "Lord Nick made it all right, didn't he? Last night after the fire? You and him?"

Emily nodded.

"Good enough! Why, you'll be rounding out with the next little lordship next thing we know!"

The thought had never entered Emily's mind, but it was more than welcome now that Rosie put it there. She ran a hand over her stomach and imagined what it would be like, carrying Nick's child, nurturing a son or daughter. Being a mother.

"You'd best get dressed," Rosie advised.

"The blue day gown," Emily said, looking forward to feeling the soft batiste envelop her like a mother's embrace. She wished she could share her happiness and her hopes with her own mother and also with the Countess, who had surely watched over her like a guardian angel. Every single venture had proved successful.

Glancing down at her hand where the blue stones sparkled in the ring Nick had given her on their wedding day, she imagined them winking at her. And she smiled back.

* * *

Nick hurried to Kendale House as soon as he had seen to his cousin's incarceration and Munford's release. Carrick's trial would not take place for a while. There would be a right to-do about it in the news when it did happen, but there was no help for it. Emily was safe now, that was all that counted.

Munford had been irate about his false arrest, but when Nick had returned the clipper ship, *Madeline,* for a mere fraction of its worth, the man had turned ecstatic. He couldn't wait to reclaim her when she returned from her current voyage to the Indies.

Nick knew Emily would be waiting for him now. Guy had laughed at him for happily grinning throughout the proceedings at the station house, but Nick could not seem to think of much besides Emily and how she had taken down not one but two full-grown men in defense of him. He wanted to crow.

It was ridiculous to take pride in such wild antics, but he couldn't help himself.

When he arrived at Kendale House, Jems, the under-butler, opened the door for him and advised him that Upton had gone, and had not been seen since the fire.

Good riddance, Nick thought as he bounded up the stairs.

When he opened the door to his old room, Emily greeted him with the sweetest smile. If he hadn't known her so well, he might have taken it at face value. Emily was up to something. "Let's have it. What have you done now?"

She wrinkled up her nose and laughed. "Not what I've done, but what I'm going to do."

He took her hands in his and drew her to him for a kiss. "And what, dare I ask, will that be?"

She ducked her head shyly. "I'm going to have a baby. A fat, raven-haired, brown-eyed little boy with no musical talent and a title hanging over his head. What do you think of that?"

Nick laughed. "Good for you! Have two while you're about it, the heir and the spare. Then you can start on the girls." He kissed her again. "Tell me, do you plan to do this anytime soon?"

She leaned back in his arms and looked up at him. "I've already begun."

"Silly widgeon, it's too soon to know that."

Even as he said it, she was shaking her head. "No, it isn't! It's a feeling I've had since I first realized it was possible."

Nick frowned. "Emily, are you quite all right?"

"Well, you'll think I'm not, but that's as may be. Take off your clothes."

"What?" he asked on a gust of laughter.

"Take off your clothes and get in bed. We have to make sure I'm not wrong about this," she warned, frowning at him now. She set about unbuttoning her own gown, her arms at an unnatural angle trying to reach the buttons in back.

"Turn around," he coaxed. "Allow me." He undid her buttons and untied the laces on her corset, then watched with interest as she promptly shed her gown and stepped out of it and her petticoats. Clad only in a thin silk shift and her stockings, Emily looked incredibly enticing. She shot him the most daring grin. "Well? Go on."

He wasted no time in stripping off his own clothes, then took her hand and walked with her to the bed. The afternoon sun streamed through the windows. Birds chirped in the cherry tree that towered up to their window. The room smelled of spring lilacs.

Though he was certainly aroused by her eagerness, Nick wanted to prolong the interlude. There was an innocence and sweetness about it somehow, as if they were offering one another all their secrets in the bright light of day. Pledging to share everything there was to share. He looked at her and saw the incredible love in her eyes that he had seen there before when she was seventeen. He knew she must see the same in his, for he felt it to the depth of his soul.

"I trust you," she whispered.

"And I *love* you. Now I know what the poets mean when they speak of love," he replied as he took her in his arms. "Now I know."

He lowered her to the bed, their bodies fitting together so perfectly he felt it would destroy the moment if he began to move too soon.

"So, do you intend to pause and read me a sonnet?" she asked, shifting sinuously against him, a mischievous note in her softly spoken question.

He kissed her neck, touching his tongue to the rapidly fluttering pulse there. "Sorry to disappoint you, love. As soon as you're too far gone with child to do *this*. Then I will read."

Epilogue

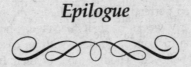

"Nicholas! Nick?" Emily cried as she came dashing down the stairs. "The most awful thing!"

He caught her in his arms the moment she swung around the newell post and nearly fell. "What's happened?" he demanded, glancing up the stairs. "Is it Guilford?"

She nodded frantically. "Yes! You must call Dr. Mershon again. Baby Guy…he swallowed my ring!" She held up her hand to show him it was missing. "I took it off to bathe him and…somehow he got it…and gulped it right down!"

"Listen. Be still and listen to me, Em." He brushed her flyaway curls from her forehead and smiled down into her eyes. "Remember, Em, when he swallowed the rock? It was much larger and everything came out in the end."

"This is not amusing!" she cried. "I can't be without that ring, not even for a day!"

He drew her down to sit on the second step and almost had to restrain her. "Take a deep breath. There now, tell me why you're so panicked. Are you worried about the baby? He's almost two, Em, not an infant. The ring will not harm his insides. It's not sharp. Trust me, you'll have it back in short order.''

She buried her face in her hands and attempted to steady herself. ''All right,'' she said finally, uncovering her face and sucking in a deep breath. ''It's all right.''

Nick frowned. It was not like Emily to carry on so. She had been perfectly calm—well, for the most part— since the early weeks of their marriage. She had made the transition to London Society with an ease he would never have believed. Though most of their friends considered her a bit eccentric, they all loved her dearly. She had been a credit to him in his work, providing opinions that deserved great consideration when presenting his speeches to the House. And what a brave soul she had been when carrying little Guilford Nicholas and giving birth to him.

But something had overset her terribly and it surely consisted of more than Baby Guy swallowing a ring. God only knew the child had ingested almost everything he could find that would fit between his teeth.

''That ring has become my talisman, you see,'' she explained haltingly. ''I sort of…depend on it.''

Nick stifled a laugh. ''Oh, Emily, surely you, of all people, are not superstitious!''

''No, well, not exactly. It's just that I feel your, uh, your mother sort of looks after me when I'm wearing her ring. I feel lost without it.''

''That's absurd,'' he declared. ''It never belonged to Mother.'' Her look of profound shock concerned him more than her silly notion. ''Why did you believe it was hers?''

She grasped his arm. ''The necklace?''

''Yours, too. I bought the set to give you as a betrothal gift the week before I kissed you and Father sent me away. I'd planned to ask you to marry me. I told you that.''

''No!''

''Yes. The moment I saw the set with gems the very color of your eyes, I spent my entire quarterly allowance and borrowed ten quid from Michael to purchase it for you. Ask him.''

She deflated like a punctured balloon. Nick slid his arm around her for support. ''So you see, it wasn't my mother looking after you from the Great Beyond. It was *you* who took care of yourself.''

Her brows drew together as she looked up at him. ''But her clothes. Whenever I wore them, I felt safer, more dignified, more like a countess. Her essence seemed to be in them somehow, shoring me up.''

''Not at all. She never even wore them, you know. She only had them done up so the dressmaker would be required to visit her once a week. The only thing I ever saw her wear in those last years were fancy nightrails and wrappers. Her maid asked for those and a few of the simpler dresses when she was leaving after Mother's death. I told her to take them. As far as I know, you haven't a stitch that ever graced my mother's form. What do you think of that?''

For a long time Emily remained silent, thinking. Then she smiled. ''I was a goose, wasn't I? But you know, Nick, I thought she was the most wonderful person. Like a queen holding court, the epitome of the English noblewoman. I think I grew to love her, yet we never exchanged more than a few words.''

Nick embraced her so that she leaned back against him and he spoke against her ear. ''You want to hear something truly ironic? I used to sit on Mother's bed and tell her of your wild antics.''

"Oh, no, you did no such thing!"

"I did. Remember that gallop across the meadow on old Bessie? How you grabbed that branch that should have raked you right off her back? I had to ride up and fetch you off it so you wouldn't drop and break both legs. There were dozens—perhaps hundreds—of tales of your almost daily scrapes. But somehow, you always landed right side up, laughing at the world. My mother lived through you, I think. She craved those stories and thought you were the bravest girl she'd ever known. I can't believe she didn't mention them to you when you visited with the vicar."

"No, she never did," Emily said, sounding a bit sad. "But she winked at me once."

Nick stood up and pulled Emily to her feet. "Let's go up to the nursery and see if our lad has found dessert for himself. I do hope you moved my old coin collection to a higher shelf. The little fellow will jingle when he walks."

She laughed and slid her arm around his waist as they trudged upstairs. "You got more mischief than you bargained for when you wed me, didn't you, Kendale?"

"I'm not complaining," he assured her with a hug. "You compensate quite well for it."

She smiled that sweet smile again, the one that always set him on guard. "I am so happy you think so," she said. "For I must warn you, there might be more on the way."

Nick closed his eyes for a moment to savor the news. He could swear he heard his mother's laughter.

* * * * *

Lookin' for some spicy Westerns seasoned
with just the right amount of sizzling
romance and rollicking adventure? Then help
yourselves to these Harlequin Historicals novels

ON SALE MARCH 2002

A MARRIAGE BY CHANCE
by **Carolyn Davidson**
(Wyoming, 1894)

SHADES OF GRAY
by **Wendy Douglas**
(Texas, 1868)

ON SALE APRIL 2002

THE BRIDE FAIR
by **Cheryl Reavis**
(North Carolina, 1868)

THE DRIFTER
by **Lisa Plumley**
(Arizona, 1887)

Harlequin Historicals®

Visit us at www.eHarlequin.com   HHWEST18

Take a jaunt to Merry Old England
with these timeless stories from
Harlequin Historicals

On sale March 2002

THE LOVE MATCH
by Deborah Simmons
Deborah Hale
Nicola Cornick
Don't miss this captivating bridal collection
filled with three breathtaking Regency tales!

MARRYING MISCHIEF
by Lyn Stone
Will a quarantine spark romance between a
determined earl and his convenient bride?

On sale April 2002

MISS VEREY'S PROPOSAL
by Nicola Cornick
A matchmaking duke causes a smitten London
debutante to realize she's betrothed to the
wrong brother!

DRAGON'S KNIGHT
by Catherine Archer
When a powerful knight rushes to the aid of a
beautiful noblewoman, will he finally conquer
his darkest demons?

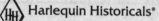

HHH Harlequin Historicals®

HHMED23

Silhouette Books invites you to cherish
a captivating keepsake collection by

DIANA PALMER

They're rugged and lean…and the best-looking, sweetest-talking men in the Lone Star State! CALHOUN, JUSTIN and TYLER—the three mesmerizing cowboys who started the legend. Now they're back by popular demand in one classic volume—ready to lasso your heart!

You won't want to miss this treasured collection from international bestselling author Diana Palmer!

LONG, TALL Texans

CALHOUN, JUSTIN & TYLER
(On sale March 2002)

Available at your favorite retail outlet.

Silhouette®

Where love comes alive™

Visit Silhouette at www.eHarlequin.com

PSLTT

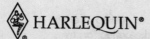

HARLEQUIN®

makes any time special—online...

eHARLEQUIN.com

your romantic life

—Romance 101—
♥ Guides to romance, dating and flirting.

—Dr. Romance —
♥ Get romance advice and tips from our expert, Dr. Romance.

—Recipes for Romance—
♥ How to plan romantic meals for you and your sweetie.

—Daily Love Dose—
♥ Tips on how to keep the romance alive every day.

—Tales from the Heart—
♥ Discuss romantic dilemmas with other members in our Tales from the Heart message board.

**All this and more available at
www.eHarlequin.com
on Women.com Networks**

HINTL1R

MONTANA *Born*

From the bestselling series

MONTANA MAVERICKS

Wed in Whitehorn

Two tales that capture living and loving
beneath the Big Sky.

THE MARRIAGE MAKER by Christie Ridgway

Successful businessman Ethan Redford never proposed a deal he
couldn't close—and that included marriage to Cleo Kincaid Monroe!

AND THE WINNER...WEDS! by Robin Wells

Prim and proper Frannie Hannon yearned for Austin Parker, but
her pearls and sweater sets couldn't catch his boots and jeans—or
could they?

And don't miss

MONTANA *Bred*

Featuring

JUST PRETENDING by Myrna Mackenzie

&

STORMING WHITEHORN by Christine Scott

Available in May 2002
Available only from Silhouette at your favorite retail outlet.

Silhouette®

Where love comes alive™

Visit Silhouette at www.eHarlequin.com   PSBORN

BESTSELLING AUTHORS

Linda Lael Miller
Kasey Michaels
Barbara Delinsky &
Diana Palmer

Lead

Covering everything from tender love to sizzling passion, there's a TAKE 5 volume for every type of romance reader.

PLUS

With two proofs-of-purchase from any two Take 5 volumes you can receive THE ART OF ROMANCE absolutely free! (see inside a volume of TAKE 5 for details)

AND

With $5.00 worth of coupons inside each volume, this is one deal you shouldn't miss!

Look for it in March 2002.

Visit us at www.eHarlequin.com

TAKE5POP